If he only knew what she was thinking...

Eve felt her face grow warm, and she tried to turn away. But Tony caught her hand, pulling her gently toward him.

She found herself standing between his legs, could feel the warmth of his bare skin. His muscles rippled, and something primitive rose inside Eve. Something even more basic than love.

He lifted his hand and brushed back the hair from her forehead. His touch was gentle and warm but his fingers trembled slightly, revealing a deeper, darker desire. His blue gaze was knowing, and bittersweet.

"What are we going to do about this?" he asked.

"I don't know."

"I don't know, either, but if you keep looking at me like that, I won't be responsible for my actions."

"I'm not...I didn't mean to..."

"No, you wouldn't," he agreed. "That's what I admire most about you. You don't play games. You're open and honest, about your feelings and everything else."

No, she wanted to tell him. *I'm not honest. Especially about my feelings. What if I told you I'd been in love with you for years?*

Dear Harlequin Intrigue Reader,

Chills run down your spine, your pulse pounds...and you can't wait to turn the page! It's just another month of outstanding romantic suspense from Harlequin Intrigue.

Last month, Amanda Stevens introduced you to a new brand of justice—GALLAGHER JUSTICE—in *The Littlest Witness* (#549). This month, Detective Tony Gallagher gets his very own *Secret Admirer* (#553) for Valentine's Day. Cupid is also hard at work in B.J. Daniels's *Love at First Sight* (#555), in which a sexy police officer has to pose as the husband of the only witness to a murder in order to protect her. Except he keeps forgetting their marriage is supposed to be a façade.

Caroline Burnes takes a break from her FEAR FAMILIAR series to bring you *Texas Midnight* (#554). Simmering passion and a remote location make for an explosive read from this bestselling author. But Familiar, the crime-solving black cat, will be back at Harlequin Intrigue soon in his *thirteenth* novel! Watch for *Familiar Obsession* (#570) in stores this June.

Finally, Rita Herron contributes to the ongoing Harlequin Intrigue amnesia promotion A MEMORY AWAY... with *Forgotten Lullaby* (#556). In this highly emotional story, not only do a man and woman commit their love to one another once, but they also overcome the odds to fall in love all over again.

Intense drama and powerful romance make for an extraspecial selection of titles this February. Enjoy!

Sincerely,

Denise O'Sullivan
Associate Senior Editor
Harlequin Intrigue

Secret Admirer
Amanda Stevens

HARLEQUIN®

TORONTO · NEW YORK · LONDON
AMSTERDAM · PARIS · SYDNEY · HAMBURG
STOCKHOLM · ATHENS · TOKYO · MILAN · MADRID
PRAGUE · WARSAW · BUDAPEST · AUCKLAND

ISBN 0-373-22553-9

SECRET ADMIRER

ABOUT THE AUTHOR

Amanda Stevens has written over twenty novels of romantic suspense. Her books have appeared on several bestseller lists, and she has won Reviewer's Choice and Career Achievement in Romantic/Mystery awards from *Romantic Times Magazine*. She resides in Cypress, Texas, with her husband, her son and daughter, and their two cats.

Books by Amanda Stevens

HARLEQUIN INTRIGUE
373—STRANGER IN PARADISE
388—A BABY'S CRY
397—A MAN OF SECRETS
430—THE SECOND MRS. MALONE
453—THE HERO'S SON*
458—THE BROTHER'S WIFE*
462—THE LONG-LOST HEIR*
489—SOMEBODY'S BABY
511—LOVER, STRANGER
549—THE LITTLEST WITNESS**
553—SECRET ADMIRER**

*The Kingsley Baby
**Gallagher Justice

HARLEQUIN BOOKS
2-in-1 Harlequin 50th Anniversary Collection
HER SECRET PAST

Don't miss any of our special offers. Write to us at the following address for information on our newest releases.

Harlequin Reader Service
U.S.: 3010 Walden Ave., P.O. Box 1325, Buffalo, NY 14269
Canadian: P.O. Box 609, Fort Erie, Ont. L2A 5X3

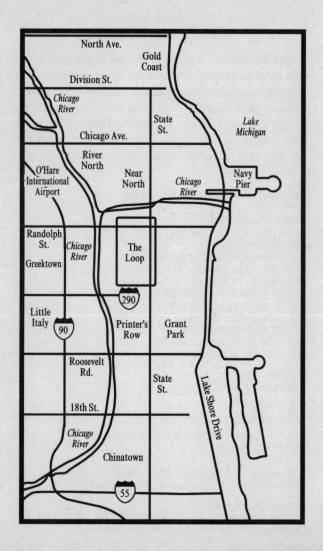

CAST OF CHARACTERS

Eve Barrett—She's been sent undercover to investigate a cop she was once in love with.

Detective Tony Gallagher—A rash of murders leads straight to his past.

David MacKenzie—Tony's attorney and best friend.

Vic D'Angelo—A cop with a grudge.

Clare Foxx—She was once Tony's partner; now she's his commanding officer. But is she also a woman scorned?

Ed Dawson—There's no room in the superintendent's squeaky-clean police force for a rogue cop like Tony.

Maria Mancini—She vowed revenge against Tony for shooting her son.

Fiona Gallagher—Tony's sister knows what's best for him.

Fisher—An informant who makes Tony nervous.

Chapter One

"Murderer!" the woman screamed at Tony Gallagher. "Look at him, you people! Take a good, long look! Ever stare into the eyes of a killer?"

In her mid-forties, with long black hair flapping about her face and shoulders and gold bangles dangling from both wrists as she gestured wildly, the distraught woman reminded Tony of a gypsy. He suspected she could be just as beguiling. Her shrieks attracted more than a fair amount of attention from people passing by on the street.

Traffic was heavy for early afternoon, and the skyscrapers lining State Street trapped exhaust fumes in the manmade canyons, adding to the thick, charged atmosphere outside Police Headquarters in Chicago.

Pointing a finger at Tony, the woman yelled to anyone who would listen, "See that man? That *cop!* He killed my baby! My Franco! Shot him in cold blood!"

Tony fished in his pocket for his sunglasses. All things considered, he would rather have been sailing on Lake Michigan this June afternoon, or stretched out on a beach somewhere. Facing a review board—and then a crazy woman—was not his idea of a great time, but he supposed the spectacle she created provided a certain amount of entertainment to some of the onlookers.

Flanked on one side by his best friend and attorney, David MacKenzie, and on the other side by his sister, Fiona, Tony started down the steps. The wind off the lake whipped Fiona's red hair into a frenzy. She peeled the fiery strands from her face as she matched her steps to Tony's and David's. Shifting her briefcase to her other hand, she squeezed Tony's arm encouragingly.

"Don't let her get to you," she murmured.

"We should have gone out the other way," David said tightly.

"Why?" Tony demanded. He yanked at his tie, letting it drape around his neck like an untied noose. "I don't have anything to hide. I was cleared in there, remember?"

"By the review board," David said. "Not by public opinion."

"Franco Mancini wounded two officers, one of them now permanently disabled. What was I supposed to do? Let him shoot me, too?"

David sighed, slipping on his own sunglasses—expensive ones, to complement his Italian-cut suit and gold watch. "No, of course not. You did the right thing. But with your record…" His words trailed off as they reached the bottom of the steps.

The woman suddenly lunged forward, and David slung up his briefcase to shield her from Tony. Two uniforms came rushing over to restrain her, but they couldn't shut her up.

"You'll pay for what you did to my Franco! So help me, you will!"

A murmur rippled through the crowd on the street, and Tony shuddered inwardly. This wasn't the first time Maria Mancini had accosted him. Her son had been fatally wounded a few weeks ago in a shootout after a robbery attempt had gone bad. Tony had been off duty and had just happened by the convenience store when the shooting erupted. Not taking the time to call for backup, he'd drawn the gunman's fire while one of the wounded officers pulled the other to safety. Then Tony had taken out the shooter.

Franco Mancini had been transported to the same trauma unit at University Hospital as the two fallen officers, but by the time Franco's mother had arrived, it was too late. He'd died in surgery.

Somehow Maria had found out that Tony was the one who had shot her son. She'd come at him in the hospital like a dark-haired wraith, and it had taken *four* cops that night to pull her off.

Tony winced, remembering the sting of her scarlet nails on his face. The bite of her words. The fierceness of her anger and grief, which hadn't abated during the three weeks he'd been suspended pending an investigation by the Internal Affairs Division.

Fiona's grip tightened on his arm as they headed down the street toward her car. The sun reflected blindingly off a nearby office building. "You did do the right thing that night, Tony. You saved those officers' lives. Ask their wives and kids if *they* think you're a murderer."

Fiona always wanted to put things right. She hated unfairness of any kind, but now that she was a practicing attorney, she was likely to get a dose of real life. Tony knew better than anyone how rampant injustice was in this world. Why else had Ashley died so young?

He frowned, not wanting to think about Ashley at all, but lately he couldn't seem to help it. The anniversary of her murder was coming up, and that date always brought out the worst in him.

It was hitting him even harder this year, probably because the suspension had given him too much time for brooding. He'd been drinking too much, hadn't been sleeping. Hell, he thought, catching a glimpse of his reflection in the car window, no wonder the people on the street had bought Maria Mancini's accusations.

David went around and opened the door for Fiona, then rested his arm on the top of her new Audi. "Why don't I meet you two at Nellie's? We can have a beer to celebrate."

Tony shrugged. "I'm back on active duty, remember? Gotta go check in."

"So how's the new lieutenant working out?"

Another sore subject. Rather than going to bat for him with IAD, Clare Foxx had rolled over, agreeing to Tony's suspension without so much as a lifted eyebrow.

"Think of it as a paid vacation," she'd told him, but they both knew what a suspension, whether warranted or not, could do to a cop's reputation. What little reputation Tony had left.

He suspected the sadistic part of Clare had enjoyed watching him being raked over the coals in the media, and he couldn't help wondering what new torture she had in mind for him today.

There'd been a time when Tony had felt closer to Clare Foxx than anyone alive. She'd been his first partner after he'd made detective, and for a while, he'd thought she might actually be able to help him exorcise the ghosts that had haunted him since Ashley's death.

But their relationship—both professional and otherwise—had ended badly. While time and promotions had passed Tony over, Clare had learned to play the game extremely well. She'd caught herself an angel somewhere along the way, and now she was his superior—literally had control over his destiny. A position she relished, Tony figured.

If there was ever a reason for not sleeping with your partner, he thought dryly, Clare Foxx was it.

"I HEARD THE NEWS," Clare said a little while later, as Tony sat in her office at district headquarters. "Congratulations."

She was dressed in a black suit with a trim jacket and above-the-knee skirt. As she came around the desk and perched on the edge, Tony caught a flash of thigh.

Damn, he thought, staring in spite of himself. Clare had been working out. Nearly ten years older than Tony, she'd held her age well at forty-one. Hell, she looked good for any age, and she damn well knew it, too.

Smiling, she tucked a wisp of long dark hair behind her ear, revealing a tiny diamond stud in her lobe. She wore a gold chain around her throat, and she played with the necklace as she talked, twisting it around her fingers.

She was a beautiful woman, but her eyes gave away her age and occupation. Dark, piercing, they were a little too hard and cynical, with deep crinkles at the corners that weren't from laughing.

Clare was a good cop, had been a good partner until she and Tony had gone and made it personal. Until it went bad. Then she'd become like every other woman he'd ever known. She'd wanted a piece of him he wasn't willing to give. Not anymore. Not since Ashley—

"So," Clare said, giving him a slow once-over, "now that the review board has exonerated you, what does Dr. Metzer say? You ready for active duty?"

No matter what the rank, it was routine procedure for a cop who had been involved in a shooting to be checked out by a staff psychologist. "Sure. My head's screwed back on straight. For the time being," he couldn't resist adding.

Clare glanced at him sharply. "That's what I'm afraid

of. You've been skirting the edge for so long, one of these days you're going to go native on us. Even Dr. Metzer won't be able to bring you back.''

''Don't sell Metzer short. Look what he did for you.''

Her cheeks colored, not from embarrassment but from anger. ''I don't have to take that from you, Tony. I'm your commanding officer, in case you've forgotten.''

''Not likely to forget that,'' he muttered. ''So what have you got for me?'' Might as well plunge right back in, get his feet wet his first day back.

''It's not going to be as easy as all that,'' she said, heading back around her desk to sit. She picked up a report and studied it for a long, tense moment. Her glasses were lying on the desk but she ignored them. ''Things are going to change around here, Tony.''

He stretched his legs in front of him. ''Meaning?''

''Just because we were…partners in the past doesn't mean you're going to get a free ride.''

''I never thought I would.'' He met her gaze.

She seemed momentarily flustered. Glancing back down at the report, she said, ''Superintendent Dawson is putting pressure on all the bureaus to clean up their acts, but especially on Investigative Services. No more tune-ups, attitude adjustments, whatever euphemism you guys are calling it on the street these days.''

''You know me better. I've never gone in for that.'' Although he wouldn't be human if he hadn't been tempted a time or two to work over a suspect, especially the ones who murdered children. He remembered the Betts case—then again, he didn't want to remember the Betts case. He'd been the one to find the child's body in the Dumpster behind an abandoned apartment building in Chinatown. The little girl's battered face and staring eyes had haunted him for months, years. But the smirk on her old man's face when Tony had gone to search his apartment had haunted him even longer.

Yeah, he could easily have done a little attitude adjustment on that psycho, but he hadn't. He might not always play by the rules, but he knew the dangers in losing control. If he ever came that close again that would be the day he'd hang it up. Walk away. Spend the rest of his life scrubbing toilets or some damn thing if he had to.

Clare's gaze softened, as if she'd decided to cut him some slack. Or maybe she was remembering little Julie Betts, too. Clare had been the one to pull Tony away from Robert Betts when they'd gone to make the arrest.

"I know you don't go that far—not even close—but you are something of a Dirty Harry, Tony, you can't deny that. You should have called for backup the other night, and you know it."

"I was more concerned with saving two lives. Three, if I could have." He hadn't wanted Franco Mancini to die. Tony had tried to persuade the man to throw down his weapon and surrender, but Franco, eyes glazed from whatever drug he'd been popping or snorting, had just kept on shooting.

Tony rubbed his forehead, where a migraine was starting to throb. The light in Clare's office was suddenly almost blinding.

"Hey, you okay?"

"Yeah, I'm fine," he said. "Let's just get this over with."

Clare frowned, and the compassion she might have felt moments earlier vanished. She said coldly, "You've got a woman threatening you because of your actions that night."

He shrugged. It wasn't the first time, and he doubted it would be the last. Still, if he were honest with himself, he'd have to admit he wasn't exactly comfortable with Maria

Mancini's vendetta against him. The woman looked pretty edgy herself.

"One of these days," Clare warned with a hint of maliciousness, "someone is going to make good on their threats against you."

He wondered if she was talking about Maria Mancini or herself. If memory served, Clare had made a few ugly promises of her own the night Tony had split. The scene had been nasty and brutal, not something he wanted to replay even in his head.

As if she were recalling that night herself, she lifted her chin, glaring at him. "You've pretty much been allowed to go your own way around here because, frankly, none of the other detectives want to be assigned with you. But like I said, things are changing. As of today, you've got yourself a new partner."

Alarmed, Tony straightened in his chair. "I thought we had an agreement. I work best alone."

She smiled. "That agreement was with your old lieutenant. Any promises you and I made to each other have long since become null and void. Isn't that right?"

Her tone and her gaze challenged him, and Tony said, "You're getting off on this, aren't you? You like making me suffer."

"You're such an easy target. You and all your pent-up angst."

He groaned. "Spare me Metzer's psychobabble. Who are you putting me with? Davis? Sanchez?" He'd give either of them a week at the most.

"She's new. Transferred from the North Side a couple of weeks ago."

She? Oh, hell... "The North Side? That's your old stomping ground, isn't it? You two pals or something?"

Clare hesitated. "I may have seen her around a few times. She worked vice."

"What happened? She get tired of wearing spike heels and leather hot pants?"

"It wore a little thin after a while," a soft voice said from the doorway behind him. "I didn't mind it on Saturday nights, but every night of the week got to be a real drag. Maybe you should try it sometime."

Tony glanced around as his new partner walked into the office. Clare gave him a derisive smile. "Tony, I'd like you to meet Eve Barrett. *Detective* Eve Barrett. I'm sure Detective Gallagher's reputation precedes him," she said dryly.

Eve held out her hand, and Tony grudgingly stood. "You don't have to do that," she said quickly. "Stand, I mean."

"So it's that way, is it?" he muttered, almost under his breath.

She shrugged. "I don't want to have to stand every time *you* come into a room."

He gave Clare a withering look, as if to say what the hell did I do to deserve this?

"Not that I don't appreciate the thought," Eve continued. "But we're going to be working together as equals. I'd like for you to treat me as you would any other partner."

He could almost see Clare smirking, but Tony wouldn't give her the satisfaction of glancing her way. "I'll see what I can do," he said, checking Eve Barrett out in spite of himself. She wore a conservative business suit, not unlike Clare's, but the skirt was just a little shorter, showing legs that were a little younger and firmer but, to Tony's mind, no more shapely. They both had great legs. Hell, he'd hit the leg jackpot in here, he thought with perverse appreciation.

Eve Barrett was thin, toned, an all-American girl with her shiny, shoulder-length brown hair and scrubbed complexion. In spite of the shield she wore clipped to the waistband of her skirt, and the faint bulge where her shoulder holster rested beneath her jacket, she looked all of twenty years old. Tony wondered how she'd ever ended up in vice. He couldn't imagine anyone looking less like a hooker.

Except, of course, for those legs…

He had a sudden vision of her in the aforementioned hot pants and spike heels, and something unwelcome stirred inside him.

As if she were reading his mind, her hazel eyes narrowed on him. "You don't have a problem working with a female partner, do you, Detective?"

He shrugged. "No. I just don't want a partner period."

Something flashed in her eyes. Anger, he hoped, but it sure as hell looked like hurt. Jeez…

She gave him a cool smile. "Well, we don't always get what we want, do we…Tony?"

The way she said his name…her voice…

For a moment, recognition teased at the fringes of his mind. Had they met before? She looked a little familiar, but surely he would have remembered that body. Those incredible legs.

"Why don't you wait outside, Eve? I'd like to have a word with Tony before you two hook up."

"Sure."

Eve gave Tony a tentative smile before she turned and left the room. He wasn't sure, but he thought he caught a whiff of her perfume as she walked by him. The fragrance was light, flowery—not at all like the heavy musk Clare had always been partial to. The floral scent was more like the perfume Ashley had worn.

Ashley…

Yes, something about Eve Barrett reminded him of Ashley, but he couldn't say what, exactly. It wasn't their looks. Ashley had been tall, willowy, blond. Drop-dead gorgeous. Eve was shorter, thin but more athletic looking. Attractive but not beautiful. Not even close.

Still, there was something about her that had momentarily taken Tony's mind off his headache. Looking back at Clare, however, the pain hit him right between the eyes.

She gave him a slow smile. "So, what do you think? Can you work with her without driving her crazy?"

Was that really what Clare wanted to know? "I'd say she has potential."

The smile disappeared from Clare's red lips. "Consider this a trial. A probation of sorts. If you screw up…"

His brows rose. "Yeah?"

"Not even the Gallagher name will save you this time."

Had it ever? Both his brothers were cops, just as his father had been before he'd disappeared almost eight years ago while investigating Ashley's murder. Tony's family had a long tradition in Chicago law enforcement, but he wasn't so sure that history had ever helped him out of a jam. In fact, maybe the pressure of trying to live up to the name—and not succeeding—had been his downfall.

Or maybe he was just a screwup, Tony conceded with an inward shrug. The black sheep of the family. At least Fiona still had hope for him.

"So how old is she, anyway?" Tony nodded toward the door. "She looks like a kid. How long was she in vice?"

"A while," Clare said evasively. "She graduated from the academy a year after you did. Top of her class, I might add. You didn't graduate top of your class, did you, Tony?"

No, but damn close. Clare might be surprised. Then again, he doubted there was much about him that would surprise her. She'd once made it her business to find out everything she could about him—and now he knew why.

Payback was hell.

"She's a good detective, so cut her some slack, will you? None of your usual male chauvinist bull."

"How many times do I have to tell you—I don't have a chauvinistic bone in my body. I just don't have much use for people in general."

"Except when it suits your purposes." Clare gave him an enigmatic glance. "One of these days you're going to fall and fall hard, Tony. I just hope I'm lucky enough to be around to stomp on the pieces."

EVE WAS AT HER DESK in the cubicle she would be sharing with Tony when she saw him come out of Clare's office. He looked thinner than she remembered, but then, the last time she'd seen him had been, what? Nearly eight years ago?

At Ashley's funeral.

He'd been so torn up with grief that day he hadn't even noticed Eve. But then, he never had.

Well, no, that wasn't exactly true. He'd noticed her before Ashley had come into their lives. They'd even shared a mild summer flirtation the year before Tony graduated from high school. But then Ashley had moved into the neighborhood and there'd been no room in his life for anyone else.

He'd been completely consumed by Ashley Dallas—and why not? She was everything a man could want in a woman. Beautiful, blond, smart. She was even *nice,* for God's sake. Eve hadn't been able to hate her, although there had been times when she'd wanted to. But Ashley had been flawless in every way. The quintessential woman. Eve hadn't been able to compete with such perfection, and she suspected Ashley's memory would be even more daunting.

The fact that Tony hadn't even remembered her told Eve how truly pointless such a competition would be.

Their two desks were shoved up against each other, and when Tony sat down, he and Eve were face-to-face. He gazed at her across the expanse. "Look. What I said in there—it's nothing personal. I just like working alone, that's all."

"I understand. Some people are like that. I've worked alone before, too," she told him.

"Yeah? How'd you like it?"

She shrugged. "I guess I'm more of a people person. I like working with a partner."

"That's fine." He stood, placing his hands on his desk and leaning slightly toward her. "So long as we understand each other. You stay out of my business, and I'll stay out of yours. None of that bonding crap—"

"I get the message," she interrupted. "Loud and clear. If I want someone to watch my back, I shouldn't count on you. Right, Tony?"

He frowned. "I didn't mean—"

"Then what did you mean?" She got up and stood facing him. "If you can't trust your partner not to bail on you, you're as good as dead out there. If that's the way it's going to be, let's get it straight right here and now."

Jeez, Tony thought. She was a lot tougher than she looked. Still, she was right. They might as well get a few things straight right from the start, even though he didn't expect her to last.

"I've never bailed on a partner. You can ask any of the detectives in this division if they'd worry about me covering their backs. You'd get the same answer from all of them. They may not like me. They may not want to have to deal with me and my bullsh—my *ways*," he amended with a begrudging shrug. "But they know, to a man—and woman—they can count on me when the going gets tough. And it will," he added ominously.

She smiled faintly. "I'm hardly a rookie, you know. I've been on the force almost as long as you have."

"How do you know how long I've been on the force?"

"Like the lieutenant said, your reputation precedes you."

He studied her for a moment, his gaze hooded and steely. She'd forgotten how blue his eyes were. Blue and almost breathtakingly intense.

Awareness tingled down her backbone. They'd been kids the last time he'd looked at her so intently, just before he'd kissed her. She'd been sixteen that summer and had never been kissed the way Tony Gallagher had kissed her, his mouth fusing to hers, his tongue entwining with hers.

Eve's mother had died when she was thirteen, and her father, an insurance adjuster, had become overprotective, resisting the reality of his little girl growing up before his eyes. She hadn't been allowed to date, but that hadn't stopped Tony. He'd come over before her father got home from work, and they'd sit on the stoop together. Sometimes they'd even go inside.

How easily he'd forgotten her, Eve thought with a measure of regret, when all these years she'd thought about him a lot. He'd been her first infatuation, and she hadn't gotten over him for a very long time.

"I'll cover your back," he said, still gazing at her across their desks. "You don't have to worry about that. But my personal life is off-limits. Do we understand each other?"

"Yes, I believe we do," Eve said, hoping her voice didn't reveal the regret she felt.

"COME ON IN, Eve, and close the door."

Eve did as she was told, then took a seat across from the

lieutenant's desk. Clare Foxx was a very attractive woman, dark, sultry looking, with the kind of body even a much younger woman would envy. She was cool and professional, qualities Eve had always admired, but there was something about Clare that was almost formidable. Perhaps it was because she had been instrumental in Eve's new assignment and was one of the few people who knew the real reason she had been sent here.

Clare sat back in her chair and studied Eve for a long, silent moment. Not since Eve had been summoned before the nuns at St. Anne's had she felt such a need to squirm.

You're a grown woman, she admonished herself. *Thirty years old and a police officer. So act like one.*

She squared her shoulders with an effort, meeting Clare's gaze. "You wanted to see me?"

Clare nodded. "How did it go out there?"

"You mean with Tony...Detective Gallagher?" Eve shrugged. "Too early to tell. He's...a bit hostile, isn't he?"

Clare gave a short laugh. "You might say that." She sat forward suddenly, folding her arms on her desk as she leaned toward Eve. "You've seen his disciplinary record. He's had his share of rips, both civilian and departmental, not the least of which was that assault charge four years ago. And now this latest incident..."

"He was exonerated each time," Eve said, maybe a shade too quickly.

Clare frowned. "Still, the media doesn't print the exoneration, only the charges. Cops like Tony make the whole department look bad."

"An active cop gets complaints," Eve argued, even though she knew Clare had a point.

Clare gave her an annoyed glance. "You sound as if

you're defending his behavior. That's not why you were brought in.''

''I was brought in to observe and evaluate. I can't do that unless I keep an open mind. I'll tell you exactly what I told my own commanding officer. I'm not going to rail-road Tony Gallagher. If that's what you want, then I may as well walk out that door right now.''

Anger flashed in Clare's eyes, but her voice was sur-prisingly obliging. ''Point taken,'' she said tightly, then added, ''You don't have qualms about this assignment, do you? It could get a little sticky, if you aren't careful.''

''I plan to be careful,'' Eve said. ''And, no, I don't have any qualms. I know what has to be done.''

Clare nodded in approval. ''A word of caution, how-ever.'' She got up and came around to lean against the desk, gripping the edge with her fingers. ''Don't let your hor-mones get in the way of doing your job.''

Eve was taken aback. ''I beg your pardon?''

''I'm talking about the effect Tony Gallagher has on women. He can be obnoxious, opinionated, frustrating as hell to deal with. But he can also get under your skin in a big way. When that happens, it's damn near impossible to get him out.'' Her gaze was very direct, knowing, and Eve stared at her in shock.

So she and Clare Foxx had something in common, after all. It wasn't a notion that gave Eve any comfort.

''I appreciate the advice,'' she murmured. ''Is that all, Lieutenant?''

''For now.'' Clare waited until Eve had gotten to the door, then she added, ''Tony Gallagher is a disaster waiting to happen. That's why you're here, Barrett. To make sure it *doesn't* happen.''

''I'll do my best.'' But when Eve opened the door and

stepped into the hall, she saw almost at once that their cubicle was empty.

Sometime after she'd been summoned into Clare Foxx's office, Tony Gallagher had decided to bail on her, after all.

Chapter Two

The second watch had already come on duty by the time Eve packed up her briefcase and purse and got ready to leave. Tony hadn't come back to the station all afternoon, nor had he called in. Eve had no idea where he'd gone off to, but she wasn't so dense that she couldn't take a hint. He was avoiding her.

She drew a long breath, wondering again if she'd made the right decision in accepting this assignment. Not that she'd had much choice. When the request came down from the superintendent himself, you didn't exactly refuse.

Still, if the brass had known about her past with Tony, would their enthusiasm for giving her this assignment have waned? Eve had considered telling them, but then figured it wouldn't have made a difference, anyway. They knew she came from the same neighborhood, knew she and Tony had attended the same school. Their paths were bound to have crossed at some point, but as Eve's commanding officer had pointed out, that made her an ideal candidate for the job. She could, in ways that counted, speak Tony Gallagher's language. An acquaintance from the old neighborhood had a better shot at gaining his trust than a total stranger.

Of course, that theory had been blown all to hell, since

Tony didn't even remember her. Now Eve was glad she hadn't told anyone about her crush on the neighborhood hunk, the few passionate kisses the two of them had sneaked behind her father's back. How humiliating to have tried to make something out of what had turned out to be a big nothing.

"Hey, Barrett," a masculine voice said from the doorway of her office. "Ready to hang it up?"

Eve glanced up, grimacing inwardly at the man who stood watching her. Vic D'Angelo was the stereotypical homicide detective—tall, good-looking and more than a little arrogant. He was tanned, toned and expensively coiffed, but his taste in clothing appeared heavily influenced by the years he'd spent watching reruns of *Miami Vice*.

In the two weeks Eve had been there, she'd learned to avoid D'Angelo whenever possible, just as she'd learned, in the two or three conversations they'd had, how much he despised Tony. "Cowboy," he called him disparagingly.

"I was just about to take off," Eve told him. She hooked the strap of her purse over her shoulder and came around the desk. D'Angelo made no move to let her by.

"A few of us are heading over to Durty Nellie's for a couple of beers. Care to join us?"

He'd been trying for days to get Eve to have dinner or drinks with him. Of course, what he really wanted was a roll in the hay. Eve knew his type all too well, and what was worse, she suspected he was of the kiss-and-tell variety. He wouldn't be able to resist boasting about his latest conquest, but it made no difference to Eve. She had no intention of going out with him, let alone sleeping with him.

As if reading her mind, he shrugged, his hand sweeping down his silk tie. "Suit yourself. It's no skin off my teeth one way or another. But your new partner's apt to be there.

Might give you two a chance to connect, although, I have to tell you, Cowboy's not exactly the friendly type. If you want to really connect…'' His oily smile reminded Eve of a street pimp she'd arrested once while working vice.

She spared him a withering glance. "However charming your offer, I'm afraid I'll have to decline."

"Ah, come on, Barrett. Just a couple of beers at Nellie's. Give you a chance to get to know some of the other guys around here, too. Who knows? You might even get to like us."

Eve hated to admit it, but he had a point. She wasn't sure how long she'd be at this station, and the more she was accepted, the better she'd blend in. Being Tony Gallagher's partner was already making things difficult for her. He was something of a pariah, though she suspected the image was one he cultivated more than he tried to live down.

"All right," she said. "I'll meet you there."

D'Angelo's grin was so insolent, Eve almost backed out. "Since you don't know where the place is, how about we ride together?" he suggested.

"Then I'd have to come back here and get my car."

"Not necessarily. You could pick it up in the morning." He let his gaze travel leisurely over her body, lingering on her legs as he released a long, appreciative breath.

When he finally glanced up, Eve gave him a cold glare. "You through?"

"You're not as tough as you try to let on, Barrett."

He stepped back to let her through the door. When Eve walked by him, his hand very deliberately grazed her derriere. She grabbed his fingers, bending the middle one back almost to his wrist, then releasing it so quickly he wouldn't have known what had happened except for the excruciating pain. His eyebrows shot skyward.

"Goddammit!" he roared, his eyes blazing with fury. "Why, you little—"

"Careful," she warned. "Next time it might be another appendage I feel like bending."

He muttered another oath, but kept his distance as the two of them walked through the noisy confusion of the squad room.

DURTY NELLIE'S WAS a typical Irish pub that had become a regular hangout several years ago for cops who worked the South Side. Although it was located near the neighborhood where Eve had grown up, she'd never been inside.

She found a parking space near the garbage bins in the back, then hurried around to the front door before D'Angelo arrived in his flashy gold 'Vette. He was the type of guy who would circle the block several times until he found just the right space, so Eve figured she had a few minutes.

The decor inside was primarily green with wood trim, and cut glass that sparkled in the subdued lighting. There was a pool table in the back, along with a dartboard that was seeing some serious action.

The patrons—mostly cops and mostly guys—sat drinking at the long, polished bar or hunched over rickety tables shoved together to make the most of the cramped space. Neon signs over the bar advertised Guinness, Bushnell's and Bailey's Irish Cream, while overhead speakers blasted an old U2 song, one of Eve's favorites.

Heads turned when she walked in, and eyes—appreciative and curious—took her measure. Most of the customers went right back to their drinking. Eve was still wearing her shield, although she'd locked her gun in her trunk. Even the ones who had never seen her before knew she was one of them and therefore commanded, even as a woman, a modicum of respect.

She spotted Tony standing at the end of the bar, leaning over a beer and a shot glass as another man stood talking to him. When the man turned toward the bar, lifting his mug, Eve caught a glimpse of his profile. She couldn't be sure, but she thought he might be Tony's brother. Nick was a couple of years older than Tony. Eve hadn't known him very well, but she remembered that of all the Gallaghers, his hair had been the blackest, his eyes the darkest blue. And his temper, even back then, had been legendary.

Taking a deep breath, Eve walked over to them. "Hi," she said over the music. "Mind if I join you?"

Both men turned at her voice. Tony barely slanted her a glance before tossing back his drink. Nick leaned his elbow against the bar, giving her a slow examination. She wondered why his scrutiny didn't offend her the way Vic D'Angelo's had.

Extending her hand, she said, "I'm Tony's new partner. Eve—"

Nick Gallagher cut her off. "Barrett, right? From the neighborhood."

Eve's mouth dropped. "You remember me?"

"Sure I remember you. You were, what? Fifteen, sixteen last time I saw you?"

Actually, Eve had been twenty, almost twenty-one, when she'd seen both Nick and Tony at Ashley's funeral. But neither one of them had noticed her that day. She'd stayed at the back of the chapel during the service and hadn't approached the family at the cemetery. Tony's grief had been too much for her to bear. She'd slipped away quietly to grieve in her own way for what might have been.

Nick smiled down at her, a slow, sexy curving of his lips that might have sent Eve's pulse racing into the stratosphere

f Tony hadn't been standing nearby. The Gallagher broth-
rs were both sexy as hell, but Tony was...

Tony.

Both sets of blue eyes were on her now, and Eve felt her
color heighten. Their perusal was very unnerving, especially the way Tony was almost glaring at her. He cocked
is head, regarding her in a manner Eve couldn't decipher.

Finally he said, "*Evie?* Hell, it *is* you."

His voice held a note of incredulity, and Eve managed
o shrug. "I wondered when you'd get around to recogniz-
ng me."

"Why didn't you tell me who you were?" he demanded.

"Wait a minute," Nick said. "You mean to tell me Eve
s your new partner, and you didn't even recognize her?
For God's sake, Tony, are you blind?"

"Well, she has changed," Tony retorted, letting his gaze
lip almost sheepishly over her features. "And it has been
awhile."

Eve smiled. "I don't wear glasses anymore, and the
praces are gone. Plus I've put on a few pounds." She gave
a fatalistic shrug.

"Yes, you have," Nick agreed. "And in all the right
places, from what I can see. You used to be almost
scrawny, as I recall. And where did all your freckles go?"

"Oh, they're still there, unfortunately. You just have to
look closely."

"Where? I don't see even one." Nick straightened from
the bar and moved toward Eve, staring down into her face
as if searching for her freckles took all of his investigative
know-how.

Behind him, Tony muttered, "Oh, please—"

Nick gave him a sharp glance. "Am I cramping your
style, Tony? Just say so, if I am."

"You always do," Tony muttered, motioning for the bartender. "But when has that ever stopped you before?"

Nick gave Eve a conspiratorial wink, then bent and brushed his lips against hers. "Nice seeing you again, Eve. And my condolences, by the way, for having to work with this punk."

Caught off guard by the kiss, Eve stared after Nick for a moment before turning to meet Tony's blue gaze. He didn't look the least bit jealous, she noticed with a flicker of disappointment. Just faintly amused. "Watch out for him," he advised.

"You're warning me away from your own brother?"

"Damn right." The bartender appeared, and Tony said, "Another boilermaker, Curly."

The man didn't have a single hair on his head. He glanced at Eve curiously. "Haven't seen you in here before."

"My first time," she admitted.

"We'll try to be gentle. What'll you have?"

"How about a Guinness?"

"Good choice."

Curly disappeared to get their drinks, and Eve perched on a bar stool. "I hope you don't mind if I join you," she said, knowing it was too late if he did.

Tony shrugged. "I guess you'd better. This crowd's starting to look pretty hungry."

She knew he was referring to the glances she'd gotten earlier, but she laughed it off. "I take it you don't get many women in here."

"Oh, we get enough. We just don't get many who look like you."

Eve's stomach fluttered at his words. She wondered if he was flirting with her or if he was actually paying her a compliment. She was confident enough to appreciate her own attractiveness, but she was also a realist. She was attractive, but not beautiful. She had neither the face nor the figure to stop traffic—not like Ashley.

The bartender set their drinks before them, and after he left, Tony leaned toward her. "Why didn't you tell me who you were in Clare's office?"

"I thought it would come to you. When it didn't..." Eve shrugged again. "It was a little embarrassing. No one likes to be forgotten."

Tony's gaze drifted over her face, stopping for one infinitesimal moment on her lips. Was he remembering that he'd given her her first kiss?

She'd been such an innocent. So naive and so impressionable. Tony had been the exact opposite. Wild, reckless, the neighborhood bad boy. But he could pour on the charm when he wanted to. Eve, fresh out of braces and glasses, didn't stand a chance.

"You were always so quiet," he said. "Always real shy, the best I remember. What made you decide to become a cop?"

She hesitated, not sure how to answer without giving too much of herself away. "In a way, I guess you're the reason. You and your family," she added quickly. "I don't know if you remember or not, but my mother died when I was thirteen. Her death hit my father really hard. He's never been particularly outgoing, so he didn't have many friends and no family to lean on except me."

She paused, taking a sip of her Guinness. "Your dad started dropping by sometimes on his way home from work. They'd sit out on the front stoop, and Detective Gallagher would talk to my father about his investigations, what was going on at the station. Just small talk, but it meant the world to my father. To both of us. Detective

Gallagher made a very big impression on me. He was a really nice man.''

A shadow flickered in Tony's eyes before he turned back to his drink. ''Yeah, he was.''

''I'm sorry for what happened to him. Your family must have been devastated.''

Tony shrugged, but a pall had suddenly been cast over the evening. Eve had just been starting her senior year in college when she'd heard about Sean Gallagher's disappearance. Coming as it had just weeks after Ashley Dallas's murder, the news had been an even more stunning blow.

Eve didn't have to struggle to recall the details. Even though she'd attended school out of state, she'd kept up with the case from the moment she'd heard of Ashley's death. Ashley and Tony had attended an end-of-the-year party at college, along with some of their friends. For some reason, Ashley had ended up leaving the party alone, and her beaten and stabbed body had been discovered early the next morning.

The murder weapon, a switchblade, had been traced back to a man named Daniel O'Roarke. He had attended the party, also, and witnesses described an altercation he'd had with Tony. The two of them had never gotten along, primarily because their families had been sworn enemies for over seventy years.

Eve hadn't known about any of that until it had all come out at Daniel's trial. By that time, Sean Gallagher, who had been the lead investigator on the case, had disappeared without a trace. The consensus at the time was that Daniel, or someone in the O'Roarke family, had murdered Sean and disposed of his body, either to keep further evidence from coming to light against Daniel, or for revenge.

Eve couldn't imagine what it had been like for the Gallaghers over the years. The not knowing had to be agonizing, she thought, watching Tony.

His gaze was downcast. He stared into his drink with a brooding frown, and Eve wondered if he was thinking about his father, or Ashley, or both. Her murder and Sean's disappearance were inseparable, and Eve felt regret prickle through her. She wished she'd never mentioned Tony's father. Because her words had reanimated Ashley's ghost.

A hand fell on her shoulder, and Eve started. She saw Vic D'Angelo's reflection in the mirror over the bar, and reluctantly she rotated her stool to face him.

"You wouldn't be trying to horn in on my date, would you, Gallagher?"

Tony glanced up. "You wouldn't be trying to hit on my partner, would you, Vic?"

"So what if I am?"

"I might not like it, that's all." Tony shrugged, but there was no mistaking the warning in his voice.

D'Angelo turned back to Eve, draping a casual arm over her shoulders. "How about we find us a table?" he said against her ear, but loudly enough for Tony to overhear. "Something a little more private."

"Tony and I were in the middle of a discussion," she said.

Tony, still leaning casually on the bar, said, "How about you and I take a little stroll outside, Vic?"

"Tony," Eve said, trying to defuse the situation. "It's okay. I can take care of myself."

"I'm sure you can, but what are partners for?" He met her gaze, his eyes so intensely blue that Eve felt her pulse quicken. It had been a long time since he'd looked at her like that, but she still felt the impact, even after all these years.

D'Angelo said coldly, "Lighten up, Cowboy. Like the lady says, she can take care of herself."

Eve glanced up at him. "And you should know, right, Vic?"

His gaze turned icy. "There's a word for women like you," he growled.

Eve lifted her brows. "Smart? Discriminating?"

Over D'Angelo's shoulder, she saw Tony grin. Their eyes met again in the mirror over the bar, and a thrill went through Eve. They'd shared something just then, she and Tony. Maybe it wasn't exactly bonding, but it was close. And that it had come at Vic D'Angelo's expense was particularly gratifying.

In the mirror, Eve saw Clare Foxx making her way through the crowd toward them. When she approached the bar, D'Angelo moved down to make room for her. "Lieutenant," he said amiably.

"Vic," Clare greeted him.

"Buy you a drink?"

"Boilermaker," she said, glancing at Tony.

Clare had taken off her jacket, and the filmy gray blouse revealed a matching lace camisole underneath. She looked very sexy. Very available. Her cloying perfume was almost an overt invitation, and D'Angelo wasn't about to pass it up. But Eve wasn't at all sure the scent was for D'Angelo's benefit.

When the shot glass and mug came, he handed her the former, saluting her with his own drink. "Here's to fast cars and loose women."

"Here's to men with big…mouths," Clare said, then tipped her head back and killed the whiskey.

D'Angelo handed her the beer chaser. "So what brings you down here, Lieutenant? I wouldn't have thought this dump was exactly your style."

Clare shrugged. "I don't mind slumming once in a while." She winked at Eve. "I just don't like to make a habit of it. Isn't that right, Tony?"

He glanced up. "Sure, Clare. Whatever you say."

Eve got the distinct impression he hadn't been listening to any of their conversation. His mind was a million miles away.

Clare was not a woman who liked to be ignored. She leaned toward Tony, touching a hand to his sleeve. "So how did the call go this afternoon?"

Before he could reply, Eve said quickly, "I told the lieutenant about the call you went out on earlier. The possible homicide down on Burley Street."

His eyes narrowed. He had no idea what she was talking about. "Yeah. Right."

"So how did it go?" Clare pressed. "When am I going to see your report?"

"Damnedest thing," Tony said. "Turned out to be a false alarm."

"A false alarm," Clare said suspiciously.

"Yeah. I'll tell you all about it tomorrow. Right now, though, I need to make a phone call."

Eve saw him move toward the back of the bar, stopping to talk with a man in an expensive-looking suit and a woman with flaming red hair.

Eve recognized the woman immediately. Fiona Gallagher had been several years behind Eve in school, but her distinctive red hair and flamboyant personality had made her well known and liked even in the higher echelons at St. Anne's. Eve had always admired Fiona's easygoing personality.

She excused herself from Clare and D'Angelo, who hardly seemed to notice her departure. They were talking in low tones, and Eve could have sworn she felt something akin to sexual vibrations emanating from the two of them. Had she been wrong about Clare's intentions? Was something going on between her and D'Angelo?

Going into the ladies' room, Eve washed and dried her hands, then ran a comb through her hair and touched up her lipstick. Staring at herself in the mirror, she tried to see what Tony saw when he looked at her. Straight, shoulder-length brown hair, hazel eyes, nice smile thanks to the braces. Nice figure, but nothing extraordinary.

She looked a little uptight, Eve decided, and wished she'd left her jacket in the car. Removing it now would be a little too obvious, so she settled for unbuttoning her beige blouse a couple of notches. Then, feeling ridiculous, she quickly redid the buttons.

The door to the bathroom opened, and Fiona Gallagher walked in. Now here was a woman who knew how to dress, Eve thought enviously, taking in Fiona's slim black pants and white tailored shirt.

Fiona smiled at Eve's reflection. "It's Eve, isn't it? Eve Barrett?"

Eve turned and smiled. "Hi, Fiona. It's been a long time."

"I almost didn't recognize you. You've changed so much."

"You haven't," Eve blurted, then added quickly, "I meant that in a good way."

Fiona laughed good-naturedly. "Even if you didn't, it's true. Not much you can change about this mop and all these freckles. Speaking of which, what happened to yours?"

Eve shrugged. "They've faded somewhat. I don't get out in the sun much these days."

"Whatever you're doing is working," Fiona said graciously. "You look great. No wonder Tony couldn't keep his eyes off you."

"I doubt it's for the reason you think." Eve turned back to the mirror to redo her lipstick even though she'd just applied it. When she couldn't get it quite right, she gave up and dropped the gold tube back into her purse. "He's not exactly wild to have me as a partner."

Fiona sighed. "Don't let him get to you. Sometimes I think he tries to see how far away he can push people, including his own family. It's just a defense mechanism, though. A way to keep from getting hurt again." For a moment, she looked as if she might have said more than she meant to. Then she shrugged. "He's had some tough blows."

Eve said quickly, "I know about Ashley. I remember how close they were."

"It'll soon be eight years since she died. Every year I keep thinking it'll get better for Tony, but when the anniversary rolls around…" Fiona trailed off, then added softly, "Maybe one of these days the right person will come along and make him realize Ashley wasn't the only woman in the world for him. Maybe she wasn't even the right woman."

"Maybe," Eve said doubtfully.

"And maybe I talk too much," Fiona acknowledged ruefully. "So come on." She took Eve's hand. "I'll introduce you to the new man in *my* life. He's pretty yummy, if I do say so myself."

Eve gave her reflection one last glance as Fiona's words echoed inside her head. *Maybe she wasn't even the right woman.*

Right, Eve thought. And the winters in Chicago were always balmy.

TONY SAW FIONA COME OUT of the bathroom with Eve firmly in tow. Eve looked a little disconcerted, as if she didn't quite know what had hit her. But that was Fiona's MO all right. A regular little bulldozer when she had something up her sleeve.

She dragged Eve over to David, who was chalking his pool cue. "David MacKenzie, I'd like you to meet Eve Barrett. Tony's new partner."

David's brows shot up as he glanced from Eve to Tony and then back again. "Nice to meet you, Eve. And my condolences."

"Those were Nick's words exactly," Eve told him.

"Which goes to show how well we both know Tony." David flashed her a charming grin, and Eve could immediately see why Fiona was so taken with him. David MacKenzie was indeed yummy. And he smelled wonderful. Expensive.

"Look, you two let someone else have the pool table, and let's all grab a table," Fiona instructed them. "I'm dying to catch up with Eve."

"Catch up?" David gamely handed his cue to the next person in line.

"We all grew up in the same neighborhood," Fiona explained. "Eve's dad still lives only a few blocks over from Mom and Gram."

Tony didn't say a word until Fiona had laid claim to a table. "I think I left my drink at the bar."

"I'll get a fresh round," David said magnanimously. "What'll you ladies have?"

"Boilermaker." Fiona shot Tony a defiant glance.

"She'll have a beer," Tony said darkly. When his sister started to protest, he snapped, "I'm not carrying you out of here again, Fiona."

Instead of a retort, she actually blushed. "Make it a Guinness," she told David.

He winked at her. "Don't worry. I'd be happy to carry

you out of here. Have a boilermaker if you like. Have two.''

''Are you trying to get her drunk, MacKenzie?'' Tony asked grimly. ''Because if you are—''

Fiona rolled her eyes. ''For God's sake, Tony, lighten up. David's your best friend. If you can't trust him with your sister, who can you trust?''

''Yeah, Tony, if you can't trust me with your sister, who can you trust?'' David taunted with a grin as he turned to get the drinks.

''What the hell are you trying to do?'' Fiona demanded the minute David was out of earshot. ''Scare him off? I finally get him to notice me after all these years, and you pull that overprotective big brother routine on me? Just for that, I *ought* to get hammered,'' she grumbled. ''I ought to get falling down, sloppy, puking drunk so that you have to baby-sit me all night. It'd serve you right.''

Tony gave Eve a long-suffering look. ''See what you got yourself into tonight?''

Eve shrugged. ''Beats staying home.''

''I'm not so sure about that,'' he muttered.

Vic D'Angelo ambled over with two mugs of beer. He sat one before Eve and the other in front of Tony. ''Compliments of the lieutenant.''

Eve glanced toward the bar. ''Where is she?''

''Had to make an early night of it.'' D'Angelo clapped a hand on Tony's shoulder. ''To tell you the truth, this place is not exactly Clare's style these days. She likes a little more class.''

Eve half expected Tony to knock D'Angelo's hand off his shoulder, but instead he picked up the beer, took a long swallow, then wiped his mouth with the back of his hand. He lifted the half-empty mug to D'Angelo. ''Have a drink,

D'Angelo. You don't strike me as the type of guy who minds leftovers.''

D'Angelo's face contorted with anger. For a moment, Eve thought he might do something stupid, like start a fight, but then he pulled off a cocky grin and raked Eve with a smoldering glare. "We'll see who ends up with the leftovers, Cowboy.''

Eve shivered and Fiona gasped. "The nerve of him! Did you see the way he looked at Eve?''

Tony said, very deliberately, "Excuse me.''

Fiona grabbed his hand. "Where do you think you're going?''

He lifted a brow. "To the bathroom. Is that okay with you?''

"Just…don't start any trouble.''

"A nice guy like me?'' He gave Eve a glance before he disappeared.

David brought the drinks right after Tony left. "Where's he off to?''

"Don't ask,'' Fiona mumbled.

"Here,'' David said, handing her a shot glass and a mug. "I brought you a boilermaker. Kill it quick, before he comes back.''

Fiona giggled. "There's nothing I like better than pulling one over on Tony.''

"You and me both,'' David agreed, distributing the remaining drinks. "How about you, Eve? Sure you don't want something stronger than beer? Might make working with Tony a little easier on the nerves.''

David was a nice guy, and Fiona was a lot of fun, but Eve suddenly felt uncomfortable sitting at the same table with them. It wasn't just because the makings of a romance were stirring, either. Like Clare and D'Angelo, Fiona and David were sending off unmistakable vibes, but that wasn't the source of Eve's uneasiness. It was her urge to defend Tony that worried her. Her desire to plant herself firmly and squarely in his corner.

And considering her assignment, that wouldn't do. That wouldn't do at all.

TONY WAITED FOR EVE outside. He leaned against his car and watched the night people come and go—the drunks, the lovers, a homeless man shuffling down the sidewalk.

He was tired tonight, almost indescribably weary, though he couldn't say why exactly. Was it the approaching anniversary that was still bothering him?

Eight years was a long time. Was he still in love with Ashley's memory, or was it the guilt that still haunted him this time of year? The knowledge that, if not for him, she might still be alive?

He closed his eyes, letting the breeze drift over him. Sometimes he had a hard time remembering what Ashley had looked like alive, but he'd never forgotten what she'd looked like in death. Her face pale. Her eyes open and staring. Her beautiful body covered in blood.

He used to see her face in almost every murder victim he saw, but not so much anymore. Not since he'd seen little Julie Betts lying in that Dumpster. Her murder had affected him in a way so profound he couldn't begin to explain it, and after that case, he'd started working alone. He found he couldn't deal with a partner after seeing something like that. He couldn't handle the camaraderie and sometimes sick cop humor that others used to deal with the nightmares. For Tony it wasn't that easy. He couldn't forget any of them. Ashley. Julie. They all haunted his sleep, because he hadn't been able to save them.

"Tony?"

He opened his eyes and saw Eve standing before him.

"You okay?" she asked anxiously.

He drew in a breath. "Just needed to get some fresh air."

She nodded. "I understand. It was pretty stuffy in there."

"Not used to bars?" he asked her.

She smiled ironically. "How could you tell?"

"Just a wild guess." He straightened from the car and stared down at her. Somehow she seemed smaller out here in the darkness. More vulnerable, although he'd seen the way she handled Vic. "Why did you tell Clare I went out on a call this afternoon?"

"Because I didn't know where you'd gone," Eve said. "I had to tell her something. She was looking for you."

"So you covered for me."

She shrugged.

"Why?" he asked softly. "Why would you do that for me?" After the conversation they'd had earlier, why would she put herself on the line for him like that?

She looked up at him, her gaze earnest. "It's like you said inside there. What are partners for?"

He ran his hand through his dark, spiky hair. "Look, I appreciate what you did. But I still don't—"

"You don't want a partner. I know."

"I work best alone, that's all."

"Maybe you just never had the right partner before. Did you ever think of that?" Her gaze looked faintly challenging.

He stared down at her for a moment, thinking in spite of himself that she just might be right. She might be the one partner, the one woman, who could stick it out with him, but he didn't think it was a chance he was willing to take. The stakes were too damned high, and he'd gambled and lost too many times in the past. Better just to go it alone.

"I'm not your enemy, Tony," she said softly.

"I never thought you were."

"Then why not give me a chance?"

How could he not have remembered her? Tony thought suddenly. She looked so pretty, standing there in the light from the bar. Like a woman who could make him forget—at least for a while. But then, the morning after always came sooner or later. That was the hell of it. "Give me one good reason why I should," he said almost gruffly.

"Because there may come a time when you're going to need someone to cover your back," she told him. "And because I'd like to be that someone, if you'd let me. You can trust me, Tony, whether you believe it or not."

Maybe he could trust her, Tony thought, his gaze riveted on her face. But maybe he shouldn't. For both their sakes.

IT WAS ALMOST TEN O'CLOCK when Eve got home that night. Early by most people's standards, but she was usually in bed by this time, reading a book or watching TV until she got sleepy.

She was turning into something of a recluse at the tender age of twenty-nine. If she wasn't careful, she'd wind up talking to herself.

"It's not as bad as all that," she muttered, picking up the remote control.

Flipping through the channels, she located a news broadcast, then lay back against the pillows, listening but not watching until she heard Tony's name mentioned. She already knew what had happened at the review board earlier that day, but she shot up in bed anyway.

He'd been caught on camera coming out of Police Headquarters with Fiona and David MacKenzie on either side of him. In a voice-over, the reporter summarized the events that had led to the hearing and Tony's exoneration.

"In spite of the outcome of today's hearing, Franco

Mancini's mother still holds Detective Tony Gallagher and the Chicago Police Department responsible for her son's death. When interviewed later in the day, Maria Mancini, accompanied by her attorney, did not rule out the possibility of a lawsuit.''

The scene switched to a dark-haired woman standing in front of a microphone, flanked on one side by a man in a suit—her attorney, no doubt—and on the other side by a group of angry-looking family members. Maria's own eyes reflected more than just anger. There was something disturbing simmering in those dark depths. Rage. Hatred. Maybe even a glimmer of madness.

Eve suppressed a shiver as she watched the woman speak. ''If we do bring suit, it won't be for the money,'' Maria insisted tearfully. ''I want justice for my boy.''

The news flashed to another story, and Eve clicked off the TV, a dark premonition sweeping over her. Maria Mancini was trouble. Eve had no doubt about that. Being named in a lawsuit against the police department was the last thing Tony needed. He was already in hot water with the brass. Hotter than he knew.

His file lay on her nightstand, and Eve picked it up, thumbing through the reports and complaints, although she'd already studied them at length. But even before this assignment, she'd known that he'd been hit with an assault charge four years ago, just after he'd made detective. He'd struck a suspect, but to Eve's mind, the circumstances had been extenuating.

If Eve had been the cop who had found the evidence underneath Robert Betts's bed, she wasn't sure how she would have reacted. But she certainly didn't blame Tony for losing control. He'd been the one who had found the little girl's body, and before that, he'd scoured the streets and neighborhoods night and day, searching for the missing child, hoping and praying he wouldn't be too late, but knowing all the while that he was.

The Betts case had come early in Tony's career. Twenty-seven was young to have made detective, let alone to be working homicide, but his phenomenal instincts—not to mention the Gallagher name—had catapulted him to prominence. He'd soon developed into one of the division's hottest and most watched detectives, but even so, Eve doubted he would have been assigned to work such a high-profile investigation if it hadn't been for his partner. Clare Foxx had been a well-known and respected detective at the time, but it had been Tony who had finally broken the case.

Eve had still been working vice at that time, but she and the rest of the department, along with the entire city, had followed the investigation, hoping and praying just like the cops who searched for the child that little Julie Betts would somehow turn up alive. The team of detectives had spent hundreds of hours on the case, combing every square inch around the victim's home and school, following up on one flimsy lead after another. Tony had taken it upon himself to widen the search, using his off-duty time to scour gutters and trash bins. And then he'd found her.

Eve closed her eyes, knowing the words in the report by heart, but picturing in her mind how it all must have gone down that day.

It had been twilight when Tony had found the child, thrown away like yesterday's useless garbage. She'd had on a pink dress, and her hair was in pigtails tied with pink ribbons. One of the ribbons was missing, and Tony had felt certain it had been taken by the killer as a souvenir or a trophy.

When the bloodstained ribbon had later been found in a shoe box stuffed under Robert Betts's bed, Tony had gone after the man's throat. Clare had managed to pull him away, but not before Robert Betts claimed his rights had been violated. He'd filed assault charges against Tony, even though he hadn't had a prayer of getting off once the DNA found on the ribbon had been matched to his seven-year-old daughter's.

In a way, the Julie Betts case was what had brought Tony back into Eve's life. After Ashley's funeral, when she'd seen how grief stricken Tony was, Eve had told herself that it was time to get over her schoolgirl crush and get on with her life. And she had. She'd graduated from college, gone to the academy and then concentrated on her career. She'd even had a serious relationship or two over the years.

But then the prominence of the Betts case, the manhunt and subsequent notoriety Tony received after the arrest, had made Eve think about him more and more. She had almost gone to see him back then, to tell him that she understood why he had done what he had. After weeks of searching, it must have killed him to find that little girl's body. Eve had a feeling he'd never gotten over it.

To most people in the department, Tony Gallagher was a rogue, a loner who didn't play by the rules. But Eve knew he was much more than that. He was a cop who cared too much. A cop—and a man—worth saving.

But the question was, did he believe that about himself?

Chapter Three

The telephone awakened Eve from a deep sleep. She thought it was the alarm clock at first and reached out blindly to slap at the button. When the ringing persisted, she rolled over and grabbed the receiver.

"This is Barrett," she said groggily.

"Eve? This is Clare. Foxx."

Eve sat up, glancing at the bedside clock. Just after four in the morning. "Yes, Lieutenant?"

"We've got a situation, I'm afraid."

Something in her voice sent a thrill of alarm racing up Eve's spine. "What is it?"

"Bill Stringer's daughter was found murdered in her apartment just under an hour ago."

"Oh, no." Bill Stringer was Vic D'Angelo's partner. Eve didn't know the detective well, but her mind instantly flashed to the picture of the young woman he kept on his desk. "Her name's Lucy," he'd told Eve proudly one day when she'd inquired about the photo. Eve remembered Bill picking up the picture and staring down at it. "Her mother and I call her Lulu. She hates it, of course, now that she's all grown-up."

Eve cradled the portable phone between her chin and ear as she began grabbing clothes from her closet.

"I want you and Tony to catch this one," Clare told her.

Eve frowned into the phone. "Are you sure? I mean…it's likely to get some attention."

"I want a woman on this," Clare said firmly. "And I want the best. I owe that much to Bill."

Eve had no delusions. She fit only half of that criteria. Which meant Clare considered Tony Gallagher the best.

So why was she trying to get rid of him?

"What's the address?" Eve threw her clothes on the bed as she picked up a pen and started scribbling.

"One other thing," Clare said, after they'd talked for a few more minutes. Her voice held a strange edge. "Is Tony with you?"

The question shocked Eve. "No, of course not. Why would he be?"

"I called him a few minutes ago and didn't get an answer." Still that odd tone. "Maybe you'd better go by and see if you can rouse him. I want both of you on the scene as soon as possible."

"I'm on my way."

THE BANGING INSIDE Tony's head matched the banging outside his apartment. For a moment, he lay drifting on the fringes of sleep, not wanting to open his eyes, but the pounding, both within and without, tortured him awake. He turned over and squinted at the clock. A little after four. Who the hell was knocking on his door at this time of morning?

"It damn well better be good," he muttered, rolling out of bed. He reached for his clothes, then realized he was still wearing the pants and shirt he'd had on the night before. The shirt was unbuttoned, and somewhere along the way he'd lost his shoes and socks.

He struggled to recall the events of last evening. He'd

gone to the pub, had a few drinks. Nick had been there. David. Fiona. Eve. That asshole, D'Angelo. Clare.

He'd waited outside for Eve, Tony seemed to recall, except…he couldn't actually remember when she'd left. He couldn't remember driving home, getting into bed.

This was bad, he thought. Real bad.

Reaching for his gun on the nightstand, he stumbled through the cluttered living room to the front door. The banging started again, and he yelled, "I'm coming, dammit."

He started to unlock the door but found the bolt hadn't been turned. Any cluckhead off the street could have come in and slit his throat for the few bucks in his wallet.

Drawing back the door a crack, he glanced into the hallway. Eve stood there, looking as fresh as a daisy in a white blouse and gray pants.

"What the hell—"

She pushed against the door, shoving it open and walking past him. "Where've you been? Clare's been trying to reach you."

"Clare…" He felt as if he were lagging at least two laps behind, trying to catch up. "What's going on?"

He saw then that Eve wasn't quite as pulled together as he'd first thought. Her hazel eyes were a little too bright, and her hair looked as if she'd combed it with her fingers. She wasn't wearing any makeup, either, and her face was pale, blanched.

"Bill Stringer's daughter was found dead in her apartment about an hour ago. She was murdered."

The pounding in Tony's ears suddenly grew louder, the pain in his head excruciating. He wiped a hand across his mouth, feeling the prickle of his whiskers. "Man," he said. "Oh, man."

"We're catching this one."

That didn't sound right to Tony. What was Clare up to? "Why us?"

"She said she wanted a woman on the case, and she wanted the best. The latter wasn't referring to me, I'm willing to bet," Eve said without rancor. "We need to get over there."

"Yeah. Sure. Just give me a minute." Tony walked out of the room, feeling as if fireworks were exploding inside his head. *This isn't good. This isn't good,* his mind kept screaming.

He unscrewed the cap off a bottle of aspirin and downed a couple without water. Stripping, he gave himself two minutes under an icy shower, standing with his hands propped against the tile wall as the water pummeled him back to semiconsciousness.

Lucy Stringer had been murdered tonight. Tony closed his eyes, shuddering. He could see her pretty face, hear her voice complaining to him that her father still treated her like a kid. "He still thinks I'm about ten years old," she'd grumbled at a Christmas party a couple years back. She'd pouted like a ten-year-old, but the look she'd slanted Tony was anything but childish. Lucy had liked to flirt, especially with cops, but everyone knew she was off-limits. Besides, she was a good kid. Never into any trouble that Tony was aware of.

He tried to remember the last time he'd seen her. At that Christmas party? No, more recently than that.

She sometimes came to the pub. She'd been there a few nights ago, hadn't she? Or was it last night?

Tony struggled to remember, catching glimpses of her in his mind at the pool table, at the bar, in the corner talking to someone…but who?

Or was all this his imagination, induced by a killer hangover?

Bad word choice, he realized with a grimace, climbing out of the shower. He dried off, pulled on a pair of jeans, then picked up his shirt, shoes, gun and wallet, and carried them all out to the living room.

Eve glanced at him in surprise.

"You're driving," he said, and walked past her out the door.

TONY FINISHED DRESSING while Eve drove them to the address Clare had given to her earlier. Eve knew the area fairly well, but she was still surprised to find that Lucy Stringer's apartment was only a few blocks from Tony's.

She glanced at him as she turned down the street. He looked like death warmed over, she thought, and grimaced at her word choice. He'd taken a quick shower, but he hadn't bothered to shave, and the stubble on his lower face was dark and thick, the shadows under his eyes almost purplish. He wore jeans and a faded CPD T-shirt, as usual not exactly the image a detective should cultivate, but then, Eve suspected his manner of dress was yet another way Tony tried to keep people at a distance.

Lucy had rented a garage apartment in a nice, middle-class neighborhood. The street was lined with police cars, and a Crime Scene Unit was pulled to the curb in front of the walkway. Eve maneuvered into a space, and she and Tony got out. As they walked across the damp grass, she could hear the faint sounds of traffic a few blocks over on the freeway, almost drowned out by the static transmission of a patrol unit radio.

She clipped her shield to her waistband as they walked by the two young patrolmen manning the yellow-ribboned perimeter. At the top of the stairs, she and Tony paused and gazed around. A mail slot had been cut in the front door, and the metal plate had already been dusted for prints.

Inside the apartment, the tiny rooms spilled over with people. The decor was typical college girl—cluttered, worn, eclectic. The only items of value that Eve could immediately discern were a computer and a stereo, and neither had been touched.

Through the open doorway, she glimpsed the dead girl lying on the bed, fully clothed, her eyes open, her arms and legs sprawled in an unnatural pose. Looking on while a Crime Scene Unit tech videotaped and narrated the setting was Vic D'Angelo.

When he saw Eve and Tony in the doorway, a curtain of rage descended over his features. Head down like a charging bull, he lunged toward Tony. Eve quickly stepped between them.

"What the hell is *he* doing here? I don't want him here."

"You don't have anything to say about it," Tony offered unhelpfully. "And by the way, what the hell are *you* doing here?"

D'Angelo was clearly in a state. Lucy Stringer had been his partner's daughter. He'd probably known her for years, maybe even since she was a little girl. Eve realized if she didn't do something to diffuse the situation and quick, both D'Angelo and Tony might end up with suspensions.

"We're following the lieutenant's orders," Eve told him, then took his arm. "Come on. Let's walk outside for a minute."

He looked as if he wanted to balk, then shrugged, a shudder ripping through his body. He wore the same black shirt and tight pants he'd had on earlier, and Eve wondered if he'd even been to bed, or if he'd been in someone else's bed when he'd gotten the call.

She guided him outside, past the crime scene tape and down the street a few steps where they could talk in private.

"I can't believe this," he muttered. "What am I going to tell Bill?"

"I know this is rough," she said softly. "You and Bill Stringer have been partners for a long time, haven't you?"

He closed his eyes briefly. "I know the whole family. His wife used to have me over for Sunday dinners. Lucy was always there, helping out in the kitchen. She was a real sweet kid. Used to have a crush on me."

He'd have liked that, Eve thought. A pretty young coed thinking of him as the studly detective.

"I don't know what I'm going to tell Bill," he said again.

"He probably already knows. I think Clare was going over there herself."

"Clare?" The name seemed to register only faintly with him.

"The lieutenant."

"Clare," he said, and drew a long breath. "She called you and Cowboy?"

Eve nodded. "We're catching this one." At the belligerent look on his face, she reached out and put her hand on his arm. "Tony's a good detective. The best. You know that as well as I do. His instincts are nothing short of phenomenal."

For a moment, D'Angelo looked as if he might fly into a fury again, but then he gave a brief shrug. "I guess I don't have any complaints with his investigations."

"What do you have a complaint with?"

He glanced down at her, scowling. "He's not the kind of man you need to get involved with, Eve."

He'd never called her by her first name before. That alone surprised Eve. "He's my partner. Who says we're involved?"

"He's dangerous. Ask Clare about him."

"I appreciate your concern," Eve said, although she didn't. She didn't like thinking that she and Tony had already become the subject of department speculation. "I can take care of myself."

He gave her a hint of the old smirk. "Yeah. I kind of figured that out." Glancing toward the street, he shoved his hands deep into his pockets. "So what am I supposed to do now?"

"Why don't you go over to Bill's? He could probably use a friend."

D'Angelo's gaze turned bleak as he stared at the flashing lights on top of the patrol cars. "I don't think I can do that. I don't think I can face him right now."

Something in his tone sent a shiver coursing through Eve. "Then go home," she said softly. "Get some rest. We've got a lot of hard work ahead of us."

He nodded absently and started down the street. Eve didn't see his car, but it had to be parked around here somewhere. He was halfway down the block before she realized she hadn't asked him how he'd known about Lucy Stringer.

Had Clare called him, too?

WHEN EVE WALKED BACK into the room, she saw Tony glance up at her, but then he went right back to work. His face was an inscrutable mask as he bent over the dead woman, cataloging the stab wounds and the bruises marring an otherwise flawless face.

There was a lot of blood. The sheets were stained almost completely red.

A wave of nausea rolled over Eve, but she fought it back.

"Landlady found her," Tony said, without looking up. "She'd gotten up to take her heart medication and saw lights on in the apartment. Said she was afraid Lucy might have been sick so she came over here to check."

''Where is the landlady?'' Eve asked.

''Downstairs. Roswell says she's not in very good shape,'' he said, referring to one of the uniforms. ''Why don't you go talk to her? I'll finish up in here.''

Eve was absurdly grateful. She hated to admit how anxious she was to get out of that bedroom. She'd never thought she was cut out for homicide, and now she knew the truth of it. Turning, she strode from the room, inhaling gulps of fresh air as she clambered down the stairs.

The landlady, Betty Jarvis, was an older woman, in her late sixties or early seventies. She sat at her kitchen table, intermittently twisting a damp tissue in her hands and lifting it to wipe at her red-rimmed eyes. This wasn't going to be much fun, either, Eve thought.

She sat down at the table and took the woman's hand in hers. ''I'm Detective Barrett. I know this is going to be difficult for you, but I've got to ask you some questions.''

IT WAS ALMOST TWO HOURS before Eve and Tony hooked back up. She'd finished her interview with Mrs. Jarvis, and Tony had already talked to the immediate neighbors, as well as the patrol officers who had first responded to the call.

They stood in the living room of Lucy's apartment as her body was lifted onto a stretcher and carried down to the coroner's van. Once the body was removed, the apartment took on an air of abandonment, a hushed quality that sent a shiver up Eve's backbone.

The CSU team was finishing up in the other rooms of the apartment, checking sink traps and trash cans. Other than the bedroom, where the victim had been found, the bathroom would take the longest. The tile and porcelain could be an especially fertile ground for trace evidence.

Eve glanced around, seeing signs of the crime almost

everywhere. The bloody bedclothes had been bagged, sealed, labeled and placed near the door, along with several other paper packets of evidence. The stack would grow as the CSU techs continued their work. Hopefully, something inside one of the bags would lead them to the killer.

Tony came over to stand beside her. "Thanks for getting rid of D'Angelo earlier."

"No problem. I didn't think this was the time or place to air personal problems."

Tony gave her a strange, probing look. "No, you're right. You did good."

"Thanks." Maybe not much of a compliment to anyone else, but it was a start, Eve thought.

"So did you find out anything from the landlady?"

Eve shrugged. "Maybe. She and Lucy were pretty tight, it seems. Lucy was like a surrogate granddaughter or something. Mrs. Jarvis liked to keep an eye on her."

"Spy on her, you mean," Tony said, frowning.

"No, I don't think it was that way." Eve paused. "I think she genuinely cared about Lucy, and from everything I've been able to gather, that wasn't unusual. Lucy was a personable young woman."

Something flashed in Tony's eyes, an emotion Eve couldn't define, but he said nothing.

"Mrs. Jarvis thought there was a possibility that Lucy may have had a new boyfriend."

"That seems to fit."

Eve knew he was referring to the setup of the crime scene—no tool marks at the front door, no sign of a struggle. It appeared Lucy Stringer had known her killer.

"Does she know who he is?" Tony asked.

Eve shook her head. "No. She never even saw him, but she said Lucy had been acting a little strangely the last few days. Secretive. And she hadn't been getting home until all hours.''

''What's 'all hours'?''

''Three and four o'clock in the morning, according to Mrs. Jarvis. She thinks Lucy may have brought him home with her a time or two.''

''Did she see a car?''

Again Eve shook her head. ''No. And she said she checked, too, but there was never a vehicle, besides Lucy's, parked at the curb or in the driveway. She thinks maybe he rode with Lucy, and then either called a cab or walked home.''

''Which means he could live nearby,'' Tony said, without expression.

Eve had thought about that, too. ''Maybe Lucy gave him a lift the next day.''

''Maybe. We'll need to find out the guy's name, which means talking to Lucy's friends and family. People she went to school with.''

''Mrs. Jarvis knew a couple of Lucy's girlfriends. I've got their names in my notebook. There's another thing.'' When Tony glanced at her, Eve said, ''A couple of weeks ago, Lucy received an anonymous love letter. She showed it to Mrs. Jarvis.''

''Was the letter signed?''

''Unfortunately, no, and Mrs. Jarvis's memory is hazy on the content. But she remembers teasing Lucy about having a secret admirer, and then a few days later, Lucy received flowers. Pink roses, and the card wasn't signed.''

''She have any idea where Lucy might have kept the letter and the card?''

''No, but she thinks Lucy's new boyfriend was the same person who sent her the letter and the flowers. Maybe that was why Lucy was so secretive about him. She didn't want his identity known.''

''Married?''

''That was my first thought,'' Eve agreed. ''But it could be someone prominent or older. Someone Lucy knew Mrs. Jarvis wouldn't approve of.''

Tony nodded, distracted. ''We'd better get the reports written up,'' he said. ''Then we can start the legwork.''

They started down the apartment stairs just as the coroner's van pulled away from the curb and headed down the street. Some of the patrol cars had already dispersed, but a few officers remained, guarding the crime scene until CSU finished up.

Silently, Eve and Tony walked down the street to her car. But instead of opening the door and climbing in, Tony sat down on the curb. He dropped his head to his knees.

Startled, Eve hesitated, then sat down beside him. ''Hey, you okay?''

He glanced up at her, his gaze dark and haunted, his expression almost tortured. Without thinking, Eve reached out and touched his arm. He jerked, as if burned, and for a moment she thought he meant to fling aside her hand. But instead he grabbed her fingers, clutching them as though they were his lifeline.

''Didn't you see it?'' His voice was like nothing she'd ever heard before.

Eve stared at him in shock. ''See what?''

''I can't believe I never noticed it before. I can't believe I never saw it.''

An icy chill rolled through Eve. ''See what?'' she repeated.

Tony's eyes closed briefly and he shuddered. ''She looked enough like Ashley to be her sister.''

A LITTLE WHILE LATER they sat behind their desks, face-to-face, typing their reports into their computers. Tony glanced up at Eve, but she didn't return his look. She'd been avoiding eye contact ever since they'd left the scene, and he couldn't really blame her. He must have sounded pretty freaked back there. What the hell had possessed him to make such an asinine comment? Lucy Stringer looked nothing like Ashley. *Nothing.*

Oh, sure, they'd both been blondes, both tall and fair. Lucy had been a pretty girl, but nothing spectacular.

What, then, had made him think even for an instant that she looked like Ashley?

Because of the wounds.

The revelation hit him like a bolt of lightning, and for a moment the last meal he'd had—whenever that had been—bubbled up in his stomach, threatening.

He hit the save button and stood. "I'll catch you later."

Eve glanced up in alarm. "Where are you going? The lieutenant will want to see our reports."

"I've got to check on something," he muttered, then turned on his heel and exited the office.

In the men's room, he ran cold water in the sink, scrubbing at his face almost brutally, as if he could somehow wash away the terrible premonition taking hold somewhere inside him.

Seven stab wounds. There had been seven vicious stab wounds on Lucy's body.

Just like on Ashley's.

THE REST OF THE DAY was devoted to searching Lucy Stringer's apartment from top to bottom, canvassing her neighborhood, interviewing neighbors, friends, relatives, anyone who might give them a lead.

They split up after lunch, Tony going to the morgue to

oversee the autopsy and Eve to talk to Mrs. Jarvis yet again. They were to meet back at the station by five o'clock for a briefing with Clare, which was to become their regular pattern over the next few days.

At the end of the second day, Clare drummed her fingers impatiently on the desk as Tony and Eve filled her in on the progress of the investigation.

"Look," she said, when the two of them had finished. "It's been thirty-six hours. I don't want this to become a mystery."

"We don't want that, either," Eve said, knowing that the lieutenant was referring to the status of a case once forty-eight hours had passed and it remained unsolved. "We're doing everything we can."

"I'm bringing Sutton and Wilson in on this. The two of you can brief them when we finish."

Tony said nothing, but Eve could feel the tension emanating between him and Clare.

"What's the status on the missing boyfriend?"

"We've talked to everyone close to Lucy. No one seems to know anything about him," Tony said.

"What about the love letter?"

"We've been over her apartment at least three times. The card from the flowers didn't turn up, either. If she threw them away, it had to have been several days ago, because we've gone through her and her landlady's trash. We've called all the flower shops in the area, but no one remembers an order for pink roses. If the suspect bought them from a street vendor, it'll be next to impossible to trace."

Clare narrowed her gaze on both of them. "Are we certain this guy even exists?"

"We've only got what the landlady told us."

When Tony glanced at Eve, she paged through her notes and read from the statement Mrs. Jarvis had given her. The older woman had seen a silhouette going up the steps to Lucy's apartment a few nights before the murder. Another time, she'd heard laughter when she went to check on Lucy. But when pressed, Mrs. Jarvis couldn't say for sure it hadn't been Lucy's voice she'd heard. Or the TV.

"I'll talk to her friends again," Eve said, when she'd finished reading from her notes. "I'll interview Mrs. Jarvis again, too. You never know. She might remember something else." That was often how it worked. Sometimes it took a half dozen or more interviews before witnesses remembered all the details.

"You do that," Clare said. "I expect both of you to bust your butts on this one. I'm catching heat from the media and the brass, so don't leave me hanging out here to dry."

But by Friday, when no new leads had surfaced, the tension at the station reached an all-time high. The specter of Lucy's funeral seemed to heat tempers to the boiling point, and Eve was almost glad to escape the investigation for an hour or two. Although she would have certainly picked other circumstances, given a choice.

She and Tony drove in separate cars to the funeral, but they met up outside the chapel. Wordlessly, they walked in together and sat down.

All through the service, Eve kept wondering how he was holding up. He was bound to be thinking of another time, another funeral. Another murdered girl.

She slanted him a glance and found that his gaze was fixed on the closed casket. He didn't even seem aware of Eve beside him, and once the service was over, the two of them went their separate ways.

By five o'clock, when Eve arrived back at the station for the meeting in Clare's office, frustrations were running high as energy waned. By five-thirty, when it was apparent Tony wasn't going to show, Clare became furious, but she went on with the meeting, venting her temper from time to time on Eve.

Since it had now been seventy-two hours, Clare had decided to call in two other detectives besides Wilson and Sutton. There would now be six detectives working full-time, and the case had become an official whodunit, with few leads and no trace evidence to speak of. The killer had been immaculate in his cleanup. Even the victim's nails had been scraped.

While Eve, Sutton and Wilson brought the new detectives up to speed, Clare paced the office in a quiet rage. After everyone else had left, she turned on Eve. "Where the hell is he?"

"I'm sure he's following up on a lead. He wouldn't have missed the meeting otherwise."

"He couldn't call in? He's a subordinate, goddammit, he can't treat me this way. He can't just blow me off like this."

Something more was at play here than Tony's having missed the meeting. Eve couldn't help wondering what kind of feelings Clare still harbored for him. At times, she appeared to almost hate him. She certainly wanted to bring him down. But there was a fine line between love and hate, Eve had always heard. And obsession was only a heartbeat away from either.

"I'll track him down," Eve said. "I'll have him call you. He can tell you about the lead himself."

Clare didn't look the least bit mollified. "It damn well better be good, that's all I can say. Don't cover for him, Eve. That's not why you're here."

"I wouldn't do that," Eve said, but that was exactly what she was doing, and she had a feeling Clare knew it.

Eve swallowed the dregs of her coffee, feeling the burn

of what might be an ulcer, and winced. One way or another, this assignment was going to get her.

A LITTLE WHILE LATER, Eve found Tony drinking at Durty Nellie's. Seeing him there made her almost as angry at him as Clare had been. She walked up to him without hesitation.

"Maybe you ought to lay off that stuff until we get a handle on this case," she said coolly.

He had on sunglasses, but she could imagine the disparaging glance he shot her. "I'm having a beer, Eve. One lousy beer. That okay with you?"

She perched on the stool beside him and glared at his profile. He wouldn't look at her. Eve couldn't help wondering why. "You missed the meeting with the lieutenant."

He shrugged. "I heard you took some heat for me. I guess I owe you again."

"I didn't do it because I wanted you to owe me. I did it because—"

"We're partners. Yeah, I know." He still didn't sound happy about it. Eve thought they'd been making headway, but now she realized that she'd only been fooling herself.

"No, we're not partners," she said almost angrily. "Partnership is supposed to be a two-way street, Tony. You can count on me, but I don't seem to be able to do the same with you."

For a moment, his mouth tightened in anger, but then he turned back to the bar and stared into his drink. "You're right. As partners go, you've been great. I mean that."

"So what's the problem?"

"The problem is me, not you."

"Tony—"

"Let it go, Eve. Okay? Just let it go for now."

It was pointless to argue. She stared at him for a moment,

then said, "So where did you go today? Can you at least tell me that?"

"I had someone to see after the funeral."

Eve frowned. "Who?"

"Bill Stringer."

So he'd gone to see Lucy's father. "That couldn't have been easy," she murmured, her anger fading. Just when she thought she had a handle on Tony Gallagher, he'd go and do something to blow her away.

"He wanted to know about the investigation. There wasn't much I could tell him. We just sat and talked for a while, mostly about Lucy." He turned back to the bar, taking a long drink of his beer. "No matter what you think, I'm not going to coast on this case. That's not going to happen. It's just…"

"I know." Sometimes you had to have a little down time, especially on cases that hit a little too close to home.

They were silent for a few minutes. The Cranberries were playing over the speakers, a song about bombs and guns and a never-ending war. The words made Eve wonder what was going on inside Tony's head. "I almost forgot to tell you. Someone called for you right before I left the station. He wouldn't leave a number, but he said to tell you that Fisher would be in touch with you very soon."

Tony's expression seemed to sharpen behind the dark glasses. "That's all he said?"

Eve nodded. "It was strange, though, because his voice sounded kinda familiar to me."

"I doubt you know this guy."

When he didn't elaborate, Eve filled the silence. "This may not be the time or place, but there's something I've always wanted to ask you."

"What's that?"

"How did an Irish guy like you end up with the name Tony?"

It could have been her imagination, but Eve thought he almost smiled. "My dad's first partner was an Italian stallion named Anthony Carlucci. Naturally, my parents figured I needed to be named after him."

"Naturally." Eve couldn't suppress a grin. "So what about your brother Nick?"

"Another partner. A Greek guy name Nicholas Acosta."

"Let me guess. Fiona is named for an Irish partner."

"Close. She's named for my grandmother."

"And your brother John is named for your dad, Sean."

"Right." Tony turned back to his beer, and Eve wondered if by mentioning his dad she'd gotten him to thinking of Ashley again.

Which wouldn't be hard, considering Ashley appeared to be constantly on his mind. *I can't believe I never noticed it before. I can't believe I never saw it. She looked enough like Ashley to be her sister.*

Eve shivered, even though the bar was quite warm.

Tony leaned toward her, saying almost in her ear, "I'll be right back."

She gave him a suspicious glare. "Sure you're not bailing on me, Gallagher?"

"Believe it or not, I've never bailed on a partner yet."

He turned and strode toward the back of the bar, where the pool table was located. But a few moments later, Eve saw that he was using the pay phone. She wondered who he was calling. A girlfriend? Clare?

The bartender was a woman tonight, a young, pretty brunette who reminded Eve unaccountably of Ashley. Maybe she was becoming as obsessed as Tony, Eve thought dryly, as she cataloged the woman's facial features, which were, after all, nothing like Ashley's.

The bartender caught Eve's eye and came over. "So what's with Lestat?" she asked curiously.

"I beg your pardon?"

She lifted her brows. "Anne Rice? Vampires? Sunglasses at night? What's with your friend?"

Eve shrugged. "I couldn't tell you."

The woman's expression perked up. Her hair was dark and curly, and one of her ears had been pierced in several places. She had a Cindy Crawford beauty mark at the right corner of her mouth, and her legs beneath her miniskirt were tanned and toned. She was very attractive, but really, she was nothing like Ashley.

"You two aren't together?" she asked Eve. "I thought for sure I sensed some vibes."

"We work together," Eve said, although she felt her stomach give a funny little lurch. Was she so transparent that even a total stranger could see how she felt about Tony?

I care about him, that's all, she told herself firmly. *He's an old friend.*

An old friend who hadn't even remembered her.

Turning on the stool to canvass the bar, Eve saw that Fiona and David MacKenzie had come in. Fiona motioned her over, and Eve, deciding it might be best to put some space between her and Tony tonight, picked up her beer and went to join them.

For the next half hour or so, she chatted with David and Fiona, who worked at the same law firm in the Loop, Eve discovered. Fiona had been at the funeral, but David hadn't gone. He hadn't been acquainted with the dead girl.

Both Eve and Fiona were in somewhat of a funk, and David did his best to cheer them up. "Come on," he complained. "You two are about as much fun as a stomach virus."

Fiona grimaced. "What a charming comparison." She sighed. "I just keep thinking about poor Lucy. She was only a few years younger than me."

David draped his arm around her shoulders. "It's a terrible thing, but you can't let yourself dwell on it."

"It's hard not to, when her murderer is still out there somewhere." She flashed Eve a glance. "Sorry. That wasn't meant as a criticism."

"I didn't take it as one."

"And I live alone, too, now that I've moved out of the house," Fiona continued.

"Most killers are someone the victim knows, isn't that right, Eve?" David said.

"Most of the time," she said noncommittally.

"See?" He turned to Fiona. "You're worrying for nothing."

"Unless, of course, I know Lucy's killer."

Both David and Eve looked at her askance. David drew back and stared at her for a moment. "This really does have you spooked, doesn't it?"

Fiona shivered. "I can't help it. It just brings back so many bad memories...."

She trailed off, and Eve saw David's arm tighten around her. He leaned toward Fiona, murmuring something in her ear, and she nodded and smiled. Eve glanced away, suddenly becoming a third wheel.

After that, she let them do most of the talking as she observed the comings and goings in the pub. She recognized several faces in the crowd including Vic D'Angelo, who was slugging back whiskey sours like the last call was just a few minutes away. He'd struck up a flirtation with the pretty bartender, and for some reason Eve didn't want to dwell on, she was glad the woman was distracted from Tony.

But the moment Clare Foxx showed up and made a bee-line for Tony at the bar, Eve had second thoughts. Maybe the bartender would have been preferable, after all.

Chapter Four

Eve had been home only about an hour when her doorbell rang. She'd barely had time to shower and dry her hair. Slipping into jeans and a T-shirt, she headed for the door, wondering who on earth would be showing up at her apartment at this hour, even though to most people nine-thirty would still be early.

Checking the peephole, she felt her heart skip a beat when she saw Tony standing in the hallway. She unlocked her door and pulled it open.

He'd taken off the sunglasses, but he still hadn't shaved. By now, he had a pretty decent beard going for him.

"Now who's bailing?" he demanded as he leaned against the door frame.

"Sorry." Nervously, Eve swiped back her hair. Her heart was still thudding. "It was getting close to my bedtime."

"You're kidding, right?" He strode past her when she stood back for him to enter.

"I'm afraid not. I need my beauty sleep."

"Seems to be working," he murmured, gazing at her with an odd glimmer in his blue eyes. "Have you had anything to eat? I'm starving."

"Actually, no," Eve admitted. She'd been toying with the idea of opening a can of soup.

"You want to go out and grab a bite?" Tony gazed around her apartment, taking in the muted tones of her decor.

Eve glanced around, too, wondering how the place struck him. Warm and homey, the way she'd intended, or maybe too feminine and fussy, with the hanging baskets of ivy and glazed pots of flowers. "I don't much feel like going out again. Why don't we just order a pizza?"

"That sounds good to me," Tony agreed. "You call, I'll buy."

"Deal."

Eve went into the kitchen to make the call. Over the bar, she could see Tony throwing off his jacket, loosening his tie, making himself at home on the mauve sofa. He let his head fall back, scrubbing his face with his hands.

What had brought him over here? Eve wondered. Was he finally starting to loosen up? Was he finally starting to accept her as his partner?

It was almost too much to ask for, she decided.

"Be here in thirty minutes," she said, coming to sit beside him.

"So why did you leave the pub?" Tony turned his head on the back of the sofa, meeting her gaze.

Something trembled inside Eve. Awareness. Attraction. Memories. She managed to shrug casually. "I guess I didn't feel much like socializing tonight."

"Yeah. I know what you mean." He watched her for a moment longer. "I've been thinking about what you said earlier. About your not being able to count on me."

"I was just angry," Eve said. "Clare came down pretty hard on us in the meeting."

"Yeah, she can be a real bi— pain," he agreed. "Still, I know I haven't been easy to work with." When she didn't say anything, he grinned. "Guess Clare's not the only one who can be a pain."

Eve smiled, too. "You have your moments."

His mood sobered. "I figured maybe that's why you left the pub without saying anything tonight. I figured you were fed up with me."

"I was just ready to come home," she said softly. "It wasn't personal."

"You sure about that?"

His gaze made Eve's stomach flutter in awareness. "Maybe I should fill you in on the meeting this afternoon," she said. "And by the way, I told Clare you'd call her."

"I talked to her a little while ago. We're cool now."

How cool? Eve started to ask. But something told her she might not want to know the answer.

THEY MIGRATED to the dining table for the pizza, and Eve finished supplying the details of the meeting while Tony ate. To her surprise, he seemed to approve of the additional detectives Clare had put on the case.

"We're going to need all the help we can get on this one."

Eve silently agreed. It didn't look good. No leads, no evidence, no anything. The mood was glum as they finished their meal and then moved back into the living room.

But in spite of the somber conversation, the barrier between them seemed to have fallen. Tony, more at ease than Eve had seen him in years, kicked off his shoes and stretched out, putting his head in her lap. "Do you mind?" He gave her a boyish grin that threatened to stop Eve's heart. "I'm tired tonight, Eve."

There was something wistful in his voice, something almost sorrowful. Without even thinking about it, Eve put her fingers in his hair, smoothing back the spiky strands.

They were not just partners, but two old friends slipping comfortably back into their relationship.

"I could go to sleep like this," he murmured. "I could sleep like this forever."

Eve didn't know what to do or say. How to react. Her memories of Tony Gallagher had once occupied such a prominent place in her heart, but she'd known her feelings for him were futile. Now here he was. And here she was. If she wanted, she could bend down and kiss him.

For a moment, the urge to do so was almost overwhelming.

What would he say? What would he do? Would he spring up off the sofa, shocked and angry?

Or would he kiss her back?

The Tony Gallagher she'd known way back when wouldn't have hesitated for a moment.

As if reading her mind, he turned his head slightly, gazing up at her. "Do you remember the first time I kissed you, Evie?"

His nickname for her made tears smart in her eyes. "Of course. That was my first real kiss. But I didn't think you'd remember."

A brief frown flickered across his brow. "I can't believe I didn't recognize you. You've changed a lot, but I should have snapped to the name."

Eve tried to act as if it didn't matter. "You and I knew each other a long time ago. We were kids. A lot has happened since then."

"True." His frown deepened for an instant, and then, with an effort, it seemed, he lightened his mood. "So that was your first real kiss, huh? No wonder you looked so shocked when I put my tongue in your mouth."

She groaned, her face coloring in spite of herself. "Don't remind me."

He grinned, and what was left of Eve's heart melted away. "You were pretty naive back then, weren't you? I couldn't believe it when you invited me to your house that day, and I found out your old man wasn't home. And then, when I got inside, you practically threw yourself at me."

"It wasn't quite that bad," Eve protested. "And besides, I was sixteen. I'd lived a very sheltered life. I was more than ready to stretch my wings a little."

"So you're saying it wasn't me who brought out the wild streak in you. It could have been any ole Tom, Dick or Harry who gave you your first kiss."

No, she thought. *It had to be you.*

"You wound me, Eve. Deeply."

I know the feeling.

He reached up and touched her hair, letting the strands slide through his fingers. "You always did have the shiniest hair. Like silk."

Their gazes met, clung, and for a soul-shattering moment, Eve was sure he would kiss her. She wanted him to so badly she could almost taste the desire, and when he turned his head away, she felt a crushing disappointment that was way out of proportion for the action.

"This isn't a good idea," he said.

"What isn't?" She swallowed past the lump in her throat.

"You. Me. Us." He still wasn't looking at her. His eyes grew bleak as he stared at the ceiling. "I've been involved before with a partner. It's great for a while, but when it ends..."

Who says it has to end? Eve wanted to ask him. But of course it would end, the moment he found out why she was really here. No words or noble intentions would make him see her as anything but a backstabber. A traitor.

"How long were you and Clare partners?" she asked him.

"A little over a year." He didn't bother to confirm or deny the insinuation in her question.

"It ended badly, I take it."

"It wasn't good."

Eve didn't want to ask any more questions. All these years, she'd imagined Ashley as the only woman in Tony's life, had never once thought she could compete with the ghost of a perfect woman. But now to think that there had been others in his life, a woman like Clare Foxx, who was still living and breathing, still wanting Tony.

Eve gazed down at him, wondering what to say to him, but then she realized words weren't necessary, after all. He was fast asleep.

"I GUESS YOU'RE WONDERING why we called you in today," one of the men seated behind the conference table at Police Headquarters said to Eve.

Actually, she had a pretty good idea, but the knowledge didn't make her any less nervous. She wasn't prepared for this meeting. The call from her commanding officer in Internal Affairs had caught her completely off guard that morning, maybe because her thoughts had been so preoccupied with Tony.

She had no idea what time he'd left her apartment last night. After he'd fallen asleep on the sofa, she'd eased away from him and gone to her own bed, where she'd been prepared to spend a sleepless night, tormented by an unsolved murder case as well as her unresolved feelings for an old flame. But she'd drifted off the moment her head hit the pillow, and she hadn't heard Tony stirring about, hadn't heard the front door open and close when he left.

Trying to tamp down a growing sense of unease, Eve

gazed around at the faces in the conference room. No doubt about it, the big guns had been called out, including the superintendent himself. Others present were the deputy superintendent of Investigative Services, a couple of representatives from the Office of Professional Standards, Eve's CO in Internal Affairs, and Clare Foxx. Open folders sat on the table before each person, but their eyes were all on Eve as she waited for her next cue.

The deputy superintendent, Louis Ackerman, motioned her now to a seat on the side of the conference table occupied only by Clare. The seating arrangement intensified the coldness of the room and reinforced the unspoken tenet that in a lot of important ways, the police department was still a man's world. The two women exchanged brief glances as Eve drew back the chair and sat.

"Sorry to interrupt your Saturday morning," Ackerman murmured.

"No problem," Eve said. "I was planning on going to the station today, anyway."

Ackerman nodded. He seemed to be the point man for the group. Tall and rigid looking with a broad, muscular physique, he had a plain face and a buzz haircut that gave him a military appearance. But in spite of his size and bearing, his presence was somewhat eclipsed by the man sitting quietly to his right.

Eve suppressed a shiver as her gaze met the superintendent's. Silver haired and perpetually suntanned, Ed Dawson was a tall man, also, but lean and very elegantly dressed. His fastidious appearance, usually called dapper by the press, had elicited more than a few political cartoons and satirical commentaries on how he spent his time on the job. One cartoon had depicted the installation—at taxpayers' expense—of a tanning bed and wall-to-wall mirrors in his office. His personal life had been rich fodder as well, ever since he and his wife divorced.

In all the time she'd worked in Internal Affairs, Eve had rarely come face-to-face with Dawson. To say that this meeting was intimidating would have been a gross understatement. Even the cops who despised him retained a certain amount of reverence for his position, and Eve was no exception.

She'd once known him in passing from the neighborhood where she'd grown up. His family and Tony's had been friends, but everything had changed after Ashley's murder. Eve had always wondered if the reason Dawson had moved his family from the neighborhood so quickly after that was because he secretly blamed Tony for his stepdaughter's death. Tony had been the one to take her to the party that night. He'd been the one to let her leave alone.

Was that Dawson's true motivation for Eve's assignment? If he still blamed Tony for Ashley's death, was he out to get him after all these years?

As if reading her mind, Dawson frowned almost imperceptibly, and Eve felt her cheeks warm. She cast her glance downward, waiting for the questions to begin.

"Tell us about the Stringer homicide," Ackerman directed. He looked up from the folder and took off his wire-rimmed glasses.

Eve glanced at Clare, whose gaze was riveted to the open file in front of her. "What exactly do you want to know?"

"Tell us about the investigation. How is it proceeding?"

"Not well," Eve admitted. "No concrete leads and very little physical evidence. No defense wounds on the body, no hair, tissue, or fiber beneath her nails. No distinguishable fingerprints other than the victim's at the scene. Whoever killed her knew how to clean up after himself."

"How would you describe Detective Gallagher's behavior at the scene?" Ackerman asked.

Eve sensed more than saw Clare glance at her. "He was thorough, professional. He did what he had to do."

"What about the altercation between him and Detective D'Angelo? How did he provoke D'Angelo?"

Nothing like a little revisionist history, Eve thought, darting Clare a look. "Detective Gallagher didn't provoke Detective D'Angelo. D'Angelo came at him."

"Are you sure about that?" Ackerman's gaze was deep, penetrating. His eyes seemed to be coaching Eve on how to respond. *Make this look good for the superintendent. Let's give him what he wants.*

At Tony's expense, of course.

Eve shrugged. "I was there. I saw what happened. Vic D'Angelo came at Tony. He was upset that Tony had been assigned to the investigation." It suddenly occurred to Eve why Clare had been so insistent that she and Tony catch the Stringer case. Clare knew of the bad blood between Vic and Tony. She knew the resentment Vic would feel over Tony's involvement. If she'd wanted to provoke Tony, push him a little closer to the edge, Vic would be a fairly reliable tool to use.

Obviously, Vic hadn't wasted a moment giving Clare his version of the events at the crime scene that night. And Clare, in turn, had reported to the bosses, all of whom seemed intent on making Tony a scapegoat for the rash of bad publicity the department was receiving. Eve knew she was expected to play the game by their rules, give them what they wanted, but what they didn't know, what she hoped they never found out, was that all along she'd had her own agenda in this matter.

"After the preliminary investigation at the scene was concluded," Ackerman pressed, "was there anything in

Detective Gallagher's demeanor or actions that raised any flags for you?''

Eve frowned. "I don't know what you mean."

"Anything he said or did that made you uncomfortable. Uneasy."

She looked enough like Ashley to be her sister.

Tony's words came rushing back to her, and Eve thought, *My God.* Was that what this meeting was all about? Had someone overheard Tony's comment that night?

Eve's mind flashed back in time. She could clearly see Tony sitting on the curb, head bowed, looking sick. And then when he'd gazed up at her, his eyes had been dark, tormented. Haunted.

Lucy Stringer had looked nothing like Ashley Dallas, other than the fact that they'd both been tall, thin and blond. Eve had seen no other resemblance between the two women, but so what? The bartender at Durty Nellie's last night had reminded Eve of Ashley, and that woman had been neither tall nor blond.

Because Tony had seen a similarity meant nothing. It had no bearing on this case, and Eve wasn't about to build a mountain out of a molehill.

She shrugged. "There was nothing in his demeanor or actions that caused me any alarm. We both did our jobs to the best of our abilities."

Ackerman leaned back in his chair, studying Eve. "And his actions since that night?"

"The same. We've both been putting in fourteen and fifteen hour days. Sometimes more."

"I understand he missed an important meeting yesterday afternoon."

Again Eve flashed Clare a glance. "Yes, because he'd gone to talk to Detective Stringer after his daughter's funeral. Detective Stringer wanted to be brought up to speed on the investigation, and Tony didn't feel he could refuse him. Under the circumstances, I would have done the same thing.''

Out of the corner of her eye, Eve saw Clare shift uneasily as Ackerman's gaze moved to her. Then he turned and said something to the superintendent, who shrugged and nodded, as if his mind were somewhere other than this meeting.

Was he thinking about Ashley, too? Like Tony, did Ed Dawson become increasingly obsessed with his stepdaughter's murder every year as the anniversary of her death approached?

Eve realized suddenly that Ackerman was addressing her again, and she had to ask him to repeat his question. ''When you transferred to IAD, you wrote on your application that you felt it was important for members of the police department to adhere to higher standards of conduct than the average citizenry, in order to command the respect and public trust necessary to perform our duties in the safest, most efficient way possible. Do you still believe that, Sergeant Barrett?''

''Yes, sir, I do.'' Referring to her rank in Internal Affairs was a subtle way of reminding Eve that her transfer to the Detective Division was transient, her partnership with Tony only a temporary ruse. She was still an IAD officer, and she would do well to remember where her loyalties lay.

''It takes a special type of individual to perform IAD responsibilities, as I'm sure you've discovered,'' Ackerman commented, letting his voice take on a note of uncharacteristic sympathy. ''You have to be a dedicated officer, maybe even a little idealistic, with a very clear sense of right and wrong. IAD is rarely the most popular unit in any police department.''

An understatement, Eve thought dryly. The officers in

IAD were usually viewed as traitors by the rest of the force, and very often hated. Noble intentions didn't cut it when a brother—or sister—police officer's career was on the line.

In the three years that Eve had been in IAD, she'd had to inure herself to the taunts and innuendos, the sometimes outright abuse by her fellow officers. But once she'd gone against the Blue Wall, there was no turning back. She'd become an outcast within the department.

Eve hadn't realized just how exiled she'd become until she'd accepted this assignment. She'd forgotten what it was like to be included in the camaraderie, the inside jokes, the drinks after a watch. She'd become a loner both at work and in her personal life, and she hadn't considered how much she'd been missing, what exactly her dedication had cost her until now.

And that was the danger of what she was doing. That was what the men in this room feared, she realized suddenly. That she would be seduced back into the Brotherhood—at least as much as a woman could be. That having won her fellow officers' acceptance—Tony's in particular—she wouldn't be able to point the finger when the time came.

"I still believe in the importance of the IAD," Eve told them. "My opinion hasn't changed since I filled out that application."

"You still believe the function of the IAD is to find police corruption and eradicate it, using whatever means necessary?"

"Within reason, yes, sir."

"You have no reservations about performing your current assignment?"

"I have no reservations about eliminating police corruption if I find it." She put the tiniest emphasis on *if*, and was rewarded by a slight lifting of Ackerman's brow.

He gazed around the table. "Does anyone else have any questions for Sergeant Barrett?"

"Just one." This from the superintendent. Eve's gaze collided with Ed Dawson's, and she shivered inwardly at the coldness of his glare, the hardness of his expression. "Are you now or have you ever been personally involved with Detective Gallagher?"

The question blindsided Eve. She hadn't expected that. "No, sir," she managed to say evenly.

"But you knew Detective Gallagher before accepting this assignment?"

"I never made any secret of that fact," Eve replied, her heart pumping like a piston.

"Were the two of you good friends, would you say?" Emphasis on the word *good*. There was no mistaking his meaning.

Eve could feel Clare's gaze on her now, and she couldn't help wondering if this line of questioning had somehow been prompted by the lieutenant.

"We knew each other in high school. After we graduated, I only saw him once or twice in passing before I accepted this assignment. We didn't keep in touch at all. As a matter of fact, he didn't even remember me, as Lieutenant Foxx can attest."

For the first time since she'd sat down at the table, Eve's gaze met Clare's. There was something in the older woman's eyes, a flash of hostility—or was it jealousy?—that made Eve distinctly uneasy. Clare was not the sort of person one wanted as an enemy. She was cold and shrewd, and could be, Eve suspected, malicious when she wanted to be.

In spite of the age difference, it wasn't hard to picture her and Tony together. They were both attractive, hard-edged, potentially explosive. Did she still carry a torch for him? Was that why *she* was out to get Tony?

"You may go now," the superintendent said softly. Eve's gaze met his once more, and again she shivered as she stood and walked out of the room.

CLARE CAUGHT UP WITH HER at the elevator, shoving open the closing doors and slipping inside. She waited until the doors had slid closed again before turning to Eve. "You okay with what happened back there?"

"What *did* happen back there?" Eve asked with a frown. "What's going on?" Both she and Clare were dressed in business suits, and Eve guessed, to the casual observer, there would be a similarity in their appearance. Working for the police department gave everyone the same hardened expression at one time or another, the same misanthropic approach to life. It was expected in men, but in women…well, the same attributes had never been considered attractive.

Eve had always tried to fight the negativism that was so much a part of her job, but even in Internal Affairs, her idealism could take only so much of a pounding before she, too, gave in to the cynicism.

In another ten years, would her eyes reflect the same wariness as Clare's? The same shrewd calculation?

Would she still be single like Clare?

"That *Tribune* article has them all foaming at the mouth," Clare said, by way of explanation. She shifted her gaze away from Eve's, staring straight ahead at the elevator doors.

"What article?"

"You didn't see the paper this morning?" Clare shrugged, still not looking at Eve. "There's a big op-ed piece about the Mancini case and about Tony's exoneration. The police department as a whole didn't come off looking too good. Plus Maria Mancini was on Pamela Griffin's program this morning,'' she added, referring to a local talk show hostess. ''Needless to say, Pamela was a very sympathetic listener. She let Mrs. Mancini rant and rave at will.''

Eve winced, remembering the dark-haired woman she'd seen on the news a few days ago. The hate and rage in Maria Mancini's eyes hadn't been faked, Eve was almost certain. Maria Mancini blamed Tony for her son's death, and she wouldn't rest until she'd exacted some sort of revenge. At the moment, it appeared to be in destroying Tony's reputation—what was left of it. Whether she knew it or not, Maria Mancini was playing right into the brass's plans.

''This is crazy,'' Eve said. ''Tony was exonerated by a review board made up of both police officers and civilians. Wouldn't it be in the department's best interests to prove that the correct decision was reached?'' She tilted her head toward the doors. ''Why are they so anxious to get rid of him? Seems to me that would only make the situation worse.''

''He was cleared, but that doesn't necessarily mean he's innocent. Not in public opinion.'' Clare paused and shrugged again. ''If Tony is caught in another transgression—and fired—it will prove that the department is willing and able to police its own. Tony's name is already high profile. His dismissal would attract a lot of media attention.''

''In other words, it's a public relations ploy,'' Eve said. Which, of course, she'd already known, in spite of the committee's lofty-sounding goals.

''Tony Gallagher is a loose cannon. There's no room in the superintendent's new and squeaky clean police force for cops like him." Eve couldn't quite tell if Clare's tone was sarcastic or not.

"Do you agree with that assessment?" Eve asked her. "Even considering Tony's skills as a detective?"

Clare turned, giving Eve a long appraisal. "His skills are immaterial. If the bosses want Tony's head, I'm more than willing to serve it up to them on a silver platter."

Her bluntness surprised Eve. "Nothing like loyalty," she muttered, deeply disturbed by Clare's attitude.

Anger flashed like wildfire in Clare's eyes, but rather than a reprimand, she gave Eve a brief smile, perhaps remembering that Eve, after all, was still IAD. Tony's actions were not the only ones that could be written up.

"Look," Clare said, her tone conciliatory for her. "We're not all that different, you and me. We both have to function in a man's world, and I suspect we both have ambitions. But I refuse to deny or be ashamed of mine, and I don't mind using a situation to my advantage. I don't plan to retire from the force a lieutenant. And I won't let someone like Tony Gallagher pull me down with him. There's no reason a smart woman can't go all the way to the superintendent's office, if she plays her cards right. Don't tell me you haven't thought about that yourself," she said coolly. "Why else would you have accepted this assignment?"

It was true. Eve did have her own ambitions. Her own agenda. But she and Clare differed in one major respect. Eve had no intention of leaving her footprints on the backs of her friends as she climbed her way to the top.

But would Tony believe that when he found out what she was up to?

Chapter Five

"You're all dressed up for a Saturday morning," Tony remarked as he watched Eve settle in behind her desk. Taking off her suit jacket, she draped it across the back of her chair. The knit blouse she wore beneath emphasized the swell of her breasts, the indention of her small waist. Had she had that body back in high school?

"One of us has to look presentable." Her gaze swept over his jeans and T-shirt before she quickly glanced away.

He leaned toward her. "Now, who do you think a suspect is more likely to open up to? Someone dressed like me or someone who looks like she just stepped out of a board meeting?"

Eve frowned, his analogy hitting a little too close to home. "There's nothing wrong with intimidating a suspect."

"No, you're right about that. But there's intimidation and there's intimidation."

She arched a brow. "Meaning?"

"Attitude will get you a lot further than a designer business suit."

"And you think I don't have the right attitude to intimidate a suspect?"

He grinned. "I think you have potential, Eve. You just need a little guidance."

She shot him a glance. "Now you sound like Vic D'Angelo. If that's the best line you can come up with—"

"Line? Come on, Eve. You don't think I'm trying to come on to you, do you? After last night?"

She blushed furiously, and Tony's grin broadened. He couldn't help it. He did enjoy teasing her. She was such an easy target, with her prim business suits and naive demeanor. How had someone like her managed to remain so untouched by police work? Sometimes Tony felt a hundred years old, and there were a lot of nights when he couldn't sleep, didn't want to sleep because of the parade of victims that haunted his dreams.

Eve was like a breath of fresh air.

He thought about their conversation the evening before, the way she'd looked at him when they'd talked about their first kiss. She'd wanted him to kiss her last night. Tony was sure of it, but for once in his life, he'd decided to play it safe. Eve was from the old neighborhood, a good girl, not someone he could toy with and then toss aside. He didn't want to be the one to take that look of innocence from her eyes.

Of course, maybe the innocence was just a false perception, a memory of what she'd once been like. She was a cop, after all, and Tony had known her, what? Twelve, thirteen years ago? She might not be anything like the Evie he'd known way back then. She might not be a good girl any longer.

Somehow that notion unsettled him, but it shouldn't have. Eve was a damned good-looking woman. She was bound to have men in her life, but had there been anyone serious? Was there someone in her life now?

Forget it, he told himself, still watching her. It didn't

matter. Eve's personal life was none of his business, just as his personal life was none of hers. He'd made that rule himself.

Still, he couldn't help wondering what kind of guy she was attracted to. Flashy, like Vic D'Angelo? A hothead, like his brother Nick? Or could she go for the plain old garden variety troublemaker, like Tony?

She glanced up, meeting his gaze only briefly before turning to switch on her computer. Instantly she seemed to become absorbed in whatever she'd called up on the screen, and she didn't look at him again. If Tony didn't know better, he'd swear she was reluctant to meet his gaze.

Because of his reference to last night? Was she embarrassed by the conversation they'd had? Or by the attraction both of them had felt?

"Speaking of last night," he said, clearing his throat. "I guess I owe you an apology. I didn't mean to zone out on you like that."

"That's okay." She didn't look up from the computer screen. "I was pretty wiped myself. It was a hard day."

"Yeah." Going to Lucy's funeral had been one of the hardest things Tony had ever had to do. At least, he'd thought so at the time. But talking to Bill Stringer afterward—that had been the real downer. What could you say to a man whose daughter had been brutally murdered?

Sorry, Bill. We still don't have any concrete leads, but we think your little girl was killed by the sicko she was sleeping with.

No. You couldn't say that.

"You gotta find him, Tony. You gotta find the sick SOB who did that to her."

Tony closed his eyes briefly, remembering Bill Stringer's anguished plea, the torment in his eyes. Tony was no stranger to that kind of pain. He knew exactly what Bill was going through. Only, when Ashley was murdered, at least her killer had been apprehended less than twenty-four hours later. At least Daniel O'Roarke was sitting on death row at this very moment. Maybe sometimes justice did prevail. It was a hope a part of Tony fervently clung to, even in his darkest hours.

He realized Eve had spoken to him, and he forced himself out of his reverie. "What's that?"

Her hazel gaze met his, then she glanced away again. "I asked what you're working on this morning."

He made a helpless motion at the stack of papers on his desk. "Just going back over our notes, trying to figure out what we've missed."

"Maybe we haven't missed anything." She looked at him again, almost hesitantly, but this time she didn't avert her gaze. "Maybe Lucy's killer was just that good."

"Which brings us back to square one," he said morosely. "Where's the motive?"

Eve shrugged. "A lover's quarrel. Jealousy."

"Crimes of passion," Tony said. "A kill in the heat of the moment. This guy knew what he was doing that night. He came prepared, and then he took the time to clean up after himself."

Eve frowned. "You think he deliberately stalked Lucy with the intent all along of killing her? Even when he sent her the love note and flowers?"

"It's possible."

"You're not thinking…" She paused, and Tony saw her shiver. "You're not thinking we've got a serial killer on our hands?"

"Even if I was thinking that, I'd keep it to myself," he said carefully. "It usually takes at least three murders to get the FBI's attention.…" He let his voice trail away as his gaze met Eve's. "But even Ted Bundy had to have a first."

Eve wrapped her arms around her middle, running her hands up and down her arms where goose bumps were suddenly visible on the surface of her skin. "You don't have any proof—"

"No proof," Tony agreed. "Just a gut instinct. Something's not right here, Eve. You can't tell me you don't feel it, too."

Seven stab wounds, just like Ashley. Should he tell Eve about that? Should he confide in her what his worst fears were? That there would be more killings. That somehow he didn't think Lucy Stringer's murderer was a stranger. That the killer was someone who knew about Ashley. About Tony. Someone he and Eve might least suspect…

"If that's true," Eve said, musing out loud, "it changes everything. The whole investigation. We may have been going about this all wrong."

"It's only speculation at this point." Tony decided he'd taken it as far as he wanted to for now. One of them needed to remain open-minded, objective. He was counting on Eve to keep him from going too far astray.

That was a switch. A turn of events he hadn't planned on. Since when had he ever relied on anyone for anything?

But somehow Eve was different. She'd proved herself not only a competent investigator, but a woman of sensitivity and intuition. Not bad qualities in a partner, so long as they both remained focused on their jobs. So long as the softness in her eyes and the remembered sweetness of her lips didn't distract him from what he had to do.

That was why he'd left her apartment so abruptly last night, when he'd awakened just after midnight. Eve's bedroom door had been ajar, and he hadn't been able to resist the temptation of glancing in on her. And then, watching

her sleep—curled on her side, hands beneath her face, looking so innocent and inviting—he'd been presented with an
even greater lure.

He'd stood gazing down at her, swamped by emotions
he hadn't dared let himself feel in a very long time. Desire,
yes, but something more. Something deeper and even more
dangerous.

Maybe Eve was right. Maybe the reason he'd always
liked working alone was because he'd never had the right
partner before. Maybe she was someone he could count on.
And if he was smart, he wouldn't do anything to mess that
up.

As if reading his thoughts, she said softly, "What time
did you leave my apartment last night?"

"Just after midnight."

"I didn't hear you go."

"I can be subtle," he teased her. "Besides, you were
sleeping like a baby. I don't think an earthquake would
have awakened you last night."

Too late, he realized he'd given himself away, and he
saw her eyes widen in surprise. "How do you—"

The telephone rang before she could ask her question,
and Tony grabbed it, muttering to himself, "Saved by the
bell, thank God."

"YOU'RE SURE YOUR MOTHER won't mind our just popping
in like this?" Eve asked worriedly. They'd parked at the
curb in front of the Gallagher house, and both of them got
out of the car.

The house brought back a lot of memories for Eve. She
used to walk home from school this way, even though it
wasn't the shortest route to her father's house on Mulberry.
She hadn't minded the extra time, though, because every

once in a while she'd caught a glimpse of Tony, sometimes with Ashley, sometimes with his brothers, sometimes alone.

Those were the times Eve had lived for, when Tony would look up from washing his car or cutting the grass and wave to her, call out her name. Smile at her. Eve would pretend that he thought about their stolen kisses as often as she did. Sometimes she'd even pretended that Ashley Dallas didn't exist.

And now she didn't.

Shivering, feeling a prickle of her old guilt, Eve let her gaze roam over the lines of the house, a post-World War II bungalow that had been added on to several times to accommodate a growing family. It was a pleasant-looking home, with freshly painted shutters and a well-kept lawn that smelled faintly of wet grass and fertilizer. The narrow walkway leading up to the house was lined with pale pink phlox, and clay pots of geraniums rested on top of the low concrete wall that partially enclosed the porch.

Eve had driven, as usual, and Tony waited until she'd rounded the front of the car before heading up the walkway toward the stoop.

"Stop worrying," Tony advised her. "We're not just popping in. I was invited, remember?"

"Yes, but I wasn't."

"Believe me, no one will care. The more the merrier is the Gallagher philosophy," he said a bit dryly. "Besides, my mother will enjoy seeing you again. She likes to keep up with everyone from the neighborhood."

Eve doubted Maggie Gallagher would even remember her. Tony hadn't, so why should his mother?

Eve slanted him a glance, studying his profile as he leaned forward and opened the door. The action brought his body against hers, and a thrill of excitement shot through her at the brief contact. Tony must have felt it, too, for he glanced back at her, holding her gaze for a fraction of a second before he pushed the door open and waited for her to enter in front of him.

The house was not unlike the one Eve had grown up in, but somehow it seemed larger and cheerier, with its haphazard arrangement of comfortable furniture, hardwood floors scuffed from years of baseball cleats and wrestling matches, and walls lined with pictures of Maggie Gallagher's family.

Eve's gaze went immediately to the photo of Tony in the foyer, taken at his graduation from the academy. He looked handsome in his dress uniform, and so young, but even then there was a hardness in his features, a resolved, world-weary glint in his blue eyes. He'd already known great pain at that age, and great loss. The love of his life had been murdered, and his father had disappeared without a trace.

Tony's picture was at the end of a row of similar photographs—his brothers, Nick and John; his father, Sean; his grandfather; and several other police officers that Eve didn't know but suspected were cousins and uncles. There wasn't a woman in the bunch, but Fiona hadn't been ignored. Shots of her were everywhere else, including a recent one that showed her proudly holding up her law school diploma.

Eve had heard laughter when she and Tony first entered the foyer, and an almost incessant buzz of chatter, but suddenly she realized everyone inside had gone silent. She could glimpse their faces through the wide, arching doorway into the living room, and they were all staring at her and Tony.

He seemed almost as reluctant as she to join the gathering, but before either of them could make an escape,

Fiona spotted them, and with David MacKenzie firmly in tow, hurried across the room toward the foyer.

"My God," she breathed, openly startled. "I can't believe you actually came." She was looking at Tony, not Eve.

He shrugged, slipping his hands into his jeans pockets. "I figured what the hell. It seemed important to Mom."

"Yes, but when has that ever influenced you before?"

"Don't start," Tony warned.

Fiona grinned. "You're right. I should just be grateful you're here, and I am. And you, too, Eve." She turned and enveloped Eve with a warm smile. "Do you remember our oldest brother, John? He and his 'significant other' are going to make an announcement tonight. It's no secret, of course. The two of them have been thick as thieves for months, but tonight they'll make it official."

"It's a family night," Eve said. "I shouldn't be here."

"Oh, don't be silly. The more the merrier."

Eve caught Tony's eye behind Fiona's shoulder, and he shrugged, as if to say, *See? I told you.* But his demeanor was distinctly uncomfortable. What made him so restless, even in his own home?

"Nikki's already here. I picked her up early," Fiona was saying. "She's John's fiancée's little girl," she added for Eve's benefit. Her eyes sparkled with mischief as she tucked one arm through Eve's and the other through Tony's, ushering them forward. "But John called a little while ago to say that he and Thea are running a bit late. Isn't that just so incredibly romantic?"

"Unless they had a flat tire," David commented dryly.

"Don't *you* start," Fiona advised. "One cynic per night is about all I can handle." She tugged on Tony's arm. "At least have the decency to not look quite so miserable," she grumbled. "For Mom's sake, if no one else's."

The chatter had resumed, but most of the eyes were still
trained expectantly on Tony and Eve, as if waiting for the
two of them to perform some sort of magic trick. At that
moment, Eve would have given a lot for the ability to disappear.

Fiona said to Eve, "Watch him for me, will you? He'll
bolt first chance he gets."

And with that, she drifted off with David who, in spite
of his earlier comment, gazed down at Fiona with a very
romantic gleam in his eyes.

Eve shifted her glance to Tony, who was starting to
scowl. Before she could say anything to him, however, his
mother, Maggie, came to the rescue. Obviously, she and
Fiona had handling Tony down to a science. *Don't leave
him alone long enough for him to disappear on us.*

Maggie kissed Tony's cheek and gave him a quick hug.
"I'm so glad you came tonight." She turned to Eve, reaching for her hand. "And you, too. Look at you! Little Evie
Barrett, all grown up! And on the police force, no less. I
couldn't believe it when Fiona told us you were Tony's
new partner!"

"I hope I'm not intruding," Eve murmured, discom-
forted herself by Maggie's effervescence. Eve's father was
always so subdued, their home very calm and quiet. The
only time there'd been this many people at the Barrett
house was when Eve's mother had died. And even then,
she and her father hadn't known many of the neighbors and
parishioners from St. Anne's who had come to bring food
and pay their respects. Eve was reminded again how soli-
tary her life was. She'd never minded until recently. Until
being presented with the alternative.

"Come with me," Maggie was saying, drawing Eve
away from Tony. Eve glanced over her shoulder and saw
that his frown had deepened. He turned and headed for the

kitchen. Eve tried to concentrate on what his mother was telling her, but her thoughts were on Tony. Was he sneaking out the back way, leaving her here to fend for herself?

"This is Tony's grandmother," Maggie said brightly, stopping before a gaily dressed woman seated on the sofa. "Colleen, this is Evie Barrett. Do you remember what a tiny little thing she used to be?"

"I do recall that sweet little face," Colleen agreed, shifting over on the faded corduroy sofa to make room for Eve. She patted the seat beside her. "Keep me company for a while. Everyone tends to ignore the oldest girl at the party."

Eve doubted that. She had no idea how old Colleen Gallagher was, but the lined face was still very attractive, the blue eyes bright with intelligence. Her vivid red hair was undoubtedly beauty salon enhanced, but the color suited her.

What was it about redheads, Eve pondered as she took a seat next to Tony's grandmother, that made everyone else pale in comparison? Her own brown hair seemed drab and lifeless, and she suspected her personality might be classified along the same lines.

"So you're Paul Barrett's little girl." Colleen stared at her unabashedly, and Eve was suddenly glad she'd left her suit jacket in the car. As it was, her skirt and blouse seemed too prim and fussy for the casual gathering, but she and Tony had come here straight from work. She wished now she'd made him let her go home and change, but she'd had the impression that if they didn't go when the mood struck him, they wouldn't go at all. And though she hadn't been all that keen on spending an evening with his family, Eve hadn't been able to pass up the opportunity to spend more time with Tony. But God only knew where he'd gone off to.

"He's probably in the kitchen fetching himself a beer."

Eve glanced at Colleen, catching the amused glint in her blue eyes. "I beg your pardon?"

"You were looking around for Tony, weren't you?"

"I just wondered where he'd gone," Eve murmured, blushing.

Colleen smiled. "It's unusual these days to see a young woman blush so easily. It's a very attractive quality, and I'll wager Tony thinks so, too."

Eve felt her face grow even hotter. "Maybe you've misjudged our relationship. Tony and I are partners, Mrs. Gallagher."

She smiled faintly and nodded. "In my day, a woman police officer was unheard of, let alone a homicide detective. But I've always thought I would have made a very effective investigator. I'm gifted with perception, you see, and I'm a fairly reliable judge of people, as well."

Eve didn't doubt it for a minute. Very little would escape Colleen Gallagher's attention, she thought uneasily. "Your husband was a detective, wasn't he?" she asked for lack of a better response.

"Yes. William was the first Gallagher to join the police force. That was nearly seventy years ago. He set a fine example for his offspring." Her accent was very Irish and very lyrical. She patted Eve's hand. "Remind me someday to tell you the story of the Gallaghers and the O'Roarkes."

Eve lifted a brow. "You mean O'Roarke, as in Daniel O'Roarke on death row?" Funny how even here, talking with Colleen Gallagher, Ashley's ghost was never far away.

Colleen nodded. "Yes, but the Gallagher-O'Roarke feud goes back much further than that. Daniel's grandfather, James O'Roarke, and my William were once best friends. They came over from Ireland together. Then something happened to tear them apart," she said sadly. A shadow flickered across her features. "They went their separate ways. William chose the law, and James turned to a life of crime."

Sounded like the plot of a novel, Eve decided, or an old black-and-white movie. She suspected Colleen, with her flaming red hair and creamy Irish complexion, was the "something" that had torn the two friends apart.

Tony came back into the room, and Eve met his gaze briefly. Her heart thumped in painful awareness as she turned back to his grandmother.

Colleen smiled knowingly, as if she'd witnessed the momentary exchange. "It's one of life's ironies, I suppose."

"What is?"

"That we can't choose who we fall in love with."

Was she referring to herself or to Eve? With an almost superhuman effort, Eve willed herself not to blush.

"We Irish can be a passionate lot," Colleen told her, "but it might interest you to know that I don't believe any woman—or man, for that matter—has only one great love of a lifetime."

Eve wasn't quite sure what to say. "Why not?"

"Because what we remember as our 'one great love' is almost always the affair that didn't work out. And usually for good reason, if we stop to think about it. Once the passion burns itself out, what is there left worth keeping?"

Eve said doubtfully, "But what if one's 'great love' dies before the passion has a chance to burn itself out? What then?"

Colleen nodded. "That does present a problem. With me, I'd only been married to William a few years before I realized that what I'd had with James was little more than a fantasy. The man I thought was the one great love of my life never really existed, you see. I embellished his memory and our passion in my mind so that it was impossible for anyone else to live up to it.

"Then I woke up one day and realized that a truly great love affair is more than just an all-consuming passion. It's friendship, perhaps above all else, that really matters. It's building a life together, day by day, sharing happiness as well as sadness. It's knowing that there is one person you can always count on, who will never let you down. Thank God I learned that before it was too late."

Eve sat quietly, not knowing how to respond, but enthralled just the same. She'd always thought of Ashley Dallas as Tony's one great love. But if Ashley had lived, would their passion have burned itself out? Would they have grown apart, eventually gone their separate ways? Would Tony have been able to move on?

But in dying, Ashley had remained the love of his life. The woman no other could ever measure up to. Eve wondered if she even had the courage to try.

Colleen leaned toward her again. She smelled faintly of gardenias, a sweet, old-fashioned fragrance that brought, for some reason, a pang of nostalgia to Eve. "I've never known a man more in need of the love of a good woman than my Tony."

They were both staring at him from afar, and as if drawn by the force of their combined gazes, he turned. He smiled slightly, lifting his beer in salute, but he made no move to join them. He remained at the fringes of the celebration, alone, aloof, still unavailable.

Eve sighed in spite of herself. "I don't think you could ever convince him of that," she said softly.

"No," Colleen agreed. "I don't imagine *I* could."

"SO WHAT'D YOU THINK?" Tony asked. They were walking down the steps toward the street, and he took Eve's elbow, holding it lightly until they reached the curb.

It meant nothing, Eve told herself, but his touch sent her pulse racing. "I had fun," she said a little breathlessly.

He followed her around to the driver's side of her car and opened the door for her. "Sorry," he said, when she glanced up at him before sliding inside. "We're equals. I shouldn't have done that."

Eve forced her tone to remain even. "Well, we're off duty tonight, so I'll let you get by with it this one time."

"Thanks." He closed her door, and then went around to climb in on the passenger side. "So you had fun, huh? Is that a polite way of saying let's get the hell out of here while the coast is clear?"

Eve laughed. "Not at all. I meant it. I enjoyed seeing your family again. I can't believe they all remembered me."

"Why not?" His expression was unreadable in the dim light from the street. "You're not so forgettable, Eve."

"I was to you."

He grimaced. "I'm not all that reliable."

"Oh, I don't know. You haven't bailed on me yet, have you?" She'd tried to say it lightly, but their gazes met before the words were out of her mouth, and something quick and electric flashed between them. Her car was a compact, small, close. Tony was only inches from her, and when he turned his head to her, when he moved almost imperceptibly toward her, their lips were nearly touching.

Eve could hear her heart hammering in her ears as she watched him. He let his head fall back against the seat, closing his eyes briefly as he groaned. "Help me, Eve."

"Help you do what?" she almost whispered.

"Help me do the right thing." He turned his head on the

seat, gazing at her in the semidarkness. "I'm a screwup, Eve. You don't want to get mixed up with me."

It was a warm night, and she'd left the windows in the car open. Distant street noises filtered in, along with the scent of roses. Somewhere down the street a dog barked, a car horn sounded, and then all grew silent. Breathless.

Eve said shakily, "I don't think you're a screwup, Tony. I think you're a man who's had some tough breaks. A man who doesn't give himself enough credit."

"I've made a lot of mistakes. I've got a lot of enemies. There are people in the department out to get me." He laughed, a sharp, bitter sound. "How's that for paranoia?"

Eve felt as if something were squeezing against her heart. He knew, she thought desperately. Somehow he knew. "Tony—"

He put a fingertip to her lips, silencing her. "I didn't want a partner. You know that. I always thought I worked best alone."

"Yes, I know."

"But I was wrong about you, Eve."

No, you weren't, she wanted to tell him. *You were right not to trust me.*

No matter how noble her intentions, her assignment still boiled down to the same thing. Tony was right. There were people in the department out to get him, and the list reached all the way up to the superintendent's office. To Ashley's stepfather. If Ed Dawson was truly Tony's enemy, Eve wasn't sure there would be anything she could do to help him.

But the very worst thing she could do at the moment was to confide in him to alleviate her own conscience. Because once Tony turned against her, pushed her away, there would be no one in his corner.

She forced a smile. "I've decided you're not so bad yourself."

He grinned halfheartedly. "Was that what you and my grandmother were talking about?"

"What makes you think we were talking about you at all?" she challenged.

"Maybe because you were both staring a hole through me," he said. "And because I know my grandmother. She's a hopeless romantic. Take what she says with a grain of salt."

Eve had no intention of doing that. She liked what his grandmother had told her. She cherished it. "Your grandmother may be a romantic, but she certainly isn't hopeless. I've never met anyone whose head was screwed on straighter."

"Too bad it doesn't run in the family."

"Yeah, too bad," Eve agreed, and when he glanced at her in reproach, she laughed.

She reached to start the ignition, but his hand closed over hers. When she glanced up at him, his eyes were the deepest blue she'd ever seen. "What I've been trying to say is that maybe it's not so bad having a partner, after all."

Her hand trembled beneath his. She cleared her throat. "It's not so bad for me, either."

"I guess that's why this other thing worries me so much." When she lifted a brow in query, he frowned. "You know what I'm talking about."

She let out a shaky sigh. "Yes, I know."

"I don't want to mess things up between us, Eve. Do you know what I'm saying? Relationships come and go, but a partner...someone you can count on..." His words trailed away and he turned his head to stare out the window. "You must think I'm an idiot."

"No, I don't. I know what you mean." *A truly great*

love affair is more than just passion. It's knowing that there is one person in all this world you can always count on, who will never let you down.

"I think your grandmother is one of the smartest women I've ever known," Eve said softly.

He glanced around, his gaze skeptical. "What brought that on?"

"Nothing." She shrugged. "It's getting late. How about I drive you home?"

He lifted their clasped hands, and, for a moment, Eve thought he meant to bring her fingers to his lips. But then he squeezed her hand and released it. "Where've you been all these years, Evie?"

"Not far." She'd always been only a phone call away, but the problem was, he'd never known it. He'd never cared, until now.

EVE SPENT MOST OF SUNDAY with her dad. They went to church in the morning, had lunch at Callahan's, then caught a matinee—a comedy that left them both in good spirits. Afterward, they went home and sat on the stoop in companionable silence as the remainder of the afternoon slipped away.

Finally at dusk, Eve rose, kissed her father's cheek and said her goodbyes before heading back to her apartment. Letting herself in, she reflected on the day as she flipped the light switch and went to check her messages. She'd enjoyed the time with her father. Paul Barrett had never been a particularly jovial man, or openly affectionate as some parents were—as Eve remembered Sean Gallagher being with his kids—but she'd never felt their relationship was lacking. Even though he never said the words, Eve knew her father loved her, knew that if she were ever in a jam, he would be the first one at her side.

Perhaps it was the time she'd spent with him today, or the visit with the Gallaghers last night, that made her feel oddly isolated now in her own apartment. Eve glanced around. Her living room reflected an eclectic though somewhat understated taste. Her furniture was a mix of antique and modern, the pieces bought individually because she'd liked them—not necessarily because they went with the rest of her decor. Eve had always thought the colorful Peruvian throw rugs at the front door and beneath the pine trunk coffee table added a festive air, the framed family pictures lining the mantel a homey quality, but suddenly her personal space seemed foreign to her, cold and empty and maybe even a little frightening.

She tried to shrug off the disquiet as she headed for the refrigerator, but halfway to the kitchen, she stopped, gazing around again. Gooseflesh prickled along her arms as she realized the source of her unease. A faint scent lingered in the air, not unpleasant but definitely unfamiliar, as if someone had been in her apartment while she was out.

Her heart thudded in alarm as she slowly turned, scanning the living room, dining area and kitchen beyond. Nothing seemed amiss, but Eve was almost certain someone had been there. But for what purpose? Her television, stereo and computer hadn't been touched. If robbery wasn't the motive, then what was?

Slipping into the darkened bedroom, Eve opened the drawer in her nightstand and removed her weapon. Even though she lived alone, she'd always been very careful about putting away her gun when she got home from work. But lately, since Lucy Stringer's murder, she'd been taking the .38 out of the drawer at bedtime and leaving it on top of her nightstand, within reach. Eve wasn't sure what that said about her or her state of mind, but now was not the time for deep analysis.

Crossing the room, she turned on the light, her gaze scouring the corners. She checked the closet, the bathroom and underneath the bed before going back out to do the same in the living room and kitchen. But once again, she detected no sign of a break-in. If her personal belongings had been rummaged through, everything had been meticulously put back in place.

Opening the sliding glass door to the tiny balcony, she carefully examined the lock. The latches on such doors were easily manipulated, but she hadn't gone to the trouble of installing a stronger bolt. Police officers were notorious for their own lax security, but now she chided herself for her neglect. Cop or not, she was a woman living alone, and she should have taken the necessary precautions.

Closing and locking the sliding door, she returned to the front door and checked the lock there, as well. Again no tool marks, no sign of a forced entry. So how had the intruder gotten in?

The same way he'd gotten into Lucy Stringer's apartment? She and Tony had assumed, since there were no marks on the doors or windows, that Lucy had known her killer. She'd invited him inside. But what if that wasn't the case? What if he was a good enough lock pick that he didn't leave any marks behind? Just like he didn't leave any prints or DNA behind to lead the police back to him.

Or even more frightening, what if he had somehow gotten a key to Lucy's apartment? And to Eve's?

A chill descended over her as she closed and locked the door, turned the dead bolt and shot home the chain lock. Fetching a broom from the tiny closet off the kitchen, she broke the handle with a hammer, then fitted the wood to the sliding door so that even if the lock was broken, the door couldn't be easily opened.

But in spite of her precautions, Eve was frightened.

Someone had been in her apartment. Someone had violated her personal space, and he'd left nothing behind but a faint, unidentifiable scent. Evidence that couldn't be analyzed under a microscope or traced back to a suspect because already it was starting to fade.

Realizing she made a vulnerable target at the window, Eve turned off the light and stood in darkness. If he was out there somewhere, watching her apartment, he would know she was home.

Would he try to get inside again?

Chapter Six

The phone rang just after three o'clock on Monday morning. Eve woke up instantly, an unnamed premonition hovering on the fringes of her consciousness. She grabbed the .38 on the nightstand instead of reaching for the phone or the alarm clock. Peering into the darkness, she let the phone ring twice more before she snatched it up.

"Barrett," she said cautiously.

"Eve?"

She recognized Clare's voice at once, and Eve's stomach clenched in alarm. "Yes?"

"A couple of students found a body about an hour ago in Grover Park. I want you to get over there and take a look."

Eve was already up, dragging clothes out of her closet. "I'll pick up Tony on my way."

"No, don't bother," Clare said, then paused. "He's already at the scene."

OFF THE BEATEN TRACK, Grover Park was a peaceful, landscaped enclave on the city's South Side. The perimeter of the park was well lit and easily accessible from the street, but deeper inside, huge oak trees and lush vegetation cast shadows over the walkways and benches.

Eve pulled her car to the curb near the patrol units and got out. The morning was damp and misty, and a cool front had moved in sometime during the night. The streets were all but deserted. The hour and the weather kept the usual gawkers and rubberneckers who accumulated at crime scenes to a minimum, and as Eve entered the park, a feeling of aloneness came over her.

She could hear voices and occasional laughter from the other officers in the distance, but the trail she followed seemed isolated, almost eerie. The steady dripping of mist from the trees reminded her of a heartbeat, and she recalled reading in high school that Grover Park, like Washington Square in New York, had once been a cemetery.

If she used her imagination, she could probably see corpses rising in the fog, she thought wryly. Even in her line of work, the occasional twinge of superstition was not unheard of, and she felt the hair at the back of her neck rise unaccountably.

Maybe her uneasiness had something to do with her experience last evening, she decided. Her sense that someone had been in her apartment. But as she glanced around, seeing only haze and shadow, she had the strangest feeling again that she was being watched from the dense foliage, that the murderer might not have fled the scene as expected, but instead was lurking in the darkness. Like he had been last night?

Her senses on full alert, Eve resisted the urge to draw her weapon as she made her way along the murky path.

The first person she saw when she finally emerged into the clearing was Tony. He left the circle of cops and came toward her.

When he saw her face, he said anxiously, ''Everything okay?''

Eve gave a shaky laugh. "I just got a little spooked back there. The trail is almost pitch-black."

He glanced over her shoulder, into the darkness behind her. "I never realized how isolated this damn park is. My brothers and I used to play here all the time as kids, but in daylight, the place seems harmless."

"It's just like any other big city park," Eve said, trying to shrug off the lingering disquiet. She nodded toward the cluster of police officers. "So what happened?"

"Some kids stumbled across a body earlier this morning. They said they were just out walking, but I have a feeling something a little more nefarious was going on."

"Drugs?"

"Maybe. By the looks of the trampled grass, there were several of them out here, but only two stayed behind to call 911. And they're not naming names. At least not yet." He paused. "Looks like the victim was stabbed to death."

Eve gave him a sharp glance in the darkness. "Do you think the kids had anything to do with the murder?"

"Not likely. You'll understand why after you have a look."

The CSU team had finished in the immediate area and the coroner's investigator was examining the body. Eve followed Tony through the group of police officers milling about the area. Portable lights had been set up, and as Eve stared down at the victim, her throat went dry. She understood instantly what Tony had meant.

"I know her," she said in shock. She glanced up at him. "I saw her at Durty Nellie's on Friday night. She was the bartender."

"Her name is Megan Riley," he said without emotion. He didn't let on whether he'd recognized the woman or not, but Eve couldn't help remembering that Megan had asked about Tony, had seemed more than a little interested in him. "We found her address in her purse. She lived a couple of blocks over on Newell."

"Was she on duty at the pub tonight—last night?" Eve amended, remembering the time.

"Nellie's is closed on Sunday nights. We're trying to track down a home phone number for the owner, or one of the other employees, see if we can pinpoint when she was last seen alive."

"I'd say she's been here at least twenty-four hours," the coroner's investigator said. "Although the cool front makes that estimation iffy."

Eve knew what he was saying. Neither rigor mortis—the stiffening of the body—or algor mortis—the cooling of the body—was an exact way to establish time of death. Too many outside variables, such as temperature, could slow or speed the process. The best way to determine time of death was to find the last person who had seen the victim alive, as Tony had suggested.

"Twenty-four hours," Eve repeated. "And the body wasn't discovered until this morning? Parks are always packed on Sundays."

"This is a fairly remote area," Tony said. "Most of the traffic is in the main part of the park, near the playground and picnic tables."

The woman's eyes were open and staring, her clothing covered in dried blood. Like Lucy Stringer, she'd been stabbed several times in the chest. A bruise darkened one pale cheek, as if a blow might have been used to stun her. She was attractive even in death, but the beauty mark at the corner of her mouth stood out starkly against her blanched skin.

There was something about that beauty mark....

Eve knelt beside the body. "What about trace evidence?"

"Almost nil," one of the CSU techs told her. "The area's been contaminated. The grass around the body was badly trampled by the kids, which means no usable prints, no hair or fibers, although we'll suction her clothing. We've got her purse, but we're not likely to find anything there, either. The guy was thorough, I'll say that for him. I'd swear he used a vacuum cleaner."

His words chilled Eve. The brutality was one thing, the cunning something else altogether. What kind of killer had the know-how to be so meticulous?

Someone who knew what the police would be looking for....

Eve drew a long breath. "I don't see any defense wounds," she remarked, glancing back up at Tony. She stood and pulled him away from the crowd of officers. "Why did Clare call us out on this?" she asked in a low voice.

"That's pretty obvious, isn't it? Two victims in less than a week, within a five-mile radius of each other. Both of them stabbed to death."

Eve frowned. "You think the same guy who killed Lucy Stringer killed Megan Riley?"

Tony shrugged. "Could be. Neither of them had any defense wounds, which suggests they both knew their killer. Both crime scenes were spotless." He paused. "We won't know for certain until we see the autopsy and lab reports, but Megan Riley doesn't appear to have been sexually assaulted, and neither was Lucy."

Eve glanced down at the body. "I thought of that myself, and it puzzles me." She turned back to Tony. The light was spotty where they stood. She could only see a portion of his face. The rest was dark, shadowed. Unreadable. For some reason, Eve shivered. "If he's not killing these women for some sort of perverted sexual gratification, why is he killing them?''

''Maybe the kill is his gratification.''

Eve shook her head. ''I don't think so. I mean, he's not cutting them up. He's not drawing it out, prolonging their pain. He does it quickly, like he wants to get it over with. Like he's not particularly enjoying it. There's no excessive stabbing. No mutilation. The faces were left virtually untouched except for some bruising. It's almost…clinical.''

''The kill is not his main objective,'' Tony said quietly, almost as if he hated to put voice to her suspicions. ''Is that what you're trying to say?''

Eve nodded, feeling a shudder of unease ripple through her. She thought about last evening, coming home to her empty apartment. She was less certain now that someone had broken in, but she knew she should probably mention the incident to Tony. For some reason, she didn't. Eve suspected it had something to do with her desire for his approval. If he thought she was prone to hysterical imaginings, would he still want her for a partner? Would she still be allowed to work on these cases?

''It's almost as if he's using them for some ulterior motive.'' Her voice took on a hushed quality in the darkness. ''These women are nothing more than tools to him. The kills are secondary to what his true agenda is.''

Tony moved slightly away from her, into deeper shadow. ''The two murders might not be related at all. We could have two killers on our hands.''

''You don't believe that,'' she challenged him. ''You knew after the first one there'd be others.'' When Tony didn't answer, Eve lowered her voice even more. ''*How* did you know?''

He rubbed his hand across his forehead, as if he'd suddenly developed an excruciating headache. "I don't know."

His evasiveness made the chill inside Eve deepen. She had a dark premonition that Tony knew—or at least suspected—more than he was telling her about these killings. Because he was trying to spare her? Because he didn't think she had enough experience to deal with it?

Well, it was true, wasn't it? She was a fraud, and Eve had never been more aware of the fact than she was at that moment.

She gazed at Tony in the darkness. "You don't think he's picking his victims at random, either, do you? There's some kind of rhyme and reason to his kills. Some kind of connection between the victims."

"If it's the same killer, then it's a reasonable assumption the two women were somehow connected," Tony agreed.

Eve grew pensive, considering the possibilities. One seemed fairly obvious. "Megan Riley worked in a bar where a lot of cops hang out, and Lucy Stringer was the daughter of a detective."

"You think a cop's doing this?" Tony sounded disbelieving, but Eve suspected the same thought had already crossed his mind. He just didn't want to admit it.

"I'm not saying anything like that. But whoever is doing this knows how to clean up the crime scene. No prints, no fibers, nothing beneath the victims' nails. Neither Lucy nor Megan suspected they were in danger until it was too late."

"That doesn't mean it was a cop."

"No, but we can talk to some of the officers who go to the pub regularly, see if they remember anyone being overly friendly with Megan. Maybe she met someone there Saturday night. A lot of the same officers probably knew Lucy Stringer, as well. At least it's a new angle to explore."

She couldn't see Tony's face clearly in the shadows, but Eve knew that he was frowning. She sensed his disapproval before he ever spoke a word. ''Do you have any idea what you're letting yourself in for?''

''What do you mean?'' she asked doubtfully.

''I'm talking about the Brotherhood, Eve. You know how it is.''

''So we're not even supposed to ask questions?''

He glanced away, letting his gaze scour the trees behind her. ''We'll ask our questions, all right. Only we have to go about it the right way. You can't go off half-cocked, putting people on the defensive. Cops don't like that.''

Eve opened her mouth to argue with him, then abruptly bit back her retort. He was right. Any perceived threat, and police officers were known to close rank, protecting their own. That had been her first lesson in IAD, and though the attitude and sometimes arrogance never failed to irritate her, she knew it was something she had to put up with. To argue further was useless and might jeopardize her assignment.

It was almost a shock to realize that the Lucy Stringer case and now Megan Riley's murder were secondary to Eve's own agenda. She was here to observe and evaluate Tony's performance on the job, not to catch killers.

But as Eve glanced back at Megan's bloodstained body, she realized that her prime objective had been changed by the murders, whether the brass liked it or not.

THEY SPENT HOURS canvassing the park and surrounding neighborhoods, searching for the murder weapon or an eyewitness, anything that could lead them to a suspect. The misty cold crawled through Tony's clothing as he combed the dense foliage in the park, using his Maglite to probe shadows and hideaways.

A few feet away from him, another cop was doing the same thing, but in some ways, Tony felt disconnected, a million miles away from the others. It wasn't yet dawn, but the horizon had lightened, glimmering for a moment between daybreak and darkness. The shadows grew longer, deeper, and the mist swirled like a living creature in the heavy wind off the lake.

He thought about Megan Riley and Lucy Stringer, and their killer.

He thought about Ashley, and her killer sitting on death row.

Was it possible Daniel O'Roarke was somehow masterminding these killings from behind bars?

Or was all this some bizarre coincidence?

Ashley had had seven stab wounds to her chest, and her face had been bruised, more severely than either Lucy's or Megan's. Her murder had seemed one of passion, almost of hatred, but there was something different and troubling about the way Lucy and Megan had been killed. Eve had put her finger on it precisely. The kills seemed clinical, passionless, cold-blooded but not mind sick.

Seven stab wounds to Ashley's heart and seven stab wounds to Lucy's heart. Tony would be willing to bet money that the autopsy on Megan Riley would reveal the same pattern.

Coincidence? Not likely, he thought grimly.

A copycat killer was a possibility, but Daniel O'Roarke wasn't the usual kind of psycho who attracted ardent imitators. Ashley had been his first victim, and then, while waiting to stand trial, he'd killed Tony's father, the lead detective on the case, out of revenge or perhaps desperation.

Or at least that was the conclusion reached by CPD and by Tony's family after Sean Gallagher had mysteriously disappeared. But without a body, without a murder weapon, without hard evidence and only supposition, O'Roarke had never stood trial for Sean's murder.

But he'd been on death row for nearly seven years for Ashley's, and now, as the anniversary of her death drew near, someone was killing again.

Tony raked a hand across his damp brow, remembering that he'd seen Megan Riley at the pub on Saturday night. He couldn't be sure, but he thought he remembered seeing Lucy Stringer there on the night she'd been killed, too. Was the pub the connection? Somehow Tony didn't think it was going to be that easy.

A dark coldness seeped through him, chilling him to the bone with a dread he didn't want to give name to. But the omen was there and had been since Lucy Stringer's body was discovered. Somehow, in some way, Tony himself was the connection to these murders.

He closed his eyes, urging his mind to return to Saturday evening, forcing himself to remember things he didn't think he wanted to remember. He and Eve had left his mother's house around ten o'clock. They'd talked for a while before she'd dropped him at his apartment, but he'd been too restless to sleep. A thousand thoughts—about Ashley, about Eve, about poor Lucy Stringer—had churned inside his head. The images had been so disturbing, he'd gone out to the pub to try and chase them away. And to keep from being alone.

He remembered seeing Fiona and David there, and he'd talked to them for a while, had a beer with them. Clare had come in around eleven or so, and Tony had seen her having a drink with Vic D'Angelo. The usual crowd had been around, but then, at some point, they'd all drifted away, and the next thing Tony remembered, he was standing alone in the parking lot beside his car.

"Need a ride?" a feminine voice queried from the shadows.

"I have my car," he said, squinting in the darkness, trying to make out the woman's features.

She walked toward him, smiling, inviting. She wound a dark curl around one finger as she stared up at him. "You're Tony Gallagher, aren't you? I've seen you in the pub before. I'm Megan Riley."

The haze in his head cleared enough to allow him to recognize her. She was the new bartender Curly had hired to give him a hand on busy nights. "What are you doing out here?" he asked, surprised to hear that his words were slurred. What in the hell was going on? He'd only had one beer, for cripe's sake.

"I got off duty at midnight." She kept on smiling and coiling that lock of dark hair around one finger as she slanted him a glance. *"If you don't need a ride, maybe you could give me one. Otherwise I have to walk home, and I don't much like being alone in the dark."*

"Where do you live?"

"In the Lake Vista Apartments on Newell."

He turned toward his car, staggered, and she caught his arm, laughing. "Hey, looks like you had a few too many tonight. Maybe I'd better drive." She reached for the handle, opened his door....

Blood roared in Tony's ears as the memory faded. Or was it a memory? Maybe he'd dreamed up the whole thing, had some sort of weird vision because of the woman's murder. But if he *had* seen her Saturday night in the parking lot, and she'd been dead for at least twenty-four hours, that might mean he was one of the last people to see her alive. That might mean...

His head began to throb as a wave of panic rolled over him. He *had* seen her that night. Tony knew it. He could still picture her smiling up at him, her fingers on his door handle, leaving her prints on the chrome....

Now why had he thought of the fingerprints? he wondered uneasily. So what if the victim's prints were on his car, or even inside his apartment? It didn't mean anything.

No, but it sure as hell would look suspicious. And given Tony's reputation, he wasn't certain how many people would be lining up to come to his defense. It would be a little too easy to believe that he'd finally gone over the edge. It happened occasionally and everyone knew it. But it wasn't something cops liked to talk about.

Tony's stomach churned sickeningly. What the hell was wrong with him? Why was the rest of the night such a blank? He had no idea how he'd gotten home, but when Clare's call awakened him just before three, he'd been lying in bed fully dressed. And his car had been in its space outside his apartment.

He couldn't remember much about the night Lucy Stringer was killed, either. He'd had some kind of black-out...just like on the night Ashley had died.

EVE WAS STANDING by one of the patrol cars on the street, talking with the first officer on the scene, when Tony emerged from the park. He'd thrown on a windbreaker earlier, but it hadn't done much to keep him dry. He looked soaked and exhausted, but what concerned Eve more was the paleness of his face, the drawn look to his features.

She walked over to him. "Find anything?"

He shook his head. "We need to get more men out here ASAP. It's like looking for a needle in a haystack in all that underbrush, but who knows? We might get lucky."

"We could use some luck," Eve said wearily. She was exhausted, too. "No evidence, no leads and now a second murder."

He glanced down at her. His features softened a bit in the day's first light, but there were shadows in his eyes. An unexplained darkness that brought another shiver to Eve. "We'll find him. Sooner or later, we'll get him."

"But what if we don't find him in time? What if someone else dies? I can't help thinking about the next victim, who she might be," Eve said worriedly.

"I know." For a moment, he looked as if he wanted to reach for her, but instead he turned away, his expression distant and bleak. "But you can't let it tear you up inside. You do your job and then you go home and you live your life. That's the way it has to be. Otherwise…"

"Otherwise, what?" she asked when his voice trailed away.

He shrugged. "Otherwise you won't last long in homicide."

Go home and live her life. Forget the way Lucy Stringer and Megan Riley had looked in death. Forget that two young women had been brutally murdered, and that the murderer was out there somewhere, planning his next kill.

Eve couldn't forget any of those things, and she didn't think Tony could, either. The shadows in his eyes had been cast by the victims he'd seen, the killers he'd chased, the violence and unspeakable crimes he was helpless to prevent. He didn't go home and live his life. This was his life.

Turning away from him, Eve scanned the handful of onlookers who had gathered at daybreak around the yellow tape that cordoned off the park entrance. They were drawn to the crime scene as flies were to honey. "Where do they all come from?" she murmured in disgust.

"Nothing like the scent of blood to bring them out of the woodwork."

Eve's gaze lingered on a woman who stood apart from the crowd. The collar of her raincoat was turned up, touching the brim of her floppy rain hat. Her face was almost completely hidden, but there was something familiar about her. Eve stared at her for a long moment, willing the woman to meet her gaze. But instead, she lifted a camera, snapped several shots in Tony and Eve's direction, then turned and disappeared down the street.

"Did you recognize that woman?" Eve nudged Tony's arm. "The one who just left?"

He glanced in the region she indicated, then frowned. "No, why?"

"I don't know," she said uneasily. "She was taking pictures."

"Probably a reporter."

"I don't think so. She seemed familiar."

A frown flickered across his brow. "Maybe she was. They're all the same, these people. You see the same faces at all the crime scenes. Death is their entertainment. They listen to police scanners like some people listen to music." He paused, then muttered, "Let's get the hell out of here. I'm going home to change, then I'll meet you at the station."

Eve looked around for his car. "Where are you parked?"

He nodded across the street, to a '69 Mustang that she recognized, with something of a shock, as the same one he'd had in high school. He'd always driven city rides until now, and she could understand why. If the car had been a horse, she would have sworn it was on its last legs. Rather than vintage and well cared for, the pale yellow Mustang appeared to have seen its better days years ago. The paint was faded and dull, with rust showing through in several places. It was the kind of car a man with very little regard for appearances or convention would drive.

Eve's vehicle, on the other hand, was a dark blue sedan—sedate, not too expensive, but respectable, reliable and perfectly conventional. She knew what her vehicle said about her.

She wondered what kind of car Ashley would have driven. Something sleek and beautiful on the outside, fast and a little dangerous on the inside? One that would openly court admiration?

Not fair, Eve scolded herself. Ashley had been a very nice person, in spite of her beauty and popularity. And if at times Eve had sensed there might be a darkness simmering beneath Ashley's brilliant surface, it had probably been due to Eve's jealousy more than any sort of insight. Nothing like unrequited love to skewer a woman's judgment of her rival.

But as Eve watched Tony head across the street, a vague memory tugged at her. She closed her eyes briefly, conjuring the image, willing it to form as it hovered nebulously on the fringes of her mind.

And then she had it. She'd been home for Easter vacation during her junior year of college and had gone out to a movie with some friends. Returning home after midnight, she'd noticed an unfamiliar car parked down the street from Ashley's house. Eve had braked at a nearby intersection for a stop sign, and as she'd gazed down the street, Ashley had gotten out of the car and run around to the driver's side. The window had come down and she'd leaned inside to give the driver one final, passionate kiss.

Eve hadn't thought much about the incident at the time. She'd assumed Tony had gotten a new car, but why he hadn't parked in Ashley's driveway, she didn't know.

But now, staring at his yellow Mustang, the same one from high school, it hit Eve, like a physical blow, that it hadn't been Tony in that car. Ashley, the perfect woman, had been out with someone else that night.

Had Tony known?

Somehow Eve was almost certain he hadn't, that he still didn't know. He'd mourned Ashley Dallas for years, probably compared every woman he'd ever dated to her, when all along, she'd never been the woman he thought she was.

Eve's heart hammered inside her as a wave of emotion washed over her. If Tony knew of Ashley's infidelity, would it make a difference in the way he felt about Eve?

Probably, but not in a good way. If she told him, he'd resent her for shattering his image of the only woman he'd ever loved.

There was no way Eve could ever tell him. Not just for her sake, but for Tony's. She would never want to hurt him like that. Besides, she didn't know for sure what she'd seen.

Turning, she headed for her own car. A few yards away, a patrol unit pulled into the street just as a white van with the call letters of a local TV station emblazoned on its panel came to a squealing stop at the curb. There was some confusion, arms waving, tempers flaring, and for a moment, no one saw the car that had been trailing the van. As the van whipped to the curb, a white car shot forward.

The tableau unfolded in slow motion then. Eve heard someone call out to Tony, but her own vocal cords were paralyzed. She stood frozen, watching the car bear down on him, until finally her adrenaline kicked in. She lunged toward the street, but it was too late.

The car clipped Tony, lifting him off his feet, and Eve heard the sickening crunch of metal against flesh as he rolled across the hood, disappearing for a split second on the other side of the car.

The driver never even looked back.

Chapter Seven

Eve sat in the emergency room waiting area at University Hospital for a good forty-five minutes before the doctor came out to talk to her. She'd tried to intimidate the nurses by waving her shield in their faces and demanding to know her partner's condition, but all they'd tell her was that the doctor was still in with Tony, and he would be out shortly to speak with her.

When she finally saw the doctor emerge from the cubicle where Tony had been taken, Eve all but pounced on him. His white lab coat was smeared with blood, but Eve had no way of knowing whether or not it was Tony's. The ER was jammed as usual.

"How is Detective Gallagher?" she asked anxiously. "Is he going to be okay?"

The trauma resident didn't look much older than Eve, and his eyes revealed the same world-weary expression she'd seen on the faces of countless cops. Battle fatigue, she called it. A young face turned old by a barrage of death and violence most lay people couldn't even begin to imagine.

His face was homely, but the turquoise eyes he trained on her were truly remarkable, in spite of the shadow of exhaustion. They reminded Eve of the Caribbean Sea, tranquil yet somehow turbulent at the same time.

"A concussion, bruised ribs—possibly fractured," he said in clipped tones. "I've ordered X rays and an MRI, and we'll know more about the extent of his injuries once I have the results. For now, he's in stable but guarded condition."

Eve didn't like the sound of that at all. His injuries were much more serious than she'd been hoping for. Somehow she'd always thought of Tony as invincible. He'd get knocked down, yes, but he'd always get right back up again. The image of him lying helpless and unconscious in a hospital bed left her shaken. She drew a hand across her mouth, trying to quell the rising tide of emotion inside her.

"Is he conscious?"

"Oh, yeah, he's alert," the doctor told her. He gave her a wry glance. "He's not the most cooperative patient I've ever treated."

No, he wouldn't be, Eve thought with a trickle of relief. If Tony was already raising hell, that had to mean he was going to be all right, didn't it?

"Can I see him?"

"Actually, I think that might be a good idea." The doctor scribbled something on a chart, then glanced up at her. He tried to look gruff, but somehow the fatigue softened the sharp edges. "He's insisting he doesn't need to stay for the tests, but I can't stress enough how inadvisable it would be for him to walk out of here now. A head wound can be a very dangerous injury, and if he does have a fractured rib, we have to be careful it doesn't puncture a lung. There's no way he can leave this hospital for at least twenty-four hours. Maybe more."

"I understand. I'll talk to him."

The doctor nodded absently, his attention already divided

between Eve and the nurse who had come up to him. The moment he turned away, Eve headed down the hallway. She knocked on the door of the ER cubicle, then stuck her head inside. "Safe to come in?"

Tony was alone and he didn't look at all happy. He was lying on the bed, shirtless, staring at the ceiling, and Eve's gaze was drawn immediately to the deep purple bruises on his side, then to the bandage covering the wound on his forehead.

"What's the verdict?" she tried to say lightly as she closed the door and walked into the room. But the sight of those bruises left her weak-kneed because she realized again what a close call he'd had earlier. And Eve had been too paralyzed with fear to help him. What if they'd been in a situation where she'd needed to use her weapon to save him? Would she have been able to respond quickly enough?

She realized now that she hadn't considered all the ramifications when she'd accepted this assignment. She was a trained cop, and she knew the correct protocol, but she hadn't been on the street in a long time. Working IAD complaints was a lot different than tracking down murderers and hit-and-run suspects.

She wasn't qualified for this assignment, and she knew it. Her own interests—and in fairness, Tony's—had compelled her to accept a duty that she'd known even then might turn out to be a mistake. And she'd been right to have doubts. What if Tony had been killed? How would she have been able to live with herself?

He gave her a long appraisal. "What's the matter? You don't look so good."

"Look who's talking," she tried to quip. "I haven't seen bruises like that since…" She was no good at cop humor, and they both knew it. The joke fell away, and she closed her eyes briefly. "I'm sorry, Tony."

He frowned. "For what?"

"I saw the car coming, but I couldn't yell a warning. I froze. You could have been killed—"

He cut her off with a muttered oath. "I thought that was what this was all about." He struggled to sit up, and Eve hurried to his side, taking his arm.

"Don't do that," she said urgently. "You should be lying down. The doctor said you could have a broken rib."

"I don't." He sat on the edge of the bed in spite of Eve's protests. "I'm just banged up a little. I know what a broken rib feels like, and believe me, this isn't it."

"Still, you shouldn't be moving around...." It was no use. He had no intention of lying back down. Eve was wasting her breath, and she knew it.

"Listen." His blue eyes met hers. Eve shivered in spite of herself at the intensity of his gaze. "You didn't do anything wrong. I didn't see the car coming. I had too much on my mind, and I wasn't paying attention. If anyone's to blame here, besides the driver, it's me."

"But—"

"No buts. No second-guessing. In case you've forgotten, you were the first one to my side."

Their gazes met again, and Eve thought fleetingly how easy it would be to lose herself in Tony's eyes, to melt in the warmth that shimmered just beneath the surface.

She realized in a flash of devastating insight that the crush she'd always had on him was fast becoming something much deeper.

Over the years, she'd been haunted by his memory, just as he had been possessed by Ashley's. Every other man in Eve's life had paled in comparison to him. She wondered, almost sadly, if she would always feel that way. If she would grow old and lonely, still longing for Tony the way he would always yearn for Ashley.

"Eve?"

His deep voice caught her off guard. Eve's gaze flashed to his face, and she wondered if he had been able to tell what she was thinking. She felt her cheeks grow warm, and she tried to turn away from him. But he caught her hand, pulling her gently toward him.

She found herself standing between his legs, could feel, or at least imagine, the warmth of his bare skin. Muscles rippled beneath the bruises, and something primitive rose inside Eve. Something more basic and simple than love.

She resisted the urge to spread her hands against his chest, to feel his heartbeat beneath her fingertips. She ached to touch him, to kiss him, but at the same time, she was afraid of revealing her true feelings. Afraid of being hurt. Afraid of taking an irrevocable step in their relationship. What they had now was something good. It wasn't love, not for him, but it was a closeness Eve didn't want to lose. If he turned away from her now…she would be crushed.

He lifted his hand and brushed back the hair from her face. His touch was gentle and warm, but his fingers trembled slightly, revealing a deeper, darker desire.

He was smiling at her now, wistfully, his blue gaze knowing and bittersweet. "What are we going to do about this?"

"I don't know."

"I don't know, either, but if you keep looking at me like that, I won't be responsible for my actions."

"I'm not…I didn't mean to…"

"No, you wouldn't," he agreed. "That's what I admire about you. You don't play games. You're open and honest, about your feelings and about everything else, and I appreciate that."

No, she wanted to tell him. *I'm not honest. Especially about my feelings. What if I told you I'd been in love with you for years? What if I told you that while you were grieving for Ashley, a part of me was already wondering if there could ever be anything between us?*

Guilt surged through Eve, and she suddenly felt ashamed of all her secrets. She no longer wanted Tony to kiss her, but instead felt like slinking away, hiding in some cold, dark place where he would never be able to learn the truth about her.

She wasn't the person he thought she was. How had she ever sat in judgment of Ashley?

The door opened, and Eve sprang away from him, grateful for an excuse to put some distance between them. She could feel Tony's gaze on her, but she couldn't meet his eyes. She focused instead on the doctor.

"When can I get out of here, Doc?" Tony asked abruptly.

"As I told you earlier, at the very least, you've got some bruised ribs and a mild concussion. I can't release you until I see the results of the X rays and the MRI, and unfortunately, we're backed up for hours. I'd like to keep you overnight, just to be on the safe side."

"Look, I don't need any tests. My ribs aren't broken, and I can live with the headache." Before either Eve or the doctor could stop him, Tony got to his feet, wincing at the pain as he reached for his shirt on a nearby chair.

"You're asking for trouble, Detective," the doctor warned him.

"Yeah, well, what else is new?" He shrugged into his shirt.

"Look, I've been here almost thirty-six hours solid," the doctor said angrily. "I don't much feel like arguing."

"Then don't."

The doctor cut Eve a glance, as if to say what are you going to do about this? And he was right. She couldn't le Tony walk out of here. She couldn't let him endanger hi health, and maybe his job.

"Cut the crap, Tony," she said with a scowl. "You don' need to prove anything here. We go back a long way, re member? I know you're a tough guy. But this just make you look stupid."

He appeared stunned for a moment, as if she had phys ically struck him. Then his expression froze, cutting of whatever emotion he might have been feeling as he gav her a long, hard glare. "Excuse me?"

"You heard me." She lifted her chin, refusing to bacl down even under the intensity of his challenge. "You won't be any good to anyone in this condition. You migh even cause further damage to yourself, and frankly, I'm no all that keen on working with a partner who has a concus sion."

He opened his mouth—to lash out at her, Eve was almos certain—but the doctor quickly took her side. "She's right And I'm afraid your CO agrees with her, Detective. I jus spoke to Lieutenant Foxx a few moments ago. She said to tell you that if you refuse to follow my orders, you'll be facing an indefinite medical leave."

Tony swore, using a word Eve had heard rarely even in the police department, but the doctor seemed completely unfazed. The ER had obviously toughened him. "We're none of us invincible or indispensable, Detective, although it's not always pleasant to come to that realization." And with that, he turned and exited the room, leaving Tony and Eve facing off.

"Thanks for the show of support," he said bitterly.

"Oh, knock off the pity party."

"What the hell is the matter with you all of a sudden?" he snapped.

Eve folded her arms calmly. "Nothing. The doctor happens to be right, that's all. You're not invincible and you're not indispensable. You can spend twenty-four hours in the hospital and the world won't come to an end."

"No," he said quietly. "But our boy just might kill again while I'm in here."

His voice sent a chill through Eve. His eyes were dark and shadowed, his words almost prophetic. "Twenty-four hours," she repeated. "That's all."

Whatever argument bubbled immediately to his lips was stifled, almost by force, it seemed to Eve. He gazed at her for a long, enigmatic moment before turning to sit on the bed. With a grimace, he eased himself back against the pillow. "Okay, you win. Satisfied?"

"It has nothing to do with winning—" Her cell phone rang, interrupting her, and Eve jerked it out of her pocket. "Barrett."

Clare said coolly, "Let me talk to Tony."

Eve handed over the phone, not bothering to ask how the lieutenant had known she would be with Tony. When she hadn't been able to get Tony on his own smashed phone, she would naturally have tried Eve. "It's Clare."

Tony hesitated for a split second, as if considering the consequences of refusing, then he grabbed the phone from her hand and lifted it to his ear. "Yeah."

He listened for a moment, his brow like a thundercloud. "You wouldn't. Dammit, Clare, that's my case—" There was another silence, then he growled, "Oh, I get the message all right. Loud and clear." Without another word, he slapped the phone closed and handed it back to Eve. She had no idea what Clare had told him, but it was obvious Tony was furious.

The phone rang almost instantly, and Eve answered it.

"You tell that SOB he better *never* hang up on me again you got that?"

Eve grimaced at Clare's tone. Tony had managed to pu them both in the doghouse. "I'll tell him."

"Look, Eve, I'm serious about this. If he doesn't sta and get those tests, he's going on medical leave, or at th very least, desk duty. I won't have him out on the stree endangering lives. If he doesn't stay put, he's off th Stringer case permanently. And that means I'll have to tak you off, too."

Eve got the point. Wherever Tony was assigned, sh would be, too. That was the whole purpose of her tempo rary transfer.

"I'll take care of it," she promised.

"You do that." There was nothing veiled about Clare' threat. "I don't have to remind you this is the very thin the bosses are worried about. One more incident an Tony's out."

"Okay." Eve glanced at him. He was lying rigidly o the bed, scowling up at her, as if she were the cause of al his immediate problems.

"Oh, and one more thing." Clare paused. "You can tel him we got the hit-and-run driver. She's already i lockup."

Eve wondered why Clare hadn't told him hersel "Her?"

"Yeah. Maria Mancini was driving that car."

EVE SPENT THE REMAINDER of the morning going door-to door in the neighborhoods surrounding the park, searchin for eyewitnesses, but nothing turned up. When she finall made it back to the station, she typed her report into th computer, and then, after lunch, met with the rest of the team in Clare's office.

To Eve's surprise, Vic D'Angelo had been asked to sit in on the meeting, and he gave her a sardonic smile when she slipped into her seat.

After leaving the hospital, she'd gone home to shower and change, and now she was wearing one of her business suits. D'Angelo ogled her legs, not even bothering to camouflage his leer. Eve tried her best to ignore him.

"Vic's not yet officially on the case," Clare explained, sipping coffee from a ceramic mug with the Chicago Police Department emblem on the side. She set the cup aside and gazed at the group of detectives assembled in her office. "He's volunteered to do some of the legwork, though, as his own caseload allows. With Tony out of commission, I'm sure you'll welcome his help."

Eve could feel his oily gaze on her, and she darted him a glance. He lifted a brow knowingly, giving her another once-over that made her skin crawl.

When Eve glanced back at Clare, the older woman's eyes had narrowed on her, as if she'd witnessed the exchange with D'Angelo and hadn't liked it. Eve wondered again if anything was going on between them. D'Angelo didn't seem like Clare's type, but then, Eve didn't really know the woman well enough to make that assumption. The only thing Eve felt certain of was that the lieutenant had it in for Tony.

As for D'Angelo, he was the type of cop who would use whatever tools he had at his disposal to ingratiate himself with his CO. And Eve was almost certain that same self-serving willingness would extend all the way to the top, if he was given the chance. If the brass—including the superintendent himself—were out to get Tony, they'd have a willing recruit in Vic D'Angelo. How far would he be willing to go to make inroads with Ed Dawson?

Realizing her mind had strayed too far off course, Eve forced herself to focus. For the duration of the meeting, she made sure she didn't make eye contact with D'Angelo again.

Until further notice, the Stringer and Riley homicides would be investigated separately, but the detectives on each case agreed to meet regularly to compare notes and share leads. Eve had been itching to interview the owner and employees at the pub where Megan Riley had worked, but now to do so would be a breach in protocol. She could be written up for interfering in an investigation, but Eve also knew that given her temporary status in the Detective Division, it probably didn't much matter. And besides, it might be worth it, depending on what she found out.

"Can I have a word with you?" she asked Clare, after everyone else had filed out of the office.

The lieutenant glanced up from her paperwork, her gaze cool and assessing. "What's on your mind?"

"I want to ask a favor."

Clare's expression instantly became shuttered. She sat back in her chair and stared up at Eve. "Did Tony put you up to this?"

"No, of course not. He has no idea I'm here. It's not what you think."

Clare arched a brow. "You're not here to go to bat for him? You seem to have become his staunchest supporter these days, and I can't help but wonder how that'll go over with the brass. Especially the superintendent. He doesn't like Tony. They go way back."

"I know," Eve said, surprised by Clare's candor. "I used to live in their neighborhood."

"I keep forgetting you and Tony have a past, as well."

Clare's smile was frosty. "But then, Tony has a past with a lot of people, doesn't he?"

"I wouldn't know about that," Eve said just as coolly. "I'm not here to talk about Tony's past or my assignment. I want permission to interview Maria Mancini."

Clare looked momentarily taken aback. "I don't think that's a good idea."

"Why not?"

"You're not a homicide detective," she said bluntly, almost smugly. "I think you're starting to forget why you were brought into this division, and that once this issue with Tony is resolved one way or another, you'll go back to where you came from." Her tone told Eve just exactly what she thought of IAD. Clare might be willing to use Internal Affairs to suit her purpose, but that still didn't mean she had to like it.

"I'm not asking to be assigned to the case," Eve argued. "I just want to talk to her."

"Gee, Eve, if I didn't know better, I might think your interest here is a little more personal than it should be."

Eve held Clare's gaze. "Meaning?"

"Meaning there's no way I'm going to let you talk to that woman." Her voice turned cold, almost menacing. "And I better not hear that you've been down to lockup."

"That's your final word?"

"It is." She flicked her hand toward the door, dismissing Eve curtly.

Eve turned and headed toward the exit, but before she left the office, Clare said without looking up from her paperwork, "It might interest you to know some strings have already been pulled, from what I hear. There's a bail hearing scheduled—" she glanced at her watch "—in about an hour. Mancini will likely be released, since she has a slick attorney and no priors. Once she leaves lockup..." Clare glanced up. "I can't be responsible for who she talks to, now can I?"

EVE SLID ONTO A BAR stool at Durty Nellie's and ordered a soft drink. Curly, the bartender, waited on her, but he didn't linger to talk. He placed the drink in front of her and started to turn away.

"It's Curly, right?"

Reluctantly, he turned back. "Actually, it's Walter."

"How did you get the nickname Curly?" Eve asked in amusement, her gaze moving to his shiny bald pate.

He ran a hand over the smoothness. "Would you believe, I used to have curly hair? Long, too. Down to here at one time." He turned, measuring the center of his back. "That was back in my hippie days."

"You from Chicago?" Eve sipped her drink, studying him curiously. She had no doubt that he knew who she was and why she was here. Still, she figured it was best to lead up gently to her questions.

Not that Curly appeared in the least fragile. He was at least six-two, and probably weighed somewhere in the neighborhood of two hundred twenty-five. A man his size would have very little difficulty subduing young, slender women, Eve thought suddenly. Even those who might put up a struggle.

As if reading her mind, Curly scowled down at her. "You don't really want to know where I'm from, do you? You're here about Megan. Just like the two homicide dicks who came in here earlier."

Eve nodded, not bothering to conceal her true intentions. "I'm sorry about what happened to her. Had she worked here long?"

"Only a few weeks. Nice kid. Hard worker."

"Pretty, too," Eve murmured, glancing at him over the rim of her glass.

"Yeah," he said. "She was damn attractive, and more than one man who walked through that door noticed her. Mostly cops, I might add."

Eve caught his point and realized again that Curly was nobody's fool. If she'd suspected him, he'd neatly turned the tables.

"Did you know Megan before she came to work here?"

"Nah. She answered an ad I ran in the paper. Walked in one day, showed me her resume, and I hired her. I figured she needed the job. She was a part-time student at the university, and she had a little girl she wanted to support."

That was news to Eve. She'd known from the meeting earlier that Megan, like Lucy Stringer, was a student at the University of Chicago, but Eve hadn't known she was a mother. That made her death seem all the more tragic.

"The child didn't live with Megan, did she?" Megan's apartment had been sparsely furnished, with no sign of a child anywhere.

"She lives with Megan's mother. Somewhere in Indiana, I think. South Bend, maybe."

"Did you give that information to the detectives who interviewed you earlier?" Eve asked.

Curly shrugged. "Maybe. I don't know. They asked a lot of questions. I don't remember everything I said. Some things I'm just now remembering."

"Like what?"

"Like the way Megan asked to have off early Saturday night. Told me she had a headache, but looking back, she seemed fine up until then. Laughing and flirting with the customers like she always did."

"You think she lied about the headache?"

"I think she had a date," Curly said flatly. "And, yeah,

I think she lied about the headache. Wouldn't be the firs
time, would it?''

"Was she seeing someone regularly?'' Eve asked. ''She
have a steady boyfriend?''

"Not that I know of.'' He paused, then glanced away.

"You sure?'' Eve pressed.

Curly shrugged. ''Look, I don't know if she had a boy
friend or not. But one of the waitresses—I don't even re
member which one—was teasing her a couple days age
about a secret admirer.''

"Secret admirer?'' Adrenaline kicked through Eve'
veins. Lucy Stringer's landlady had said something along
the same lines. Lucy had received flowers and a love note
from some anonymous admirer a couple of weeks before
she was killed. That note still hadn't turned up, nor any
other clues leading to the identity of the admirer-stalker. I
was looking more and more evident that the same man had
killed Megan Riley. But the same question remained: if he
wasn't seducing these women, why was he killing them?

"Can you find out which waitress made that comment?'

"I guess I can try.''

"It'd be a big help.'' Eve paused, then said, ''You eve
see Megan leave here with a customer? Ever see a custome
act, maybe, a little too interested in her?''

Curly frowned. ''Like you said earlier, she was a pretty
girl. A lot of the customers were interested in her. A lot o
them came on too strong, but then, that's not unusual fo
cops, is it?''

If he really had an aversion to cops, as he sounded, i
was strange that he should be running a cop bar, Eve de
cided. She might be way off base, but something about
Curly aka Walter struck her as odd. Durty Nellie's wa
something of an institution on the South Side, but Eve had
been away from the neighborhood for a while. She didn'

know how long Curly had owned it. But she was sure going to find out.

"Let's go back to Saturday night. When did Megan first tell you she had a headache and that she wanted to leave early?"

"Right before she did leave. Around midnight."

"You didn't see her leave with anyone?"

"That would have been a little obvious, wouldn't it? I mean, if the guy was going to kill her."

"So you think she had plans to meet someone?"

He shrugged.

"Was there anything unusual about Saturday night?" Eve persisted. "Anything that might have alarmed Megan? A customer that got a little too aggressive, anything like that?"

"No more so than usual." Curly took a dish towel and started polishing the teak bar. "Megan knew how to handle the customers. She liked cops."

Cops again. Eve frowned. "Not everyone who comes in here is a cop."

"That's true." He stopped polishing the bar and leaned toward her slightly. "But Saturday night, the place was crawling with them. Not just the usuals, but some of the big boys. The brass."

"Like who?"

"Would you believe, the superintendent himself?"

Eve stared at him in shock. "Ed Dawson was here on Saturday night?"

Curly shrugged his beefy shoulders. "It wasn't the first time. He drops in every once in a while to slum with the beat cops and the patrol officers. Remind them that he's still one of them. From what I hear, he does that with joints like this all over town."

The door behind her opened, and Curly's glance slid over

Eve's shoulder. He frowned slightly, in what looked like annoyance, then went back to his polishing. Eve saw the newcomer in the mirror behind the bar as he approached her, and she stiffened.

Vic D'Angelo straddled the bar stool next to Eve's. "Little early for cocktails, isn't it?" He nodded toward the drink in front of her. "I never would have suspected you of drinking on the job, Barrett. Maybe you're not such a tight ass, after all."

"Yeah, I am," she said. "Not your type at all."

He grinned. "Sure you are. You just don't know it yet. It takes some women a little while to warm up to me. But when they do…" His voice trailed off suggestively and his grin broadened.

Eve had met cops like Vic before. Macho. Cocky. Self-absorbed. She knew how to handle them, how to avoid them, how to put them in their place when the situation warranted it. But there was something about Vic D'Angelo that left her feeling…violated somehow.

It takes some women a little while to warm up to me…

When Eve had been in here on Friday night, Vic had been flirting with Megan Riley. And he'd known Lucy Stringer since she was a child. He'd even told Eve that Lucy had once had a crush on him. But…what if it had been the other way around? What if he'd come on to Lucy and she'd rebuffed him, maybe even threatened to tell her father? An accusation like that could ruin a cop's career, not to mention a friendship.

Eve knew she was reaching, but she also knew she couldn't afford to throw away any possibility. A third woman's life might depend on her insight.

"So what are you really doing here, Barrett? This isn't your investigation. Seems to me you're turning into a reg ular little Dirty Harriet. Your partner's bad habits must be rubbing off on you.''

She glanced up at Vic, her smile benign. ''I don't know what you're talking about. I just stopped in here for a Coke. What are *you* doing here?''

His grin was sly. ''I'm here for the same reason you are. A Coke.'' He leaned toward her, his warm breath fanning her neck. ''Don't worry. I won't tell if you won't.''

Eve shrugged, not about to make a bargain with the devil.

''So did you find out anything?'' Vic asked casually.

She shrugged again. ''Megan left here around midnight on Saturday night. Curly said she told him she had a headache, but he thinks she might have been going to meet someone.''

D'Angelo's eyes flickered, whether in surprise at her detective work or in alarm, Eve didn't know. ''He say who she was going to meet?''

''No. He didn't see her leave with anyone, and he can't remember her talking with anyone in particular.''

''Except for Cowboy, of course.''

Eve shot him a glance. ''What are you talking about? Tony wasn't here on Saturday night.'' She knew that for a fact, because she'd dropped him at his apartment after they'd left his mother's house.

''Oh, he was here all right. Came in kind of late.'' D'Angelo cocked his head, staring at her. ''What? You mean he didn't tell you?''

Eve schooled her expression to remain placid. ''Why should he? He was off duty Saturday night. What he does on his own time is none of my business.''

''Unless, of course, someone turns up dead.''

''You're not trying to imply Tony had something to do with Megan Riley's murder,'' Eve said coldly.

"I told you once he wasn't the type of man you wanted to get involved with. I told you he was dangerous, remember?"

"Yes, I remember," Eve said. "What's your point?"

He gave her a sidelong glance. "Don't say I didn't warn you, that's all."

Chapter Eight

After Eve left the pub, she decided to drive over to Maria Mancini's house and take a chance that the woman was already out on bail. Although Clare had given her explicit orders not to try and see Maria in lockup, Eve took the lieutenant's parting words as permission to approach the woman on her own turf.

Of course, there was no guarantee Eve would be able to make any headway with Maria Mancini, but for Tony's sake, she felt she had to try. The woman had tried to kill him earlier. If something wasn't done to somehow diffuse her rage, make her see that he wasn't the bad guy in this situation, Eve was very much afraid Maria would try again. And next time she might succeed.

Heading east on Roosevelt, Eve crossed the Chicago River and then turned north, into Little Italy, one of the oldest Italian communities in the city.

When she had been younger, and on the rare occasions when she and her father had been fortunate enough to get tickets to a Bears game at Soldier Field, they would always drive up early so they could have lunch at Grisanti's, one of the family-owned Italian restaurants along Taylor Street. It had been years since they'd done that, and Eve felt a touch of nostalgia as she passed by the University of Illinois, taking the same route she and her father had driven along years before.

She'd gotten Maria Mancini's address from the computer before leaving the station, and as Eve made her way along the narrow streets, she studied the numbers posted on the houses. Finding the correct address, she parked down the street, not wanting to alarm Maria or give her time to duck out if she saw Eve's car.

Getting out, Eve swept the street with a cautious gaze. It was a lower middle-class neighborhood, but the houses looked well cared for, the yards neatly tended. A rose bush bloomed near Maria's front stoop, and as Eve climbed the steps, she inhaled the heavenly aroma, letting the perfume drift through her senses.

She rang the bell, waited a few seconds when no one answered, then pressed the button again. Lifting her hand, she knocked loudly, and as her knuckles made contact with the wood, the door swung inward.

Eve was immediately on her guard. In this day and age, everyone in large cities knew to secure their premises. But Maria Mancini—or someone—hadn't even taken the time to make sure the latch had caught, much less engage the lock. It was as if she'd been coming or going in a great hurry.

Her unease growing, Eve tried to get a look inside the house through the narrow opening. "Mrs. Mancini? I'm Detective Barrett with CPD. I'd like to talk to you."

When no one answered, Eve glanced over her shoulder, then with the toe of her shoe, shoved the door open wider. "Mrs. Mancini? Are you in there? Is everything all right?"

Eve had always marveled at the stupidity of cops who put themselves in compromising situations. A few weeks ago she would never have contemplated entering a house without a warrant or probable cause, but her instincts were telling her something wasn't right about this setup. The front door had not only been left unlocked, but hadn't been pulled shut. What if someone was inside the house besides Maria Mancini? Someone who didn't belong there?

Eve drew her weapon as she entered, feeling the inevitable adrenaline kick she knew she would never get used to. She stood in the tiny foyer, her gaze darting about her immediate surroundings. Two steps led down to a living room that was cluttered and shabby, but somehow made quaint by the fringed lampshades, faded silk upholstery and old-fashioned upright piano in a place of honor near the wide picture window.

Beyond the living room was the dining room, with its heavy mahogany table and hutch, and a swinging door that would lead to the kitchen. Directly in front of Eve, a narrow staircase led to the second floor, and to her right, a glass door opened into a tiny office.

The groomed order of the office was in direct contrast to the rest of the house. Where newspapers and books, even a stray shoe or two, littered the living room, the office was almost compulsively organized. Eve ignored the little voice inside her head that screamed for her to get out of that house before she got herself caught. Instead, she stepped slowly into the office.

The surface of the desk was cleared of everything but a telephone and a stack of files, neatly placed at the corner. A computer sat on the credenza behind the desk, facing the window, and it occurred to Eve that she had no idea what Maria Mancini did for a living. Real estate? A writer? Some kind of business she ran from her home?

More than a little curious, Eve opened one of the folders on the desk. It took her a moment to realize what she was looking at, but then, as she riffled through the pile of papers, the information became all too clear. Maria Mancini had been copying old newspaper articles—either from the library or from the Internet—about Tony.

Eve's heart tripped in apprehension as she studied the pages more carefully. The first few sheets were photocopies of articles Maria had gleaned from the local papers, including Franco's obituary and a picture of Tony coming out of police headquarters with David MacKenzie and Fiona the day he'd been cleared. A red X had been drawn through his features.

As Eve continued to search, she spotted several articles concerning the Julie Betts case, and then, toward the bottom of the stack, pieces about Ashley.

Frowning, Eve scanned the headlines, but she barely glanced at the picture of Ashley, not wanting to be reminded of her almost ethereal beauty. Instead, Eve concentrated on an article about Sean Gallagher that linked his investigation and subsequent disappearance to Ashley's murder.

Another article had an accompanying photo taken at Ashley's grave site. This picture Eve felt compelled to study, and she recognized immediately Ed Dawson, Ashley's stepfather; Annette Dawson, Ashley's mother; and Eddie Dawson, her stepbrother. Behind the family stood the Gallaghers—Sean, grim faced and stoic; Maggie, wiping a tear from her eye with a white hankie; John, Nick, Fiona and then Tony, who stood apart from the rest of his family, wearing dark glasses to hide his grief.

Tearing her gaze from Tony's image, Eve scrutinized the photo, recognizing several other faces in the crowd, including more police officers and, she realized in surprise, David MacKenzie. Fiona had mentioned that David and Tony had been roommates in college—closer than brothers, she'd said—and as Eve studied David's expression in the picture, she noticed that, unlike the other mourners, who seemed mesmerized by the flower-shrouded grave, his gaze was trained on Tony.

Were there other faces in that photo too blurry and distant to recognize? Eve wondered. Vic D'Angelo? Clare Foxx? If they'd known Ed Dawson back then, it wouldn't have been unusual for them to attend his stepdaughter's funeral. And somewhere in that crowd Eve stood. The knowledge that they were all somehow interconnected—and maybe had been for years—was disquieting.

But where did Maria Mancini fit into the equation? Eve couldn't shake the notion that something more was going on here than a deranged woman's fascination with the cop who had shot her son.

At the bottom of the stack Eve found another picture, not a copy this time, but an actual photograph, taken near Lucy Stringer's apartment on the night she'd died. Tony sat on the curb, his head in his hands, while Eve sat next to him, her heart in her eyes. The camera had captured everything. Ruthlessly. Tony's anguish. Her own secret longings.

Eve felt sick at her stomach, not only because her feelings had been exposed in such a manner, but because Maria Mancini had been at the crime scene that night, taking pictures, just as she had been earlier this morning, when Megan Riley's body had been found. Eve had no doubt that the woman she'd seen at the park entrance, wearing a raincoat and hat, had been Maria Mancini. But how had she known Tony would be there?

Eve started to close the folder and return it to its place, but then rummaged through the contents again, searching for the article concerning Ashley's murder. Where moments earlier she'd shied away from looking at Ashley's picture, Eve made herself study it now.

Over the years, she'd tried to convince herself that her

memory had embellished Ashley's beauty. No one could be that perfect. But staring at the image, Eve realized that far from exaggerating Ashley's looks, her memory had tricked her into dimming them. No wonder Tony had been so crazy about her. What man could resist the almost silvery-blond hair, those pale blue eyes and a porcelain complexion unflawed except for the tiny beauty mark at the corner of her mouth.

A beauty mark...

Voices sounded outside the front door, and Eve jumped, realizing that she couldn't afford to be discovered by Maria Mancini.

Closing the folder, Eve glanced around the office. The only way out was through the door that opened to the foyer, where she would run straight into Maria. But if Eve stayed put, the woman would see her through the glass door.

Eve's assignment was to make sure Tony didn't break any more rules, and if he did, to report his transgressions to the powers that be. But now Eve was in a delicate situation herself, and her only way out was to put herself in Tony's position, figure out what he would do.

Hide! came the immediate response. *Deal with the consequences later.*

Wasting no time, Eve ducked into a small closet just as the front door opened and Maria Mancini entered the house. She came straight into the office. Through the louvered closet door, Eve could see the woman walking around her desk, placing a package on the surface, then gazing at the stack of folders and frowning as if she somehow knew they'd been disturbed. Just like Eve had known someone had been in her apartment the other night.

Maria Mancini lifted her dark head, glanced around the room, and then Eve could have sworn she started for the closet to search inside when the phone on the desk rang.

Hesitating for a split second, Maria answered. She listened for a moment, then said, "I haven't been home that long. I had to go next door to get a package my neighbor signed for."

There was silence, then, "No, I know I have to be careful. I won't go back out again until I hear from you. I'll do exactly what you say, only…when can we meet?"

They spoke for a few more minutes, Maria's portion of the conversation cryptic and vague. Eve thought she might be talking to her attorney, but something about the woman's tone made Eve wonder if she'd had an accomplice early that morning, someone who was helping her in her plan to get even with Tony. Or to destroy him.

When Maria finally hung up the phone, Eve held her breath, praying the woman wouldn't come near the closet. When Maria finally exited the room, Eve let out a sigh of relief. She opened the door, glanced out and then hurried to the foyer.

She could hear water running upstairs, and she assumed Maria was preparing to take a shower. Going back into the office, Eve picked up the phone and dialed the code that would automatically reconnect the number that had last called in. She let the phone ring several times before finally hanging up.

Slipping out the front door, Eve walked down the street to her car. Glancing back at the house, she saw a curtain move in an upstairs window, as if Maria Mancini were standing up there watching her.

Had she known all along that Eve was inside?

EVE MADE ONE MORE STOP before going to the hospital to visit Tony. Walking in from the street entrance, she nodded to the uniform at the desk in the lobby. They exchanged greetings, spoke for a few moments, then Eve headed for the annex. The records and files section was on the fourth floor, and the officer on duty had ready the file that she'd phoned in earlier to request.

"You can sign it out," he informed her.

Eve was a little surprised by how easily accessible Ashley's file was to her. She'd almost expected it to still be restricted, as it had been for years. But the officer didn't even seem to realize the importance of the file he handed her.

Eve tried to act just as nonchalant, but the thick folder and packet of photos seemed to burn into her skin, and as she drove to the hospital, the file's presence and its content was almost as disturbing as if Ashley's ghost was riding shotgun beside her.

Eve had never been prone to wild bouts of imagination or jitters, but something was spooking her lately. Whether it was the murders, Maria Mancini's obsession with Tony or Eve's own suppressed emotions, she couldn't say for sure. But she had a bad feeling they were all connected, just as all the people who had been at Ashley's funeral were linked. And at the center of it all was Tony.

He was lying on his back, propped against a couple of pillows, when she walked into his hospital room. He muted the TV as she came toward him, and Eve saw that he'd been watching the news.

"So, how are you?"

He shrugged, his expression grumpy. "No broken ribs and only a mild concussion. Just like I said this morning."

Eve smiled, trying to cheer him up. "Well, it's always best to be on the safe side. You'll be out of here in no time."

He glowered at her. "Spare me the Little Mary Sunshine routine. I can't take perkiness and orange Jell-O all in the same day."

"Fair enough," Eve said. "I'll try to work up a bad mood, just for you." Which wouldn't be hard, considering everything she'd just learned. "I guess you heard about Maria Mancini."

"You mean that she's out on bail? Yeah, I heard. The reporters have it all screwed up, as usual. They're making it sound like I somehow goaded her into running me down. She's the victim, all of a sudden, just like that crackhead son of hers who shot two good officers."

Eve had never heard such anger in his voice. Maybe it was because being confined to a hospital room had a tendency to make one feel helpless. Or maybe because he'd almost been killed and no one seemed to care. No one except Eve.

She pulled up a chair and sat down beside his bed. "Listen, I need to talk to you about something. I need your advice. I think I've done something really stupid."

His glance turned wary. "What?"

"I sort of broke into Maria Mancini's house."

Tony's brows shot skyward. "You *what?*"

"I wanted to talk to her about you," Eve tried to explain. "I wanted to make her see your side of things. When I got there, her front door was open. I thought something might have happened to her. So...I went in."

Tony's gaze narrowed on her. "Why would you think something had happened to her?"

"Because of the murders, the publicity...I don't know." Eve shrugged, realizing her excuse sounded lame, even to Tony. "Okay, maybe I just wanted a chance to have a look around her house. Maybe I thought I could learn something about her. The point is, I did it. I went inside her house when she wasn't home and I searched through some of her things. And I think she may know."

"Damn. You mean you were busted?"

"Not exactly," she hedged. "I slipped out, but I think she may have seen me from an upstairs window. What do you think I should do?"

Tony scratched his head, eyeing her suspiciously. "This doesn't sound like you, Eve. What the hell's gotten into you?"

Seems to me you're turning into a regular little Dirty Harriet. Your partner's bad habits must be rubbing off on you.

Frowning at the memory of Vic D'Angelo's warning, Eve said almost angrily, "The woman almost killed you this morning. It was no accident—I don't care what she says now. Is it so hard to understand why I'd want to question her? Maybe even have a look around her place?"

"No," Tony said bluntly. "It's not hard for *me* to understand. I would have done the same thing. And that's what worries me. You're not me. And you don't need to get involved in this mess because of me."

She folded her arms. "Yes, I do. We're partners, aren't we?"

Their gazes met, and Eve saw something that might have been gratitude flicker in his eyes. Something that might even have been admiration. But was that all? She thought of the folder on the front seat of her car, and the memory of Ashley Dallas was suddenly so strong between them, Eve could almost smell her perfume.

She sighed, running her fingers through her hair. "Okay, I know it was a stupid thing to do. It wasn't like me, and the first time I bend the rules, I get caught." She paused, shaking her head. "I don't know what came over me."

"I'm a bad influence on you," he said dryly.

She shrugged. "You weren't there, twisting my arm. I just hope you don't get burned by the fallout if Maria Mancini decides to file a complaint."

He gave her a half grin. "Don't worry about me. IAD complaints I can handle."

But Eve did worry. Maria Mancini had tried to kill him, Clare was out to get him, Vic D'Angelo hated him and Ed Dawson might harbor the darkest of all threats against him. And as superintendent of the police department, Dawson would certainly have the power to execute his revenge. Eve should know. Her current assignment came straight from the top.

"How well do you know Ed Dawson?" she asked Tony suddenly.

He glanced at her in surprise. "He's the superintendent. We don't exactly rub elbows at the country club."

"No, but he used to live in our neighborhood," Eve said. "He and your father and uncle were friends, weren't they?"

Tony shrugged. "They had a beer together now and then, I guess. What are you getting at?"

"I don't know. I've just been thinking." She got up and paced to the window to stare down at the roof of the parking garage. This wing of the hospital faced the wrong direction to have a view of the lake, but Eve could imagine the sailboats and yachts putting into dock for the evening as the sun began to set and the wind picked up.

"What did he think of you back then?" she asked Tony. "Did he approve of your seeing Ashley?"

He didn't answer her right away, and Eve wondered if he was thinking about Ashley, about her murder, about how much he still missed her. Maybe he was still feeling guilty, because he hadn't been able to save her.

After a moment, he said without emotion, "He didn't like me. Not that I much blame him. I had a pretty wild reputation back then, but I don't think he would have approved of anyone Ashley dated. She was his stepdaughter, but in some ways, he was much closer to her than he was to his own son. It was funny because his son, Eddie, and Dawson's second wife, Annette, got along great. It was almost like they traded kids once they got married.''

"Did he ever try to get Ashley to stop seeing you?"

"Probably."

Eve glanced over her shoulder. "She never told you?"

"Ashley had a mind of her own. She wouldn't have cared what Dawson said, or what her own mother said, for that matter. She would have found a way to see me. And I would have her."

Eve had known that, of course. Neither Ashley nor Tony had ever made a secret of their feelings. But hearing it from Tony, even after all these years, didn't lessen the pain. He'd been as crazy about Ashley as Eve had been about him. Only, Ashley had returned his feelings.

"What's going on, Eve?"

She'd turned back to the window, deep in thought, and when Tony spoke, his voice was very close. She hadn't heard him get up, hadn't heard him cross the floor on bare feet to stand behind her. When she turned, he loomed over her, tall, muscular, no less imposing because of the bandages.

He wore pajama bottoms that rode low on his lean hips, making Eve almost tremble with awareness. He'd been a boy when she'd first fallen in love with him, but even back then, her attraction to him had been powerful. So potent, in fact, she hadn't been able to forget the feel of his mouth on hers, the way his arms had tightened around her, crushing her to him in a teenage flurry of passion.

How would his kiss affect her now that he was a man, and a dangerously seductive one at that? She was a woman, a little more experienced to be sure, but no less vulnerable to his touch. No less uncertain of his feelings for her. If he kissed her now, would she be able to stop it there, as she once had? Eve didn't think it wise to put her willpower to the test. Not where Tony was concerned.

"What's this all about?" His voice was deep, almost husky. "Why all the questions about Ashley?"

"I don't know. I guess I'm just curious."

He stared at her for a moment longer, searching her face. "I don't think so. You're onto something, Eve. What is it?"

She sighed. "It may be nothing. A wild theory, that's all." Although maybe not so wild. Because Eve knew for a fact there were people in the department out to get Tony. She was supposed to be one of them.

"Just tell me," he commanded softly.

"Maria Mancini has been collecting newspaper articles about you. I saw them today. Everything was there, Tony. Her son's death. The Julie Betts case. She even had articles about Ashley's murder and your father's disappearance. It's obvious the woman is obsessed with you, but I can't help thinking something else may be at work here."

He frowned down at her. "What do you mean?"

"She received a phone call while I was hiding in the closet in her office. It sounded like someone was warning her to be careful. I thought it was her lawyer at first, but now I'm not so sure. What if someone is helping her get revenge against you, Tony? What if they're using her to make you look bad?"

If he thought Eve's conjecture absurd, he didn't say so. He moved beside her, staring out the window as he seemed to consider what she'd told him. "And you think Ed Dawson has something to do with this?"

Eve cast an uneasy glance over her shoulder. Discussing the superintendent even in private was not something she could take lightly. She lowered her voice. "I can't help wondering if he blames you for Ashley's death, for letting her leave the party alone that night. You said yourself they were very close. She was like his own daughter. Her death was bound to have devastated him, and now he's in the ultimate position of power. He could do you a lot of harm if he wanted to.''

''But why wait until now? Ashley's been dead for nearly eight years.'' Tony was still staring out the window, not looking at Eve. She wondered what he was really thinking.

''I don't know why he would wait,'' she said. ''Maybe because you've only now given him ammunition, with Franco's shooting and all the bad publicity surrounding it. And maybe I'm way off base. But you do…stir passions in people, Tony.''

''Do I?'' He glanced at her then, his expression guarded. But there was something in his eyes, something dark and sensual that hinted at that passion.

Eve moistened her lips, her senses heightened by his gaze, by his closeness. ''What happened between you and Clare?'' When he didn't answer, she said quickly, ''Look, I'm not asking out of idle curiosity. I'm trying to figure out if something really is going on here. I'm worried about you, Tony.''

He shrugged, but his gaze sharpened. ''Don't worry about me. I'm not worth it.''

''Yes,'' she said simply. ''You are.''

He smiled at that, and Eve could have sworn he almost raised his fingers to touch her face. Instead he rubbed a hand across his forehead, turning back to the window to stare out. ''It was pretty…intense between us for a while. But it cooled fast when Clare got too possessive. She'd accuse me of coming on to younger women, sleeping with them. Her jealousy almost wrecked both of our careers.''

''How?''

He hesitated. "She pulled her gun on me at a bar one night. There were witnesses. We managed to keep it quiet, but after that…" His voice trailed away, and he scowled out at the twilight. "Clare's a good cop. She lost control that once, but it happens to all of us sooner or later."

His defense of the woman brought a prickle of jealousy to Eve, but she tried to remain cool and objective. "Still, I've seen the way she looks at you. I don't think she's ever gotten over what happened. Sometimes I think she almost hates you."

"Yeah," he said wearily. "Sometimes I think she does."

Eve knew she'd pressed him as far as she could on the subject. Tony wasn't the type to kiss and tell, and in some way, his loyalty to Clare made Eve admire him all the more. "So what about Vic D'Angelo? Why is there so much bad blood between the two of you?"

"That's easy. D'Angelo was the lead investigator on the Julie Betts case. He was crucified for weeks in the papers for incompetence, and it got worse after I found the body and Clare and I made the arrest."

The Betts case had been high profile, just the kind Vic D'Angelo would have reveled in, Eve thought. And then Tony, on his first homicide case, had stolen D'Angelo's thunder by doing what D'Angelo couldn't—finding the little girl's body, which had then led to the arrest and conviction of her killer.

No wonder D'Angelo was so bitter. His handling of the Betts case must have severely set back what had once been a promising career. He couldn't move up in the ranks now unless someone pulled strings for him. Or unless he somehow proved himself. Was that why he wanted in on the Stringer and Riley investigations?

"Any one of those three could be working with Maria Mancini," Eve mused. "How else could she have known you would be the investigator called out on the Stringer and Riley murders?''

''What are you talking about?''

Eve quickly explained about the photo that had been taken at the Stringer murder scene, and how she was sure Maria Mancini was the woman she'd seen that morning snapping pictures at the park—just before Tony had been run down.

Eve touched Tony's arm. ''You have to be careful, Tony.''

''You worry too much,'' he said gruffly, but she could tell that he couldn't dismiss her warning as easily as he might have liked. ''And some people might say you do have a wild imagination.''

''Maybe I do,'' she agreed. ''But promise me you'll be careful, anyway. No more rule breaking. From here on out, everything has to be by the book.''

''Does that go for both of us?'' he teased. When she started to protest, he held up his hand. ''I'm not trying to blow you off. I appreciate your concern, Eve. I really do. It's been a long time since I thought anyone cared.''

''That's not true. You know your family adores you.''

''Maybe.'' He stared down at her, his expression hardened. ''But I've never given them anything but grief. I've never given anyone who cared about me anything but grief.''

''Is that a warning?''

He was facing her now, gazing down at her. Eve tilted her head, staring back into his blue eyes and feeling as if the world had stopped spinning suddenly and was waiting, as she was, for something that might never happen.

When he lifted his hand to touch her hair, she let out a shaky breath. ''I don't think you should do that.''

''What?''

Touch me. Kiss me. Make me want you even more.

She heard his breath catch softly, as if she'd spoken the words out loud. "Evie…"

"And don't call me that," she all but snapped. "I'm not that teenage girl you once knew. I'm a grown woman. Your partner."

"I know that," he said almost grimly. "But you haven't changed as much as you might think. You're still beautiful."

"I'm not. I never was."

When he didn't say anything, she forced her gaze to meet his. He was still staring down at her, but his eyes had taken on a darkness that made her tremble.

"You are beautiful," he insisted. "Don't you know that? Don't you know the affect you have on men? On me?"

But I'm not Ashley, she cried inwardly. *And I never can be.*

"You could have had any guy you wanted back at St. Anne's," he told her. "But you never gave anyone a chance. You didn't seem interested."

Because the only guy I wanted didn't want me.

"I guess I was shy," she said.

"And now?" He tangled both hands in her hair, holding her face still, and Eve's heart started to pound.

"Now I'm too busy. And you're my partner. We can't—"

He lowered his head toward hers. "I have to do this, Eve. You know that, don't you?"

She closed her eyes in answer. He touched his mouth to hers, skimmed her lips with his tongue, and then the world started to spin again, faster than Eve could ever have imagined. She almost gasped when he deepened the kiss, grinding his mouth against hers, tasting her, exploring her, making her want him almost desperately.

Winding her arms around his neck, she pressed herself to him, feeling the heat of his skin through her clothing and thrilling to it, wanting more of it.

Tony did gasp out loud, and for a split second, Eve thought he'd gotten as carried away as she. But then, as he pulled away slightly, she realized she'd hurt him. Embarrassment washed over her, and she tried to stagger back from him. "I'm sorry. I forgot—"

He caught her arms, pulling her close again. "It was worth it." He turned her so that she was leaning against the wall, and he planted his hands on either side of her, trapping her. Their bodies were barely touching, but when he kissed her again, Eve had never felt so...possessed.

She kept her hands to herself this time, but her palms itched to feel his bare skin, to touch every inch of his hard body, to pull him closer and closer.

Tony wasn't the least bit restricted. One hand left the wall to caress her jawbone, sweep along her neck and then dip lower.

How was it possible to want someone this much? Eve wondered. To need so urgently what she'd done without for so long?

Because it was Tony. Because this was what she'd dreamed of for so long, yearned for. This was why she'd so readily accepted an assignment that she'd known might make him hate her in the end. Because she would have risked anything to be close to him again. To have this little bit of heaven...just one more time.

"Should I go lock the door?" he murmured against her ear.

His voice brought back a modicum of reality. Eve strained to tear apart the veils of passion, to think rationally. "I don't know," she whispered. "I can't seem to think."

"I don't want you to think."

He kissed her again, but Eve broke away. "I don't have...I'm not prepared...are you?"

He sighed deeply, brushing his lips across her cheek, nibbling her ear. "I don't suppose the nurse would bring us...nah. Bad idea."

Eve almost laughed in nervous relief. "I don't want to be anywhere near here if you ever get the nerve to ask her."

"She is a little intimidating. Attila the Hun, I like to call her." Tony straightened the collar of Eve's blouse, tucked back a strand of her hair. He gazed down at her, shaking his head briefly. "You're still a good girl, Evie. You know that? The nuns at St. Anne's would be proud of you."

Not if they could read my mind, Eve thought. Then a new voice made her jump.

"What's going on here?"

Chapter Nine

Tony had no idea how long Clare had been standing in the doorway of his hospital room, or whether or not she'd witnessed what had just happened between him and Eve. He shot Eve a glance, saw the color heighten in her cheeks, and then he turned, momentarily placing himself between her and Clare.

"You're about the last person I expected to see." He gave Eve another few seconds, then walked over to the bed and sat down, leaning back against the pillows and stretching out his legs.

"Why?" Clare's eyes were coolly assessing. "Because I made you follow the doctor's orders this morning? You're not holding a grudge, are you, Tony?"

"No more than you are," he muttered.

She came to stand beside his bed, her gaze going from Tony to Eve and then back again. She was nobody's fool. Even if she hadn't seen the kiss, she'd have to know something was going on. The air was almost electric, and as Tony let his own gaze linger on Eve, his awareness of her deepened.

She *was* beautiful, he thought almost in wonder. How was it he'd never noticed that before?

Back in high school, he'd thought her a cute girl, sweet

and shy—in other words, a challenge. But he'd been wrong about her. Once he'd gotten to know her a little better, he'd sensed there was more to her than met the eye. She'd had depth and sensitivity, traits uncommon in teenage girls and very much underrated by teenage boys.

She'd been more than just sweet, but sincere, honest, trustworthy—the kind of girl who usually wound up being your best friend. And *cute* hadn't exactly been the right word to describe her, either. Even now her quiet good looks had a tendency to go unappreciated before they suddenly hit you right between the eyes. Tony was still a little stunned by the blow.

He wondered fleetingly if their innocent flirtation back in school might have gone further if Ashley hadn't moved into the neighborhood and literally taken his breath away. Ashley Dallas hadn't been just another beautiful girl, she'd been a fantasy. The kind of woman men dreamed of. And for a while she'd been Tony's.

But if he were honest with himself, he'd have to admit their relationship hadn't gone much beyond the physical. He wondered sometimes if their attraction would have survived and matured over the years, or if they would have eventually gone their separate ways.

Ashley had been his first love, maybe even the love of his life. They'd shared a bond that couldn't be severed even by death, but when Tony thought of his life now, he had a hard time imagining her sharing it with him. Would she have remained by his side all these years, steadfast and loyal, through all his ups and downs? Would he have been able to count on her the way he knew he could Eve?

He'd been watching her for a long time, and his scrutiny hadn't gone unnoticed by either Eve or Clare. Eve had a hard time meeting his gaze. "I should be going," she murmured, clearing her throat.

"Did you tell him about the meeting today?" Clare was looking at Tony, not Eve, and her eyes glimmered with what he hoped was amusement, but suspected was not.

"I didn't get to it." Eve walked around the bed and picked up her purse. For a moment, she and Clare were standing almost shoulder to shoulder. Clare was the taller of the two, the more glamorous, with her dark hair and smoldering eyes.

Eve was thinner, more athletic looking and wholesome, with her shiny brown hair and hazel eyes. Clare was sexy, Eve was sensual. The distinction surprised Tony—not because of the difference in the two women, but because he'd made it. Because he appreciated it.

He had a feeling the distinction Clare herself would make was their age. Eve was younger by at least ten years, and no one would be more aware of that fact than Clare.

"I thought you might want to give him the details of the meeting yourself." Eve hooked her purse strap over her shoulder, looking as if she couldn't wait to get out of that room. "I've gotta run."

"Hot date?" Clare's gaze was still on Tony.

"Something like that." Eve finally glanced at him. "I'll see you tomorrow."

Something like that? Did she really have a date, or had she only said that for Clare's benefit?

The thought of Eve out with someone else, someone like Vic D'Angelo, gave Tony a feeling he didn't much care for. But then, he should give her more credit. She wasn't the type to go for a slickmeister like D'Angelo. She'd date someone with more class and style, a professional, maybe.

But somehow that notion didn't give Tony any comfort, either. He realized gloomily that he didn't want Eve dating, period.

She'd barely gotten out the door when Clare said, almost casually, "So are you two sleeping together yet?"

"What the hell kind of question is that?"

She smiled, her gaze flickering over him. "I know you too well, Tony. I know how you work. I've been on the receiving end of all that charisma, remember?"

"Charisma?" He gave a short laugh. "Yeah, I'm Mr. Personality, all right. That's why I'm so popular with the brass."

"She's not your type, you know. She doesn't know how to handle you."

Tony cocked one brow. "Oh, and you do?"

"I learned the hard way, remember? You're out for one thing and one thing only, and when the good times are over—" she snapped her fingers "—poof! You're outta there."

Her description hit a little too close to home. Had he really been that self-centered, that careless with people's feelings? Maybe, but he'd never set out to deliberately hurt anyone. He'd been too busy trying to keep from getting hurt again himself.

"You start an affair with Eve, you'll end up breaking her heart," Clare warned.

The last person in the world he'd ever want to hurt was Eve. But tonight, he'd pushed the bounds of their relationship. If Eve had let him, the affair would have started here, tonight, on this hospital bed.

But no matter where it started, Tony's past experiences told him one thing. It would end badly. No good could come of sleeping with your partner, not in the long run. If his past with Clare hadn't taught him that, then he was a bigger idiot than he imagined.

"You're not in love with her, are you?" Clare's tone

held a note of wonder, and she gave him an odd look, one that sent an unexplainable chill down Tony's back.

He shot her a derisive glance, trying to ignore the cold glitter in her dark eyes. "Me—in love? You forget who you're talking to."

She gave a harsh laugh, but her gaze was still suspicious. "Yeah, I guess I did at that. You're not that kind of guy, are you, Tony? I pity the poor woman who ever really falls for you."

"Thanks," he said dryly. He'd had about enough of Clare and her worldly wisdom. And he didn't want to talk about Eve anymore, either. Not with Clare. He felt oddly protective of Eve, and he didn't think Clare had her best interests at heart.

He smothered a yawn. "What time is it, anyway?"

Clare glanced at her watch. "A little after eight. Look, I won't keep you long, but I need to discuss something with you." She was all-business suddenly, her tone brisk. "I thought you might like to know that I'm letting Vic D'Angelo in on the Megan Riley investigation."

Tony sprang up in bed, ignoring the pain in his ribs. "You're *what?*"

"I'm surprised Eve didn't tell you."

Eve knew about this? "Since when?" he demanded.

"Since this morning. Look, Vic is a good investigator. We can use him on this case."

Tony swore under his breath. "Vic D'Angelo couldn't find his—"

"Okay, I get your point. You don't need to get graphic." She folded her arms, and Tony groaned inwardly, recognizing that stance. When Clare went all-stubborn, there was no point arguing with her.

"Why are you doing this?"

She shrugged her shapely shoulders. "I just told you. Vic is a good investigator—"

"Have you forgotten about the Betts case?" His tone was incredulous, disgusted. "You were there, Clare. You know how he blew that investigation."

"He made mistakes," she conceded. "We all do. That was four years ago, Tony. Everyone deserves a second chance."

"And that's why you're doing this? To give him a second chance? I thought our main objective was to find the killer."

"Or killers. We don't know that it's only one yet." She paused. "That's why I'm keeping the two investigations separate for now, but if at some point the evidence merges the two cases, you and Vic may have to work together. Can you handle that?"

"What's my choice?" Tony said bitterly.

"You don't have one." Clare smiled, her expression bordering on smug. She had him and she knew it. And she loved it. "Unless you want desk duty for a while."

She started to turn away, but Tony's hand shot out and snared her arm. "What's going on, Clare?"

She glanced at his hand on her arm, then lifted her brows. "What do you mean?"

"You're up to something. You don't want to help Vic D'Angelo. He either has something on you or you're using these cases to try and get rid of me. My guess is it's a little of both."

She shoved his hand off her arm. "You always were on the paranoid side."

"Yeah. With good reason, as I recall." He struggled to tamp down his anger, smiling back at her instead, because he knew that would get to her more. "You're forgetting something, aren't you? I know you pretty damn well, too.

I know how you operate. How you think. Something's going on with you, Clare, and it's only a matter of time before I find out what it is.''

Something flashed in her eyes before she lifted her chin, glaring at him with an intensity—and a hatred—that made Tony's blood run cold. "You never did know me. That was your problem. You underestimated me, and that was the first in a very long line of mistakes you've made, Tony."

TONY AWAKENED to complete darkness. The door to his room was shut, and the sliver of light creeping in from the crack at the bottom did nothing to illuminate the gloom. But he knew someone was there. Knew, without seeing even a shadow, that he wasn't alone.

"Don't turn on the light," a masculine voice cautioned. "And don't press the call button, either. I'm not here to hurt you."

The hell he wasn't, Tony thought, trying to clear his head of the pain medication he'd been given earlier. Where was that damn button?

"Who are you?" He found the cord, and as unobtrusively as he could, began to pull the button toward him.

"Fisher."

Tony's fingers froze on the cord. He knew that name, recognized the voice now that he'd had time to think. The man was an informant Tony used on occasion, but he knew nothing else about him. Fisher would call out of the blue from time to time, always refusing to meet face-to-face. He'd give Tony whatever information he had, then disappear again, as if he were nothing more than a shadow.

Tony peered through the blackness, trying to get a look at the man's face. He considered turning on the light in spite of Fisher's instructions, but he couldn't be sure the man wasn't armed.

Tony eased up in bed. "You left a message for me the other day at the station, but you never called back."

"I got tied up."

With what? Tony wondered, but knew better than to ask. "How did you know I was here?"

The man didn't say anything, but Tony sensed his shrug. He was playing it cautious tonight. Okay. Tony knew how to play the game, too. He could be patient—up to a point. "What are you doing here? Visiting hours were over a long time ago, but then, I don't figure this is exactly a social call, is it?"

"I came here to warn you." Something about the man's tone sent a shiver creeping up Tony's spine. The voice was familiar, yes, but also disturbing in a way he hadn't noticed over the phone. Tony could tell the man was trying to disguise it, but there was something more…something almost eerie in the way he spoke.

"Warn me about what?" Tony asked warily.

"Those two girls who were murdered. There's a connection."

The hair on the back of Tony's neck rose. "What do you know about those murders?"

"Only what I read in the paper, hear on the streets. Both of them young, pretty coeds. Both of them stabbed seven times in the heart. Seven times," the man repeated, his voice almost raspy.

As far as Tony knew, none of the details of Megan Riley's autopsy had been released to the press. So how had Fisher known about the seven stab wounds? Was her murderer standing in this very room?

"Let me turn on the light," Tony said easily. "I like to see who I'm talking to."

"You don't need to see me," the man said gruffly. "I'm not the killer. You know that."

"Give me one good reason why I should trust you."

"Because I've never given you any reason not to. My information has always been solid. And right now, I may be the only person you can trust, Tony."

The way he said his name…

Tony fought back an irrational instinct to do exactly as the man said—to trust him. He scowled into the darkness. "How do you know how many times she'd been stabbed?"

"I've got friends inside."

That didn't surprise Tony. A lot of informants were plugged into the police department as well as the criminal element on the street. That's what made them so effective…and so dangerous. They worked both ends.

"All right," Tony said. "Tell me about the connection."

"I don't need to tell you. You already know."

"Then why are you here?"

The man paused. "Because I hear things about you, Tony."

"What things?"

"You've got a lot of enemies."

"That's not exactly a news flash," Tony said irritably. "What does it have to do with the murders?"

"You knew both victims. Both of them were stabbed seven times in the heart." Fisher hesitated, his voice lowering to almost a whisper. "Just like Ashley Dallas."

Sweat beaded on Tony's forehead. His stomach knotted with a cold, unnamed fear. "How do you know about Ashley?"

"She died just like the other two. Seven stab wounds to her heart."

"You're not suggesting the same man killed all three women." Tony's heart was pounding so hard now he wondered if Fisher could hear it. It took a lot to scare Tony these days, but he was suddenly terrified, not of what the man would do to him, but of what he was going to tell him. "He couldn't have, because Daniel O'Roarke's on death row."

"Yes," the man said almost wearily. "I know he is. So that leaves Lucy Stringer and Megan Riley's killer."

"Are you saying you know who he is?" The cloak and dagger atmosphere was getting to Tony. He wanted to leap out of his bed, grab the man and shake him until he confessed everything he knew.

Or maybe what Tony really wanted to do was turn tail and run, not look back, not hear another word of what the informant was going to tell him.

"I don't know who the killer is," Fisher admitted. "But I know why he's killing these women. He's killing them to get to you, Tony. Someone's setting you up."

Tony's eyes were becoming accustomed to the dark. He could see the man's silhouette now. He was leaning against the wall, his face hidden beneath the bill of a baseball cap. Tony couldn't see his expression, but he knew Fisher was looking at him, knew their eyes were connecting in the darkness.

The chill inside Tony spread. "How do you know that?"

"Think about it," the man said almost urgently. He'd almost forgotten to disguise his voice, and for a moment, recognition rippled through Tony, then faded, leaving him more uneasy than ever. "Two women murdered within a week of each other, in the exact same manner. Seven stab wounds to the heart. You knew both of them. Sooner or later someone else is bound to make the link back to Ashley."

"I didn't kill them." Tony was shocked to hear that his own voice had gone hoarse, almost unrecognizable.

"No, but someone wants to make it look as if you did. Your suspension was probably the trigger. You were portrayed in the media as a rogue cop, a loose cannon, someone who could very easily go off the deep end, if provoked. And the anniversary of Ashley's death is only a few days away. Everyone knows you never got over her murder.''

Tony could feel the noose tightening around his neck, even as they spoke. He no longer doubted the man's word. He'd been feeling the same thing himself for days. Eve had said as much tonight, only she'd been focused on Maria Mancini. She hadn't taken it the next step. She hadn't considered—hadn't wanted to, maybe—that *everything* was connected, even the murders. That whoever was out to get Tony would stop at nothing, would even kill innocent women, to exact his revenge.

Who hated him that much?

It wasn't a question Tony particularly liked pondering. He had enemies. He knew that. But politics on the force was one thing. This was just plain…sick. The thought of Megan Riley and Lucy Stringer killed in cold blood because of him…

A wave of nausea rose inside him, and he wiped his hand across his mouth, surprised to find that he was shaking.

''If you don't find him, he'll kill again,'' Fisher warned. ''He'll keep on killing until he gets what he wants.''

''What's that?'' Tony asked, but he already knew the answer.

Fisher paused. ''You dead, or behind bars for the rest of your life. Just like Daniel O'Roarke.''

It seemed to Eve that she must have just fallen asleep when a nightmare awakened her. She'd been dreaming about the killer, a nameless, faceless shadow bending over her bed, stabbing viciously at her pillow while she watched, terrified, from the shadows.

Time and again he raised the knife and plunged it into

the softness he thought was her flesh. One, two, three, four, five, six, seven...

Eve caught her breath as the sound inside her head became real. She realized that a noise and not the dream had awakened her, and she sprang up in bed, listening. The cadence matched the knife thrusts in her dream—one, two, three...

She grabbed her gun from the nightstand, thumbing off the safety as she crawled out of bed, shivering in her pajamas and bare feet. The noise sounded again. Someone was knocking on her door. Relief trembled through her until she glanced at her bedside clock. It was after two in the morning. Who would be at her apartment at this time of night?

Easy, she warned herself as she slipped through the darkened rooms. The killer wouldn't come knocking on her door. Then again, maybe he would. Maybe that was how he'd gotten inside Lucy Stringer's apartment. He'd knocked, and Lucy had innocently answered the door.

Eve wasn't that naive, or so she liked to think. She glanced out the peephole, seeing little more than a shadow on the landing outside her door. "Who is it?" she called softly.

"Tony."

Tony! What in the world—

She started to open the door, then stopped herself. "Why aren't you in the hospital?"

"Open the door, Eve. I need to talk to you."

She kept the chain lock on as she eased open the door. Tony stood on her landing, the dim light from the security lamp casting shadows across his features. He gave her a dry smile. "Wanna see my ID?"

"Very funny."

She closed the door and slid off the chain latch to let

him in. He brushed by her, then waited until she'd relocked her door. Turning, she let her gaze slip over him. He was wearing faded jeans, ragged at the hem and knees, and a long-sleeved gray shirt over a black T-shirt. He must have gone home to change before coming over here, because he hadn't been wearing those clothes yesterday morning when he'd been taken to the hospital.

Speaking of which…

"What are you doing out of the hospital?" she asked him again. "Has something happened?"

He shrugged, but the gesture was far from nonchalant. He looked wired, edgy. And the shadow of his beard made him seem a little threatening.

It's just Tony, she tried to reassure herself. *You've known him all your life.*

But she hadn't really. She'd been in love with him for years, or the memory of him, but Eve realized suddenly that she didn't really know him anymore. People changed in eight years, and Tony had been through a lot.

She shivered unaccountably as his blue eyes met hers, reminding her all too vividly of the kiss they'd shared earlier, of the way she was dressed at this moment.

"What's happened?" she persisted. "Why'd you leave the hospital?"

"I never should have been there in the first place," he muttered. "It was Clare's way of getting to me. I'm fine, and besides…" He trailed off, rubbing the back of his neck. "I needed to see you."

His gaze slid down her, lingering, knowing, almost ravishing. Eve was suddenly aware of the gun she held at her side. "Let me go change, and then I'll put on some coffee. We can talk."

"I'll fix the coffee." He tore his gaze from her and

glanced around. "If you don't mind me tinkering around in your kitchen."

"No, go ahead."

In her bedroom, Eve put her weapon away, then grabbed her robe. *Better get dressed,* something warned her. She didn't trust Tony, and she didn't trust herself. No use tempting fate.

Pulling on jeans and a Bulls T-shirt, she went back out to join him. He hadn't even started the coffee, but was standing instead at the dining room table, leafing through the file she'd left there earlier. And the photographs.

Eve's heart rolled over. She'd stayed up past midnight reading Ashley's file, even forcing herself to study the crime scene photographs. She thought she'd put them all away, but had she? Had she left any of the pictures lying on the table where Tony couldn't help but see them?

As she started toward him, she tried to convince herself that all the pictures had been put back in the envelope, out of sight. But when he looked up, his face told her what he'd seen. He glanced away from her.

"What are you doing with Ashley's file?" His voice was ragged, edged with anger.

Did he think Eve was prying into something that wasn't her business? She walked over to him. "I'm sorry, Tony. I shouldn't have left it out. I thought I'd put everything away—" She broke off when she saw the photograph lying on the table. Ashley, bloodstained, pale, beautiful even in death. Tony couldn't have missed it.

Eve reached over and gently turned the picture facedown. She almost expected Tony to stop her, but instead he gazed at her, his blue eyes deeply haunted. "What are you doing with that file?" he asked again, then paused, as if gathering his control. "I thought it was restricted."

"I expected it to be, too," Eve admitted. "But the case

was cleared. Daniel O'Roarke is still in prison. I guess there's no longer any reason for it to be restricted.''

"Somehow I figured Dawson would have taken care of that.''

"Maybe it was released to me by mistake.'' Eve watched him for a moment. "Does it bother you that I've seen it?''

He walked into the living room and stood with his back to her. "You were bound to see it sooner or later, I guess.'' He turned around to face her. "You've made the connection, haven't you? That's why you wanted the file.''

She looked down at the folder, knowing exactly what he meant. "Ashley's murderer stabbed her seven times. In the heart.''

The tension in the room was almost palpable. Eve held her breath as she waited for him to speak.

"Yes, but that's not all,'' he said in that same tense voice. "Lucy Stringer looked like Ashley. Same coloring, same build.''

"So did Megan Riley.'' When Tony frowned, Eve said quickly, "The first time I saw her at the pub I thought she looked like Ashley, but I couldn't figure out why. She had dark hair and was shorter than Ashley. I didn't understand the resemblance until I saw Ashley's picture at Maria Mancini's house yesterday. I started putting it together, and that's when I went to get her file. And then tonight, when I studied the crime scene photographs, it hit me all of a sudden why Megan had reminded me of Ashley.''

Tony was staring at her as if she was out of her mind. "What are you talking about, Eve? Megan Riley didn't look anything like Ashley.''

"Yes, she did. *I* saw it, and so did her killer.'' She lowered her voice to almost a whisper. "It was the beauty mark. They both had beauty marks in the exact same place.'' Almost inadvertently, she touched the corner of her mouth, and she saw Tony's gaze move to her lips.

"I never even thought of that," he said almost numbly.

"Are you sure?" When he glanced at her, Eve said, "Why didn't you tell me you were at the pub Saturday night, Tony?"

He shrugged. "I couldn't sleep after you dropped me off. I went out for a drink. One drink, Eve. That's all."

"You don't have to explain to me how much you had to drink. I'm not your keeper. But what I don't understand is why you didn't tell me you were there. That you'd talked to Megan Riley that night."

He cocked his head slightly. "Is that an accusation?"

"Of course not. But I can't help wondering why you didn't tell me. I'm your partner, Tony. Don't you trust me?"

"Do you trust me?"

"Yes," she responded instantly.

"You don't have any secrets from me? Nothing you need to tell me?"

Her heart landed with a thud in her stomach. What was he driving at? Did he know about her assignment? "I don't know what you mean."

"Why didn't you tell me Vic D'Angelo was put on the investigation?"

Was that what had him so upset? "I understood it wasn't official. Clare said today he'd be helping out when his own caseload allowed."

Tony shook his head. "No, he's in, all right. Up to his neck. What I can't figure out is what he and Clare are up to. Why they're thick as thieves all of a sudden."

Eve wondered if he was jealous. "You think he and Clare are going to use these investigations to try and undermine you?"

"It wouldn't surprise me. They've both got a score to settle. Question is, how far would they go to settle it?"

She stared at him in shock. "You don't think…you *couldn't* think…"

"What?"

"That either of them are somehow involved in these murders."

His gaze hardened. "I don't know what to think. I knew both of the victims, Eve. I talked to Megan Riley the night she died. For all I know, I may have talked to Lucy Stringer, too."

Eve gasped. "For all you know?"

He turned away from her. "I've been experiencing some…blackouts."

"Blackouts?" Eve was suddenly more scared than she'd ever been in her life—but not of Tony. She was terrified for him. She walked over and put her hand on his arm. "What kind of blackouts? Tony?"

He took a deep breath. "I don't know. When you came to my apartment the night Lucy was found dead—I couldn't remember driving home, getting into bed. I couldn't remember anything except…I had these vague flashes of Lucy at the pub, or in some bar, talking to some guy. I don't even know if it was me she was talking to."

Eve's heart stopped beating for a split second as she realized what he was saying. Then it crashed against her chest, stealing her breath. "And the night Megan died?"

"Same thing."

"Oh, my God."

"Eve." He turned suddenly, grabbing her arms. "I didn't kill those women. You have to believe me."

"I do believe you." She didn't hesitate even a fraction. "But, my God, what you're saying…someone is setting you up.…"

"And he's not through yet."

"He?"

"Or she," he said grimly. "The point is, the killer's not ready to point the finger at me. He's waiting for something."

"What?"

Tony's eyes closed briefly. "The anniversary of Ashley's death, I think."

The hammering in Eve's chest matched the memory of her nightmare. In her mind, she could see the shadow bending over her bed, chopping at what he thought was her dead body.

One, two, three, four, five, six, seven...

Chapter Ten

Eve put on the coffee while Tony went into her bathroom to wash his face. When he came back out, his hair was damp, his eyes slightly bloodshot, as if he'd dunked his whole head in cold water.

Gratefully, he took the coffee she offered him. "It's not decaf," she warned.

He shrugged, as if he couldn't care less, and Eve knew why. Neither of them were going back to sleep tonight, anyway.

His gaze was so intense, Eve's breath quickened almost painfully. It was not the most appropriate time, but she couldn't help thinking about last evening, when he'd kissed her in his hospital room. She'd dreamed of that kiss, yearned for it, but now she almost wished it hadn't happened. She wanted him more than ever, but he seemed so far out of her reach. If she touched him now, she had the distinct feeling he would flinch away from her, because Ashley's presence was almost tangible.

"What's happening to me, Eve?"

"That's what we have to figure out." Eve resisted the urge to take him in her arms, to draw his head to her bosom and comfort him as best she could. But there was work to do. A killer to find. And now was not the time to succumb to temptation. She didn't want to listen to the little voice that told her there might never be a right time.

"Let's sit down," she said softly.

When he complied, Eve sat on the sofa beside him, placed her cup on the coffee table and then curled her legs beneath her. "Tell me about that night, Tony."

He didn't have to ask which night she meant. They both knew she was talking about the night Ashley was killed. Tony let his head fall against the back of the sofa. He closed his eyes, and for a moment, Eve wondered if he would talk to her at all.

For the longest time, they sat in silence, but finally, he began to speak.

"I didn't want to go to the party that night." He was staring at the ceiling, and Eve saw him swallow, as if the words left a bitter taste in his mouth. "Ashley and I argued about it. I didn't belong to the fraternity hosting the party, but David did. He wanted both Ashley and me there, and she wanted to go. She was the fraternity's sweetheart or poster girl or whatever the hell they called it. I didn't really fit in with that crowd. They were mostly rich kids, and I was a little older. I don't know if you remember or not, but I didn't go to college right after high school. I bummed around for a year, not knowing what I wanted to do. Then when Ashley started at the university, I guess I figured it was a good way to keep an eye on her." He gave Eve a derisive glance. "Great reason to pursue higher education."

Eve shrugged. "You graduated."

"Yeah. Somehow." He drew a long breath and released it. "Anyway, the frat house was packed that night. Most of the people I didn't even know, but my cousin Miles was there and Eddie Dawson. A few others from the neighborhood."

"Wait a minute," Eve said. "The superintendent's son was at that party? I didn't see his name in the file."

"No, you wouldn't. Dawson kept it out of the official police report."

"He did *what?*" Eve couldn't believe what she was hearing. "He deliberately withheld evidence from a murder investigation? My God, Tony."

He glanced at her. "It happens all the time, Eve. You know that. And he wasn't the superintendent then."

"Oh, and that makes it all right?"

"I didn't say that. But investigations are not always black and white. We all make judgment calls."

"Still…"

Tony put his cup on the end table beside the sofa, then turned back to Eve. "Look, not to defend Ed Dawson, but he wasn't the only one who screwed around with that report."

"What do you mean?"

"Eddie Dawson's presence at the party wasn't the only thing left out."

"What else was?" Eve felt chilled all of a sudden and grabbed an afghan from the back of the sofa to wrap around her shoulders.

Tony hesitated. "For one thing, I had a blackout that night. I couldn't account for my whereabouts at the time of the murder."

Eve tried to school her expression, but she felt cold all the way to her bones. Why had Tony never told her about these blackouts? Did he still not trust her?

Maybe with good reason, considering her own secrets.

"What happened?" she asked, almost in dread.

He closed his eyes. "We kept arguing at the party. I remember Ashley had on a black dress, short, tight, sexy as hell. She looked great. There wasn't a guy at that party who could keep his eyes off her, let alone his hands. I was drunk and jealous and acting like a jerk—'' He broke off. ''I thought she was flirting too much, and it was driving me crazy. When I saw her talking to Daniel O'Roarke, I just…lost it.''

''You knew Daniel before the party?'' Eve almost said ''before Ashley's murder.''

''Our families go way back,'' he said grimly.

''Your grandmother told me about the feud.''

Tony shrugged. ''That was part of it, I guess, but mostly I didn't like the way O'Roarke was always coming on to Ashley. She said she couldn't stand him, either, but sometimes I wondered. He had money, looks.…''

Eve thought about the time she'd seen Ashley getting out of that strange car. Had she been with Daniel O'Roarke that night?

Tony sighed, dragging his fingers through his hair. ''Anyway, I got into a fight with him. We threw a few punches, and Ashley was furious. She slapped me.'' He winced, as if he could still feel the sting of her hand against his face.

''What happened then?'' Eve asked softly.

''She wouldn't speak to me after that, so I went upstairs to David's room. He'd moved out of the dorm and was living at the fraternity house by that time. I only meant to wash my face, maybe lay down for a few minutes, but when I woke up, hours had passed. The party was still going on downstairs, but Ashley was nowhere to be found.''

Because she was already dead, Eve thought. She'd been murdered only a few yards away from where Tony lay passed out. The knowledge of that must have eaten him alive all these years.

''Miles and David were both still downstairs. They were surprised to see me. They thought Ashley and I had left together hours before. When we started asking around, we discovered that Daniel O'Roarke was missing from the party, too. That's when I knew something was wrong.''

"What did you do?"

"I had this terrible feeling something had happened. Don't ask me how I knew, but I did. I remember grabbing David, shouting at him that we had to find her because I knew she was in trouble. He tried to calm me down, but then someone came rushing in, screaming they'd seen a woman's body outside, covered in blood.''

Eve put a hand to her mouth, wishing he didn't have to relive this, but knowing somehow it was important for both of them to hear it. That night was irrevocably linked to what was going on now.

"Did you go outside?" she asked him.

"I had to. I had to see her." He drew a ragged breath. "It was bad. I can't—''

"I'm sorry you had to go through that," Eve said softly. "I know how much you loved her.''

"I just kept thinking, why? Why did it have to happen to her? She was so beautiful, Eve. So young.''

"I know.''

"I was in shock, I guess. I wanted to hold her, but David kept pulling me back. I think he even hit me. We were all pretty close to the edge, but at least Miles had the presence of mind to call my dad and my uncle. They were both detectives, and when they arrived on the scene, they took control. They tried to keep Miles and me out of it as much as possible.''

Eve said almost fearfully, "How did they keep you out of it? What else was left out of the report, Tony?''

"Like I said, I couldn't account for my whereabouts at the time of the murder.''

"But you were upstairs—''

"I couldn't prove it. No one saw me. My own cousin thought I'd left the party with Ashley." Tony turned and stared at Eve. "Who is always the first suspect in a murder investigation?"

"The spouse or boyfriend," she said almost numbly.

"Exactly. My dad knew that better than anyone. So he tried to protect me."

"But you weren't guilty. You didn't need protecting."

"A lot of innocent people go to prison, Eve. You know that."

What Eve was hearing went against everything that she believed in as an IAD officer. And yet at the same time, she could understand wanting to protect someone you loved. Wasn't that what she wanted to do for Tony?

"I know how this must sound, but it didn't affect the outcome of the investigation," he said. "The murder weapon was found in the bushes nearby, and Daniel O'Roarke's fingerprints were all over it. Spots of blood on Ashley's dress matched O'Roarke's DNA. He was arrested later that same day, and there's never been any doubt in my mind that he was the killer. I think he was responsible for Dad's disappearance, too. Daniel O'Roarke got exactly what he deserved."

And the killings now? Eve wanted to ask. Who knew enough about the past to link Lucy Stringer and Megan Riley's murder to Ashley's? Almost anyone in the police department could have had access to Ashley's file, Eve thought.

She glanced at Tony. "Was there anything else left out of the report?"

He stood abruptly and walked over to the sliding glass doors, staring out. After a moment, Eve got up and followed him. She stood at his side, peering out into the darkness.

The silence in the room was tense, electric. Eve's heart was suddenly pounding inside her chest, because she somehow knew this night would change her relationship with Tony forever. Either he would turn to her for help, or he would turn away from her, because of the intimacy of this conversation.

He stared down at her, his expression almost raw. "You want to know what else was left out of the report? How about the fact that Ashley was pregnant?"

EVE LOOKED AS IF she'd been physically struck. Her eyes widened.

Tony scrubbed his face with his hands. He knew exactly how she felt. He still felt a little stunned every time he thought about it. "She'd told me earlier that night that she had something important to tell me, but I was too busy picking a fight with her to listen. And then it was too late."

Eve said in a whisper, "I'm so sorry."

He turned back to the window. "Sometimes I can't help thinking what it might have been like if…things had been different. Whether the baby would have looked like me or Ashley. Whether he would have been a cop."

"How…why was that information left out of the police report?"

Tony shrugged. "Because Ed Dawson wanted it that way. He was trying to protect Ashley, and I guess he didn't think it would have any bearing on the case against Daniel O'Roarke. I didn't even know about it myself until Dad told me a few weeks later."

Without a word, Eve walked back over to the sofa and sat down. She looked exhausted suddenly, and Tony wondered if he'd made a mistake in coming here. If he shouldn't have unloaded all this on her at once.

"It's not a very pretty story, is it? I wasn't there to protect Ashley or the baby."

"You can't blame yourself for what a killer did. None of it was your fault. You have to know that."

He crossed the room and knelt in front of her. There were tears in her eyes, and Tony felt something inside him start to melt. "Do you want me to leave?" he asked softly.

She shook her head. "I don't want you to leave. I don't want to be alone."

"I don't want to be alone, either."

He lay his head on her knees, and after a moment, he felt her fingers in his hair, stroking him, soothing him. Tony closed his eyes. With very little effort, he could fall asleep, and for him, that said a lot.

EVE WAS COLD. She shifted her position and her stiff muscles protested. Lifting her head, she glanced around. She'd fallen asleep on the sofa, her neck at an awkward angle and her legs curled and cramped beneath her. Tony was asleep on the floor, his long legs stretched out, his head tilted back against the sofa as he snored gently.

Eve got up and slipped into the bathroom, starting the shower and then climbing in to let the hot spray pound away the twinges in her muscles, the cobwebs in her mind. It was still early. She had plenty of time before her shift started, so she didn't hurry, but allowed herself the luxury of a leisurely shower before getting out to blow-dry her hair and put on her makeup.

Once inside her bedroom, she dressed carefully in rust-colored slacks and a matching Oriental silk blouse. She placed her jacket, holster and purse on the bed while she slipped on her shoes. Glancing around the room, she stopped finally and drew a long breath. She was ready to go and she still had time to spare. Time to think, which was what she didn't want to do.

She sat on the bed, and then, unmindful of her fresh clothes, lay back against the mattress and flung her arms over her head as she stared at the ceiling. Ashley had been pregnant with Tony's child. Why did that knowledge bother her so much?

Eve had known they were in love, had always assumed they would have gotten married if Ashley had lived. At some point, they would have had children. But those were all abstract images, because Ashley hadn't lived. But now to find out that she'd been carrying Tony's child before she died—that was a bond between them that could never be severed.

Both Ashley and the baby had been brutally murdered, and Eve didn't lose sight of the horror for even a moment. The child would have been seven years old now. She could picture Tony going to Little League games, playing catch in the backyard. She grieved for him. But...

A part of Eve ached for herself, too, because she knew that this loss was not something Tony would ever get over. Ashley had been his first love and would have been the mother of his child. What he felt for Eve couldn't ever come close to that.

She rose finally and went out to awaken Tony, but he was already up, reheating the coffee she'd made hours earlier.

"That's got to be awful." She passed him in the narrow kitchen and stood at the sink. "I'll make some fresh."

He took a drink and grimaced. "No, don't bother. It's better than what I usually have."

Eve busied herself with the carafe and water anyway, reluctant to meet his gaze. She sensed him behind her, but didn't turn. When he placed his hands on her arms, she closed her eyes, breathing deeply.

"What's wrong, Eve?"

"Nothing."

But the tremble in her voice gave away her emotions, and Tony's grip tightened on her arms. "Maybe I shouldn't have told you what I did."

"No, I'm glad you did. It's important for me to know everything. These cases—"

"I'm not talking about the cases. I'm talking about us." Gently he turned her to face him. "I feel as if I've hurt you somehow."

Eve tried not to look at him, but his gaze was too compelling. Too caring. She said reluctantly, "I don't know what's wrong with me. The way I feel…it's so stupid.…"

"Nothing about you could ever be stupid." He put his hand under her chin, tilting her face up to his. "Tell me."

She closed her eyes briefly, feeling tears smart behind her lids. "Maybe I should tell you. Maybe you should know you're not the only one who has kept secrets all these years."

A shadow flickered in his eyes. "What are you talking about?"

She turned back to the sink, pouring soap into the carafe. Her hands were trembling. "Back in high school, when you used to come over to my house, when we would…talk out on the porch or in my room—those times meant a lot more to me than they did to you. I liked you, Tony."

"I liked you, too." She heard something that might have been a smile in his voice. "I especially liked kissing you, as I recall. I still do."

Eve's heart started to pound at the memory. "I mean, I really liked you. I had a crush on you. I was devastated when you started going out with Ashley. Why do you think

I went out of state to college? Because I didn't want to see you with her. Because I thought if I could get away from here, I could finally get over you.''

She heard the soft intake of his breath. "I didn't know."

Eve shrugged. "I didn't want you to know. It was embarrassing, the way I felt, because you were so crazy about Ashley. You were in love with her. And I was just—'' She broke off with a derisive laugh. "You didn't even remember me that first day in Clare's office. That pretty much said it all, didn't it?''

He didn't answer her, but instead slipped his arms around her waist, pulling her against him and holding her close. Eve tensed at first, then closed her eyes and let her head relax against his shoulder.

"I *was* in love with Ashley," he finally said. His breath was warm against Eve's cheek. "She was my first love, but...I'm starting to wonder why you weren't.''

EVE DROVE TO THE STATION while Tony went home to shower and change. She was in their office, going through case files, when Clare stuck her head inside.

"You heard from Tony this morning?''

Almost instantly, he appeared behind her. He breezed past her, taking off his sunglasses and saying with a goading grin, "You come down here just to welcome me back? I'm touched, Clare.''

To Eve's surprise, Clare didn't rise to the bait. She looked tense, almost shaken. "I need to see you both in my office. Right now.''

Tony and Eve exchanged glances as they followed Clare down the hall.

"Close the door,'' she said as she sat down behind her desk.

Tony closed the door, and then he and Eve took seats across from her.

"I'm not going to beat around the bush," Clare said grimly. "I just got a call from a friend of mine at District 15. Maria Mancini was murdered last night."

Eve felt the bottom drop out of her stomach. She glanced at Tony, but he was staring straight ahead, at Clare. "How?"

Clare glanced up at him. "She was shot."

"Not stabbed," Eve heard herself murmur in relief.

"No," Clare said. "We don't have any reason to believe her murder has anything to do with our cases. But you have to know, Tony, the media is going to be all over this. You have an airtight alibi, since you were in the hospital last night, but I want you to keep a low profile, anyway."

The momentary relief Eve felt fled at Clare's words. Tony hadn't been in the hospital last night. At least not all night. She shot him a glance, but he refused to look at her.

"When was she killed?" he asked Clare. "Do they know?"

"Sometime after midnight was as close as my friend could tell me." She paused, then said, "You don't have anything you need to tell me, do you, Tony?"

He shrugged. "Like you said, I was in the hospital last night."

Clare's gaze was measuring, maybe even a little disbelieving, Eve thought. Did she know Tony had left the hospital? Was this some kind of test?

Back in their own office, Eve grabbed Tony's arm. "Why didn't you tell her about last night?"

He scowled down at her. "Are you crazy? You know why I didn't. Someone is setting me up for these murders, Eve. If I told Clare I left the hospital last night, what do you think her reaction would be?"

''I don't know—'' Eve started to say, but Tony cut her off.

''She would have suspended me. Again. And once that happened, I would be on the outside, Eve. I wouldn't have any way to protect myself. You know that as well as I do.''

''Yes, but aren't you forgetting something? You put me in a position of having to lie, too.''

''Neither one of us lied. I *was* in the hospital last night. And all you have to do is keep quiet. You didn't see me. You're not involved in this.''

''But I am involved,'' she said in frustration. She raked her hands through her hair. ''Don't you see what you've done? We can't tell the truth now. I can't tell Clare you were with me. Depending on time of death, I could have probably provided you with a real alibi, but that's gone. No one would believe me if I came forward now. They'd think I was trying to protect you.''

''Just don't say anything,'' Tony advised. ''Let me handle it.''

''How?'' she demanded. He started toward the door, and Eve grabbed his arm again. ''Where are you going?''

''To the crime scene.''

''Are you crazy? Didn't you hear what Clare said? You have to keep a low profile. The media will be all over you.''

He took her hand from his arm and held it for a moment. ''I'm not going to sit around here and let someone railroad me for something I didn't do. I'm going to find out who's behind all this, Eve. Are you with me or not?''

Did she really have a choice? ''You know I am, but I just wish…''

''What?''

She shook her head. ''Nothing. Let's go.''

He gazed down at her, his features softening for a moment. "Did you really have a crush on me back in high school?"

"That can't really be a surprise," she said dryly.

"I honestly never knew."

"Not even after I invited you over when my father was out? Not even when I practically threw myself at you?"

"I guess that should have been a hint," he said with a rare grin. "But you were always so shy. I guess I just thought—"

"That I was suddenly ripe for the picking?"

His smiled turned ironic. "Something like that. You were sixteen and never been kissed, so I assumed you wanted me to teach you a few things. And you *were* a fast learner, as I recall."

Eve started out the door, saying over her shoulder, "I still am," but so softly she wasn't sure Tony heard her.

THEY SHOWED THEIR SHEILDS to the two uniforms guarding the perimeter of the crime scene, then stepped over the tape and headed for the front door of Maria Mancini's house. Once inside, they split up. Tony went upstairs and Eve walked into the office, introducing herself to the lieutenant on the scene and explaining why she was there.

"What kind of connection?" he asked with a frown, when she told him she thought Maria Mancini's murder might be linked to a case she was working on.

When she wouldn't elaborate, he said, "You people on the South Side seem to think you can waltz all over my crime scene without giving me any answers. I don't much care for your attitude."

Eve flashed him an apologetic smile. "Sorry, but you know how it is. The case is extremely sensitive."

The smile seemed to get to him. He softened almost grudgingly. "What is it you want to know?"

"I guess for starters, do you have any leads or eyewitnesses?"

"We're still canvassing the neighborhood, but we haven't turned up much so far. The crime scene was pretty clean, too."

"Where was she found?"

"Upstairs, in her bedroom. Looks like she might have been surprised in her sleep."

"How'd the killer get inside?"

He shrugged. "Beats me. No sign of a forced entry. Looks like he must have had a key."

"Did she live here alone?"

"Yeah. Her son was killed a month or so ago. Maybe you heard about it."

Eve nodded vaguely. "What about the murder weapon?"

"My guess is a .38, but we'll have to wait for ballistics."

A lot of cops used a .38 caliber weapon, including Eve. She glanced around. "Mind if I have a look about the place?"

He hesitated. "I guess not. We've pretty much got everything out of here we need. You weren't as fast as the other guy."

Eve glanced at him sharply. "What guy?"

"The other detective from your area. He was Johnny-on-the-spot right after we got the call. A real pain in the ass type, if you know what I mean. Told me to get in touch with him as soon as I got the autopsy report. *Told* me, mind you. Didn't bother to request." He shook his head, muttering an expletive.

Eve nodded sympathetically. "Did you catch his name?"

"D'Angelo. Vic D'Angelo. You happen to know the jerk?"

EVE AND TONY DROVE OVER to the Navy Pier for lunch before going back to the station. It was out of the way, but

Eve thought a change of scenery might do them both good.

They ate at a restaurant near the Crystal Gardens, with a magnificent view of the city skyline and Lake Michigan. Eve watched the mesmerizing rotation of the fifteen-story Ferris wheel as she and Tony ate their angel-hair pasta.

As the meal progressed, he seemed to relax.

"So who do you think did it?" she finally asked him, reluctant to break the mood.

He shrugged. "Who knows? It's not our case. Not even our jurisdiction, but I wouldn't mind running a little background check on Maria Mancini, anyway. See if we can turn up any potential suspects."

"You think her murder is connected to the others?"

Tony frowned, glancing out the window toward the horizon, which was dotted with sailboats. "She doesn't fit the MO. She was older, didn't live in the same area, and she was shot, not stabbed."

"But she was connected to you," Eve pointed out. "And she was at both crime scenes taking pictures. I still can't figure out how she knew you would be there."

"She had a police scanner in her bedroom, a pretty sophisticated model. Obviously she knew the code."

Every police department in the country had its own radio code, which was used to dispatch and communicate with units quickly and efficiently without being understood by civilians monitoring the broadcasts. But obviously Maria Mancini had been well informed, and Eve still wasn't willing to dismiss the possibility that she had been working with someone on the inside.

"One of the uniforms said the scanner was turned on when they found the body," Tony said. He glanced up. "He said they could hear the other units being dispatched to the scene when they found her. Pretty ironic, isn't it?"

Ironic and sad, Eve thought. For some reason, Maria Mancini had been compelled to lie in bed at night monitoring police calls, unaware that one of those calls would eventually be for her.

Eve remembered the phone call Maria had received yesterday, while Eve had been hiding in her closet. She'd asked the other party when they could meet, and Eve couldn't help wondering now if the person Maria had been talking to was the same one who had helped her keep track of Tony's whereabouts. The same one who had entered her house sometime after midnight and shot her to death.

Because she knew too much?

"Did you know Vic D'Angelo was at the scene this morning?"

Tony scowled. "D'Angelo? What the hell was he doing there?"

"That's what I'd like to know." Eve paused, then said, "Actually, what I'd really like to know is how he found out about Maria Mancini's murder so quickly."

Tony gave her a knowing look. "You starting to think D'Angelo could be involved in all this somehow?"

"I don't know. I do know he has a grudge against you."

"He hates my guts."

Unfortunately, Eve suspected that was true. She'd told Tony once that he inspired powerful feelings in people. Vic D'Angelo. Clare Foxx. Maria Mancini. Even Ed Dawson, the superintendent of police.

But would any of them be willing and able to murder innocent women just to point the finger at Tony? It was a very disturbing thought.

They finished their meal in silence, and then Tony paid the bill. When Eve protested, he said, "You can catch the next one. I'm not being chauvinistic, Eve. I just want to buy you lunch, okay?"

She smiled. "Can't argue with that."

They took their time heading back to the car. Eve stopped in front of the huge carousel—another Navy Pier attraction—admiring the hand-painted horses and chariots. "Would you believe, I've never ridden a carousel?"

"Then you haven't lived," Tony said dryly. "Tell you what. When all this is over, I'll bring you back here and buy you a ticket. Only we'll come at night, when the Ferris wheel is all lit and they have the fireworks show over the lake. Deal?"

Eve smiled and nodded, but she had a bad feeling that when all this was over, carousels and fireworks would be the last thing on Tony's mind.

Chapter Eleven

Eve was summoned to police headquarters on State Street the next day. A secretary led her to the same conference room where she'd met with the contingent a few days ago.

Taking a deep breath, she opened the door and stepped inside. But rather than facing the half-dozen men in dark suits who had been assembled before, there was only one man sitting at the table now.

Ed Dawson smiled slightly as Eve closed the door. "Please sit down, Sergeant Barrett," he invited cordially, motioning her to the seat across from him.

He was impeccably dressed as always, his silver hair slicked back, his complexion still smooth and deeply tanned. He had to be in his late fifties, but he obviously took good care of himself. Eve could smell the subtle notes of his expensive cologne as she rolled out one of the chairs and sat down.

He folded his hands together on the table. This time he made no pretense of studying the file in front of him, nor did he beat around the bush. He said, in an almost matter-of-fact tone, "Do you think Tony Gallagher is involved in these murders?"

The question caught Eve completely off guard. She

gaped at him for a moment before gathering her poise. "No, sir, I don't."

"No doubt whatsoever?"

"None."

"I don't understand how that can be, Sergeant Barrett."

Eve sensed a trap. "What do you mean?"

"Even though you're acting as his partner, you can't be with the man twenty-four hours a day. In fact, my guess is that you weren't with him when any of these women were killed."

"I wasn't with a lot of other people during that time, either," she pointed out.

"No, but a lot of other people don't have Tony Gallagher's problems." He gazed at his hands for a moment, then back up at Eve. "Do you know why you were chosen for this assignment, Sergeant Barrett?"

"Not exactly. I assume my record had something to do with it."

"It had a great deal to do with it. You've been in Internal Affairs now for, what? Three years? Four? You've garnered yourself quite a reputation. As Deputy Superintendent Ackerman mentioned the other day, it takes a special kind of person to succeed in IAD. You have to have a very clear concept of right and wrong. No equivocation."

Eve thought about the way she'd entered Maria Mancini's house without a warrant. There had been a time when such an action would have been unthinkable for her. But somehow on the street, matters weren't always as black and white as she'd once thought they should be, and she couldn't help worrying how she would handle her duties once she returned to Internal Affairs.

She glanced up at Dawson. "I still have a clear concept of right and wrong."

One brow rose as he watched her. "You would have no

hesitation in reporting back to your commanding officer if you had incriminating information regarding Detective Gallagher's whereabouts at the time one or all of these murders were committed?''

The knot in Eve's stomach tightened. "I don't have any such evidence."

"That's not what I asked you."

"What exactly are you asking me…sir?" she added almost hesitantly.

"You know something isn't right here. You sense it, don't you, Eve?" He'd never used her first name before. If he'd meant to put her at ease, it didn't work.

Their gazes met, and Eve suppressed a shiver. "I don't understand why you called me in here today."

"Would you believe me if I said I was worried about you? That I felt it was my duty to warn you?"

"Warn me?"

He got up and paced to the window. His back was to Eve, but she could see his profile, the rigid set of his jaw and chin. When he glanced back at her, his eyes had grown very cold. "I remember you from the old neighborhood. Does that surprise you?"

"Yes." Although the Gallaghers had been friends with the Dawsons, Eve and her father had barely been acquainted with them.

He turned to face her. "You knew my daughter, Ashley."

Eve's heart thudded against her chest. "Not very well, but I do remember her."

He came back to the table and sat down. "She was a lovely girl. Her mother and I were devastated when she died."

Where was this going? Eve murmured something sympathetic, but Dawson acted as if he didn't hear her. He sat back in his chair and studied her for a long moment. "Tony was there the night she was murdered. Did you know that?"

"Yes."

His gaze froze her from saying anything more. "Revenge and money are powerful motives for murder. But there's one motive even stronger. Do you know what it is?"

"Sex. Passion. Jealousy."

"All of the above," he agreed. "Did you know Ashley was going to break up with Tony?"

Eve almost gasped. "She told you that?"

"I sensed it. She had…a number of admirers. I think she was getting a little tired of Tony."

"Who were these admirers?"

For the first time, he looked down at the folder on the desk in front of him. "Daniel O'Roarke, for one."

"Then doesn't that give *him* the motive we just talked about?"

"Maybe." Dawson touched a finger to his chin. "But you can imagine how Tony would have reacted if he'd found out about Ashley's…flirtations. She was a beautiful girl. The kind of woman a man can't easily let go of."

Eve felt a shiver of something indefinable as she gazed at Ed Dawson. He referred to Ashley as his daughter when in fact she'd been his stepdaughter. Nothing wrong in that, so long as his feelings for her hadn't crossed over the bounds.

But there was something about the way he spoke of her…

Something in his eyes…

"Why are you telling me all this?" Eve suddenly couldn't wait to get out of that room, to get as far away from Ed Dawson as she could. Regardless of what his feelings for Ashley had been, there was something about him

Eve didn't like. Didn't trust. He was the kind of man who might wait years to exact a revenge that constantly ate away at him.

"I like you, Eve. You're intelligent, conscientious, savvy. The kind of woman who could move up in the ranks quickly." He paused, his gaze flickering over her. "Depending, of course, on the outcome of your current assignment."

EVE THOUGHT ABOUT DAWSON'S implied threat all morning, and every time she looked at Tony, she worried about how he would react when he learned the truth about her. And he would learn the truth. There was no way Eve could keep her assignment from him indefinitely. But she had to pick her own time to tell him, and right now, her instincts were warning her to wait until they'd apprehended the murderer. If their suspicions were true and Tony was being framed, then he needed a friend on the inside now more than ever.

After lunch, Eve decided to have another crack at Lucy Stringer's landlady. Ever since Curly, the bartender at Nellie's, had mentioned that Megan Riley had had a secret admirer, Eve couldn't shake the feeling that she'd missed something in Betty Jarvis's statement.

It had been over a week since Lucy's body had been found by Mrs. Jarvis, and as Eve pulled her car to the curb, her gaze went instantly to the garage apartment where Lucy had lived.

The crime scene tape had been removed, and there was no outward sign that a brutal murder had taken place inside. Both Mrs. Jarvis's house and the adjacent garage apartment looked almost picturesque in the drizzle that had started to fall.

Eve got out of her car, but rather than going to the front door, she followed the drive around back, to the steps that led up to Lucy's apartment. The door to the apartment was closed, the blinds pulled, but the clay pots of geraniums on every other step somehow made the place look inviting. A very deceptive image.

She heard her name called and turned. Mrs. Jarvis, holding a jacket over her head, came out of the house and beckoned to Eve.

"Detective Barrett, isn't it?"

"How are you, Mrs. Jarvis?"

"I'm feeling much better." The woman hesitated, then said, "For a moment, I thought you were one of those awful sightseers. You wouldn't believe the way they stop by here and stare up at Lucy's apartment, like it's some sort of sideshow or something." She shuddered, but Eve suspected it had very little to do with the chilly rain. "Won't you come in, Detective?"

"Thank you." Eve held the back door for Mrs. Jarvis, then followed the older woman inside.

Mrs. Jarvis hung her jacket on a peg in the kitchen. "Would you like a cup of coffee? Tea?"

"No, I'm fine, thank you. Mrs. Jarvis, I know we've been over that night several times already, and I hate to put you through this again, but if you wouldn't mind, I'd like to ask you some more questions."

Mrs. Jarvis motioned Eve to the table and then sat down across from her. "I've told you everything I can remember."

"I'm sure that's true, but there's still one thing that bothers me. You told me that Lucy received flowers and a love note from an anonymous admirer a couple of weeks before she was killed."

Mrs. Jarvis nodded. "Lucy and I both thought it was so romantic—" She broke off, glancing at Eve in alarm. "But he was probably the one who killed her, wasn't he?"

"It's possible."

"He was one of those stalkers you read about. A man who becomes obsessed with a certain woman. Poor Lucy." Mrs. Jarvis's eyes grew shadowed. "In my day, a secret admirer was something we girls would giggle and tease about, but nowadays there's a lot of sick people out there."

Eve nodded sympathetically. "You said Lucy showed you the letter. Have you remembered anything more about it?"

"Not really. It wasn't mailed to her, you know. He slipped it under her door one night. But I told you that didn't I?"

"Yes, but just keep going as if you're telling me all this for the first time."

Mrs. Jarvis's brow wrinkled in concentration. "The note was very poetic, the best I remember. He talked about destiny and karma. Things like that." She sighed.

"When you say poetic, do you mean an actual poem?"

"No, no, it wasn't a poem. Nothing rhymed, or anything like that. It was just the way the note was written. I remember Lucy saying that it was unusual for a man to be so sensitive. She said he knew all the right things to say to a woman. She was very intrigued by him. Especially after he left those flowers for her."

"Tell me again about the flowers."

"Roses," she said with another sigh, as if she still couldn't quite let go of the fantasy she and Lucy had spun that day. "He left them at the top of the stairs, by her front door. Most men would send red roses, but these were pale pink, the most beautiful shade I think I've ever seen. Very feminine."

Eve glanced up. "Feminine?"

"Delicate," Mrs. Jarvis amended.

But her first instinct had been to say feminine.

"Mrs. Jarvis, you said Lucy had started seeing someone shortly before she died—this admirer, you thought—but she never told you his name. You never saw him."

"Just a shadow once on the stairs."

"And you said you heard voices in her apartment."

"Well," Mrs. Jarvis hedged, "I'm not sure I actually heard *his* voice. It may have been the TV or stereo. Lucy loved to play music."

"What about the shadow on the stairs?"

"Oh, I saw that all right."

"But was he tall or short? Thin or heavy?"

"I really couldn't tell. Like I told you before, it was just a shadow. I couldn't see any details."

"Could it have been a woman?"

Mrs. Jarvis glanced at her in surprise. "A woman?"

"Lucy's admirer knew the right things to say to a woman. And she sent pink roses. *Feminine* was the word you used."

"Oh, but I didn't mean—"

"Think about it, Mrs. Jarvis. Did Lucy say anything that might indicate her admirer was a woman instead of a man?"

"Oh, my word," Mrs. Jarvis said in a whisper. "Times really have changed, haven't they?"

EVE WAS STILL GONE when Tony got back to the station. He was just about to clear away the stack of folders on his desk and call it a day when Clare walked in without knocking.

"I need you to come down to my office, Tony."

He glanced up from the file he'd been reading, saw the expression on her face and scowled. "What's going on?"

"I don't want to talk in here." She glanced over her shoulder as if she were afraid of being overheard. The watch change outside made the squad room even noisier than usual, but Tony knew there were always prying eyes and ears.

"Can't this wait until morning? It's been a long day, Clare."

"This can't wait." She turned on her heel and left the room.

Tony had no choice but to follow her. He automatically closed her office door and turned to face her. Rather than taking a seat behind her desk, she leaned against the edge. She looked tense, almost rattled, and Tony had a sudden premonition that the ax was about to fall.

"What's going on?" he asked her again.

"Sit down, Tony."

"I don't need to sit. Just tell me what the hell this is about."

"I think you'd better sit," she advised. Her dark eyes flicked over him, but Tony couldn't tell what she was thinking.

He shrugged and sat. "Satisfied?"

Her knuckles whitened as she gripped the edge of the desk. "This is serious, Tony."

"Okay, let's have it."

"Where were you night before last between the hours of midnight and five in the morning?"

Busted, he thought with a sinking feeling in his stomach. "You know where I was."

"You left the hospital sometime after midnight, didn't you?"

He didn't say anything.

Clare leaned toward him, her eyes flashing. "You better come clean with me, Tony. I can't help you if you don't. Your car was seen a couple of blocks from Maria Mancini's house around twelve-thirty on Tuesday morning. How do you explain that?''

His stomach sunk lower. ''I can't.'' Which was true. He hadn't left the hospital until one-thirty, after he'd spoken with Fisher.

''What happened to your car after you were taken to the emergency room?''

''One of the officers on the scene drove it back here to the station, and then my brothers picked it up Monday afternoon and parked it at the hospital. I wanted to have a ride first thing Tuesday morning when I was released.''

''Did they give you the keys?''

''Yeah.''

''Does anyone else have a set?''

Tony thought about that one. His mother had a set, and maybe Fiona. But neither of them would have taken his car without asking him first, and they sure as hell wouldn't have driven to Maria Mancini's neighborhood.

He glanced up at Clare. ''It wasn't me driving that car.''

''You were in your hospital room all night?''

Tony hesitated, then said, ''I left around one-thirty. My car was parked in the parking garage right where Nick and John told me they'd left it. Someone else must have taken it.''

Anger flickered in Clare's gaze. ''So you lied to me yesterday.''

Tony leaned toward her. ''I know how this looks, but I didn't have anything to do with Maria Mancini's death. Come on, Clare. You know me better than that.''

She stared at him for a long, tense moment, then got up and rounded the desk to her chair. ''Your car is being impounded, Tony. I hope for your sake it's clean.''

His mind shot back to the night Megan Riley was murdered. Had she been in his car? What about Tuesday morning? It looked as if someone had taken his car and driven to Maria Mancini's neighborhood. Had her murderer deliberately planted evidence to tie Tony to the crime?

"I'm going to have to ask you for your weapon," Clare said.

"Clare, you know me better than this. I didn't kill anyone. I wasn't anywhere near that house on Tuesday morning."

"Your gun, Tony."

"Dammit, this is a railroad job, and you know it."

"I know I've got a job to do, and I intend to do it," she said grimly. "Now, are you going to hand over your gun or are we going to have a situation on our hands?"

He gave her the Smith and Wesson without a word.

She slipped it in a bag and put it in her desk. "You still have your father's .38 at home?"

He scrubbed his forehead with his fingertips. "You know I do."

"I'm going to send Wagner with you to get it," she said. "Or if you'd rather, we can get a search warrant."

He rose. "You're making a big mistake, Clare. While you're pulling this crap on me, the real killer's still out there. He's getting away with it."

"Nobody's going to get away with anything." Her gaze hardened on him. "And I mean nobody."

He leaned over her desk, planting his hands on the surface. "I'm going to find out who's behind this, Clare. One way or another."

Something that might have been fear flashed in her eyes before she blinked it away. She allowed herself a smile. "You're hardly in any position to make threats or promises, Tony. Under the circumstances, I think it might be best if you take a few days off. You understand, don't you?"

"Oh, I understand all right. You've wanted me out for a long time, haven't you, Clare?"

She shrugged, but her expression wasn't as cool as she might have wanted. "This isn't personal."

"Like hell it's not."

"Instead of blaming me for your troubles, you might want to get yourself a good lawyer," she advised. "Because I think you're going to need one."

SOMETHING WAS GOING ON, Eve thought as she walked toward her and Tony's office. People were glancing in her direction and the squad room was almost unnaturally quiet. But the moment she closed the door to the office, she heard the drone of voices start up again. Were they talking about her?

"Don't be paranoid," she muttered, turning on her computer.

She was halfway through her notes when Vic D'Angelo opened the door and walked in.

She glanced up at him. "Don't you believe in knocking?"

He shrugged. "Sorry. Just wanted to offer you my support. Too bad about Cowboy."

Eve's stomach fluttered in apprehension. Had something happened to Tony? "What are you talking about?"

D'Angelo looked surprised. "You don't know? Your boy's in a lot of trouble, Eve."

"What kind of trouble?"

"Seems he's just a little too trigger happy for his own good."

"What's that supposed to mean?" Eve snapped, but her heart was hammering in her throat as she rose and faced him. "What's going on, D'Angelo?"

"You used to call me Vic," he complained.

"Tell me, damn you!"

He looked slightly taken aback by her language and by her anger. "Okay, okay. Look, I only know what I hear through the grapevine. Rumor has it your partner is about to be arrested for Maria Mancini's murder."

Eve gasped. "That's ridiculous!"

Vic smirked. "The lieutenant doesn't seem to think so. She's impounded his car and confiscated his weapons. That sounds pretty serious to me."

"When did this happen?" Eve asked in alarm. *Tony could be arrested for murder.* The words were like a litany inside her head.

"He was escorted out of here a little while ago," D'Angelo told her. "And to tell you the truth, I didn't see a lot of people lining up out there to come to his defense. Cowboy's burned a lot of bridges around here. Now he's going to have to suffer the consequences."

DURTY NELLIE'S WAS PACKED for a weeknight. Eve scanned the crowd, searching for Tony. She saw Fiona at a table in a corner and headed over.

Leaning down, she said over the music, "Have you seen Tony?"

Fiona took Eve's hand and drew her down to the chair beside her. "I was hoping he was with you. I'm worried to death about him, Eve."

"You know what happened then?"

Fiona nodded. "David told me. Tony called him from the station. David went straight over, but Tony had already left, and we haven't heard from him since. David thought he might turn up here. What's going on, Eve?"

"I wish I knew." She glanced up as David came over with two drinks.

"Hi, Eve. Can I get you a drink?" He sat down, sliding Fiona's glass in front of her.

"No, thanks. I'm looking for Tony."

David grimaced. "Join the party." He took a sip of his beer, staring at Eve over the rim. "Do you know the details?"

"Barely." Only what Vic D'Angelo had relished telling her. She filled them in on what she knew.

David leaned across the table toward her. "Did you know Tony left the hospital sometime Tuesday morning?"

She hesitated, then nodded. David was Tony's attorney. He couldn't help him unless he knew all the facts. "He was at my place."

Fiona glanced at David. "That means it couldn't have been his car that was spotted in Maria Mancini's neighborhood."

"What time did he get to your place?" David asked more cautiously.

"Two, two-thirty." If either of them thought such a late night visit strange, Eve gave them credit for trying not to show it.

"Maria Mancini was killed somewhere between the hours of midnight and 4:00 a.m. Tony claims he left the hospital at around one-thirty. If he got to your place at two-thirty, we've got an hour he hasn't accounted for."

"Maybe it was closer to two," Eve said.

"You said two-thirty." When she started to protest, David held up a hand. "Look, the time line is important. We've got to figure this thing out as closely as we can. It's for Tony's own good."

"All right, it probably was closer to two-thirty," she admitted, feeling like a traitor.

"The hospital is, what? Twenty minutes from your apartment? At that time of morning, there wouldn't have been much traffic.''

''Okay, so that narrows it down to forty minutes. He couldn't have gotten all the way to Little Italy, somehow managed to get inside Maria Mancini's house, shoot her and then drive all the way back to my place. There just wasn't enough time.''

David and Fiona exchanged glances.

''What?'' Eve demanded.

''It's your word, Eve,'' David said. ''No one else saw Tony at your place. And your credibility may have been compromised.''

''How?''

''For one thing, you didn't set the record straight yesterday when Tony let Clare Foxx believe he'd spent the entire night in the hospital. And for another...'' He paused, looking uncomfortable. ''It's obvious you have strong feelings for him.''

Eve stared at him in shock. ''He's my partner. There's nothing going on between us.''

''That's why he came to your apartment at two-thirty in the morning?''

''Yes,'' Eve said almost angrily. ''It is. He had something he wanted to discuss with me.''

''May I ask what?''

She shrugged. ''He wanted to talk about our cases. There's nothing unusual in that, is there?''

Something flickered in David's eyes. He leaned toward her again. ''What time did he leave?''

She glanced from Fiona to David, feeling helpless. ''He didn't leave. He spent the night. But nothing happened,'' she insisted.

''Can you prove that he spent the night?''

''What is this?'' Eve all but exploded. ''Why do I feel as if I'm being interrogated here?''

''Because you're forgetting to think like a cop,'' David said grimly.

Fiona took Eve's hand. ''David's playing devil's advocate, Eve. You know as well as we do what a prosecutor, let alone the review board, would do with your testimony under the circumstances.''

Were her feelings for Tony that obvious?

''So what do we do?'' she asked almost desperately.

''First we have to find him.'' David leaned toward her, his gaze intense. ''Then we figure out exactly what the hell the two of you are going to say.''

Chapter Twelve

Tony was sitting on Eve's steps when she got home. "I've been out looking for you," she said almost accusingly. "So have David and Fiona. Where've you been?"

He rose. "Driving around, trying to figure things out."

Eve glanced over her shoulder at the parking lot. "How'd you get here?"

"I borrowed my mother's car. Look, can we go inside? I need to talk to you."

Eve nodded and started up the stairs. Tony followed her inside and closed the door. "You heard what happened?"

"I heard Vic D'Angelo's version," she said. "Clare was already gone by the time I got back to the station. What *did* happen, Tony?"

"Someone reported seeing my car in Maria Mancini's neighborhood on Tuesday morning. Clare started asking questions, and I admitted that I'd left the hospital that night. But, Eve, she already knew."

"How?"

He shrugged, raking his fingers through his hair. "I don't know. But if someone stole my car that night, there's no telling what kind of evidence was planted."

This was bad, Eve thought. Very bad. "D'Angelo said your weapons were confiscated."

"That's another scary story," Tony told her. "When I went to get my father's .38 from the closet, the gun had been moved. Not much, but enough so that I noticed. Don't ask me how, but someone got into my apartment, took the gun and then brought it back. My guess is it was the weapon used to kill Maria Mancini. When the ballistics tests are run, you can bet I'm going to look guilty as hell."

Eve rubbed her forehead, trying to think. Trying not to let panic overtake her. "Okay, someone was able to get inside your apartment. He was able to steal your car from the hospital parking garage. That could mean it's someone who has had access to your keys at one time or another."

"Unless he's one helluva lock pick."

"I've thought about that, too," Eve said. She paused. "I never told you this, but when I came home Sunday after visiting my dad, I had a feeling someone had been in here. There was no evidence of a break-in, no tool marks, nothing. But I couldn't shake the feeling that someone had been here."

Tony stared down at her in alarm. "Why didn't you tell me?"

She shrugged. "I thought it was probably my imagination. And besides, you've had enough to deal with."

"Eve." He took her arms. "This is serious. If he was inside your apartment once, he could get in again."

"I know, but if he wanted to hurt me, he could have waited for me that night and ambushed me. He didn't."

"No," Tony agreed, his voice grim. "But maybe it was because the timing wasn't right. Maybe he was here casing the place, figuring out all the details he would need to commit another perfect murder."

Eve shivered violently. "Thanks for that image."

He gripped her arms. "You're a police officer, Eve. You

know what we're dealing with here. You can't afford not to take this seriously.''

"I do. Believe me, I take this very seriously.''

He gazed at her for a long moment, his eyes dark, troubled. Then suddenly he pulled her against him and wrapped his arms around her. "Eve, Eve. What would I do if anything happened to you? I couldn't stand it.''

The ragged edge to his voice shocked her. She pulled back a little to stare up at him. "Nothing is going to happen to me.''

He threaded his fingers through her hair. "No, you're right. I won't let it.''

When she would have moved away from him, he held her. He moved his thumb across her lips, and her mouth parted willingly.

"Tony—''

"I know. There's a million reasons why I shouldn't have come over here tonight. Another million why you should send me away.''

"I can't,'' she said hoarsely.

"I guess I was counting on that.''

His thumb continued to stroke her lips, until Eve caught his hand and turned her mouth to kiss his palm.

His gaze deepened on her. "You have no idea how much I need you right now.''

"I'm here,'' she said in a jagged whisper. "I've always been here.''

"Then what a fool I've been not to know it,'' he said with a note of wonder.

HER BEDROOM WAS COOL and shadowy—a little frightening, Eve decided as she and Tony undressed in silence. But then, when they came together again, the ghosts seemed to flee, and she wouldn't let anything else matter except the touch of his hands on her body, the whisper of his lips against her hair, the sound of his voice throbbing in her ear.

He wrapped his arms around her, pulling her close, and they stood in the darkness, kissing, caressing, letting their bodies become intimately familiar.

Eve thought about the first time he'd kissed her, so many years ago. A lot of things had happened to both of them since then, and in some ways, they were two different people. And yet that memory was still precious to her, still vital to her. She knew she wouldn't be here now if not for that kiss. Because from the moment Tony's lips had first touched hers, Eve had known there would never be anyone else.

Her heart pounding, she let her fingers travel at will over his body. Through his hair, across his shoulders, against his chest. His lips found the pulse in her throat, and she tipped her head back, giving him the access they both craved.

After a while, he carried her to the bed, and they lay down face-to-face, kissing over and over until Tony broke away and gazed at her in the darkness.

"Where've you been all these years, Evie?" His voice still held that note of wonder, as if he couldn't quite believe what was happening between them.

"You asked me that once before, remember?"

"I guess I'm wondering why it took me this long to find you again." His hand rode the line of her hip, trailed down her thigh.

Eve shivered. "Maybe you weren't looking."

"Maybe I wasn't," he agreed, his voice husky with passion. "But I'm damned if I can figure out why."

HER SKIN GLEAMED PALE in the moonlight slanting in from the window, and Tony took his time with her. His hands moved over her, finding the spots that made her tremble, made her sigh, made her moan softly in the darkness. She was incredibly sensuous, attuned to his every touch, and he felt his own control slipping as she clutched at his shoulders, murmuring his name.

He'd been with women in the past, women he'd admired, respected, might even have loved if he'd given himself half a chance. But it had been a long time since he'd felt as close to anyone as he did to Eve. He wondered if he ever had. She was his best friend, his partner, and now his lover, and he knew that he would trust her with his life. She meant everything to him.

She drew him to her, taking his face in her hands and kissing him deeply. Tony groaned against her mouth, moving over her, fitting his body to hers.

"I'd do anything for you, Eve. You know that, don't you?"

She sighed. "I never thought…I can't believe…"

"What?"

"I've waited so long for this to happen."

"I think I've been waiting for it, too, Evie. I just didn't know it."

EVE HAD FORGOTTEN ABOUT Tony's injuries. He lay on his back, and when she propped herself on her elbow to stare down at him, the moonlight struck him just right. The bruises still looked so raw and tender, Eve knew she must have hurt him.

"I forgot you were hurt," she said softly. "I should have been more—"

"Gentle?" He gave her a knowing grin. "In that case, I'm glad you forgot. Because you were—" he pulled her to him and kissed her "—incredible."

"I was?"

He trailed his fingers through the curtain of her hair. "So beautiful," he murmured.

Eve caught her breath. "You make me feel beautiful. I'm so—" She almost said, "I'm so in love with you," but she didn't want to scare him away. Instead she said, "I'm so glad you came over tonight."

"Will you still feel that way in the morning?"

"Will you?"

"I could never regret being with you, Eve. No matter what happens."

He drew her to him again, and she rested her head on his shoulder, draping one arm across his chest. *No matter what happens.* She took comfort in his words as they lay in silence.

Outside her bedroom window, shadows moved. Eve shivered, and instantly Tony's arm tightened around her.

She closed her eyes and tried not to think about her assignment, or about a killer who still lurked out there in the darkness.

She tried not to think that come tomorrow, Tony could be arrested for murder.

EVE WOKE UP EARLY. Sometime during the night, Tony must have pulled the covers over them, because they were snuggled beneath the quilt, his arms wrapped tightly around her. As quietly as she could, she slipped out of his embrace and pulled on her robe, belting it around her as she walked into the living room.

Wondering if there had been any overnight developments that she and Tony needed to know about it, Eve lowered the volume on the TV and flipped through the channels until she found the local news. The lead story dealt with the national political scene, focusing on a front-runner who had suddenly dropped out of the presidential race. Eve yawned as a Washington pundit tried to make sense of the decision.

His voice droned on and on until she felt herself drifting off. But when she heard Tony's name, her eyes flew open and she bolted upright on the sofa.

His picture flashed on the screen behind the news anchor, and Eve reached for the remote, turning up the volume a notch so she could hear what the man was saying.

"Sources in the Chicago Police Department have confirmed for this station that Detective Tony Gallagher is a suspect in the murder of Maria Mancini, a forty-three-year-old real estate agent who was found dead in her home on Tuesday morning. Gallagher was suspended last month following the shooting death of Mancini's son, twenty-two-year-old Franco Mancini, a robbery suspect. In a bizarre twist to this story, Maria Mancini was arrested early Monday morning for a hit-and-run incident that sent Detective Gallagher to the hospital. His injuries weren't serious, but it's believed revenge could be the motive.

"Detective Gallagher has come under fire several times in the past for misconduct, and sources inside CPD have revealed that he has recently been the subject of a sting operation conducted by the Internal Affairs Division."

The picture of Tony flashed off the screen, replaced by a shot of Eve and her IAD commanding officer coming out of Police Headquarters. Eve gasped when she saw the image. She felt as if the floor had dropped out from under her. There was no doubt in her mind that someone had deliberately leaked the information to the press. But who? And perhaps more importantly, why?

"Four years ago, Detective Gallagher was hit with assault charges, and Channel Five has also learned that he may have been involved in suppressing crucial evidence in the brutal slaying of his girlfriend eight years ago."

Eve saw a movement from the corner of her eye, just before she flicked off the TV. But she knew she was too late. Tony had heard everything.

He was standing in the bedroom doorway, fully dressed, as if he'd been on his way out. Eve wondered fleetingly where he'd been headed. For the longest moment, he said nothing. Then slowly he moved toward her. Eve rose.

"Why?" was all he said, but that one word conveyed a sense of betrayal that made Eve's heart plummet.

"I can explain—"

"Just tell me one thing. Is it true? Are you IAD?"

"Tony—"

He walked straight past her.

"If you would just listen to me…Tony, please—"

He opened the door before glancing back at her. "I don't think you and I have anything else to say to each other, Eve. And right now, I don't even want to be in the same room with you."

Chapter Thirteen

Eve didn't think she would ever forget the look on Tony's face when he'd walked out the door. *I don't even want to be in the same room with you.*

She closed her eyes, willing away the searing pain in her heart, but Eve knew the ache would be with her for a very long time to come. She'd betrayed him and now he never wanted to see her again. Could she blame him?

Eve had known all along it might come to this, but somehow she hadn't let herself think too hard about the consequences of her assignment. Deep down, she'd managed to convince herself that everything would work out in the end because her intentions had been noble. She'd never wanted to deceive him. All she'd wanted to do was help him.

But after seeing his face, the look in his eyes, Eve knew he would never believe her, no matter what she said.

She tried to beat back her panic as the full impact of the situation hit her. Who would help Tony now?

Someone was out to get him, set him up for murder. And now that he'd turned away from her, there was no one in his corner, no one watching his back.

Who had leaked Eve's assignment to the press? Who else had known that crucial information had been suppressed in the investigation into Ashley's murder?

The answer was almost too obvious. Ed Dawson knew all of those things, and he was certainly in a position to feed information to the press. Had he set both Eve and Tony up?

After she'd showered and dressed, Eve headed over to Tony's place. She had no idea what kind of car he was driving since his Mustang had been impounded, so she didn't know whether or not it was in the parking lot at his apartment. But if he was home, he didn't answer her knock. Eve scribbled a brief message on the back of an envelope and slid it beneath his door. "Please call me. We have to talk. Please. Just hear me out. Love, E."

She agonized for a moment over "love," but then decided not to cross it out. She did love Tony, and one way or another, she was going to prove that to him.

"How did that picture get on the news?" Eve demanded as she stood in front of her CO's desk in IAD.

Lieutenant Hadling shrugged. "I'm as much in the dark as you are, Eve. I have no idea where that leak came from."

Eve had an idea, but making accusations against the superintendent was not something she could do lightly. "My assignment is compromised. I can't go back there."

"No one is blaming you for any of this, Eve."

She glanced at Hadling in surprise. "What do you mean?"

"We knew Gallagher was dangerous, but we had no idea he was that far gone. I'm just glad you weren't harmed."

When his implication sank in, Eve said incredulously, "What are you talking about? Tony didn't kill anyone. He's being framed."

Hadling glanced up with a frown. "Framed? By whom?"

Eve hesitated. "I have my suspicions." She put her

hands on his desk and leaned toward him. "Look, what they said on the news this morning—that Tony may have suppressed evidence in the Ashley Dallas investigation. Who else would have known about that? If we can figure out where the leak came from, we can probably figure out who's setting Tony up. It may even tell us who the real murderer is."

Hadling shifted in his chair, obviously uncomfortable with the conversation. His gaze moved to the door, then back to Eve. "If I were you, I'd be careful throwing around accusations like that."

"I'm not accusing anyone." Eve straightened, still staring down at him. "But I am going to find out who's behind all this. If it's the last thing I do."

MIDMORNING, Fiona managed to track Eve down at her old office in Internal Affairs. Eve hated hearing the note of accusation in her friend's voice. "Why'd you do it, Eve?"

"Because I was ordered to, for one thing." Eve sighed. "I honestly thought I could help him, Fiona. He's made a lot of enemies in the department. They were out to use him as an example, and I didn't want that to happen. I thought I could stop it."

"I don't imagine Tony saw it that way."

"He wouldn't even let me explain this morning," Eve said worriedly. "He left the apartment without a word."

Fiona hesitated, then her voice softened. "Don't worry. He'll turn up. He just needs some space."

"I hope you're right." Maybe if he'd gone off somewhere to be alone and think, he might eventually realize that Eve had never meant to betray him.

"David and I are both in court for the rest of the day," Fiona told her. "But he suggested that the three of us meet at the pub after work. If Tony still hasn't turned up, maybe we can figure something out.''

DURTY NELLIE'S WAS a lot less crowded than it had been the night before. Eve felt all eyes on her as she walked into the pub, and she wondered if the cold shoulder she seemed to be getting was due to her imagination or because the news about her had spread.

Traitor, she could almost hear them thinking. *Snitch.* All the derogatory terms she'd heard in her tenure in IAD.

David was standing at the bar, and Eve walked over to him. He was the only person in the pub who looked glad to see her. ''Hi, Eve. Want something to drink?''

''Just a Coke,'' she told him. ''I'll grab us a table.''

When he brought over the drinks, Eve said, ''Where's Fiona?''

''She's coming. She decided to drive over and see if her mother had heard from Tony. Plus I think she wanted to make sure Maggie and Colleen were handling the situation okay.'' He glanced at her. ''I take it you haven't heard from him today.''

''I think I'd be the last person he'd get in touch with,'' Eve said gloomily.

''You can see his point, can't you?'' In spite of his blunt words, David's smile was sympathetic. ''Finding out about you must have been quite a blow, coming on top of everything else. Especially considering the way he feels about you.''

''The way he feels about me,'' Eve repeated almost numbly. She took a drink of her Coke. ''He hates me. He despises me. He thinks I betrayed him.''

''He'll get over all that in time. He'll come to realize what Fiona and I both knew from the start. You're the best thing that's ever happened to him, Eve.''

She wanted desperately to believe him, but at the moment, Eve couldn't see it. In hindsight, she thought the best thing might have been to level with him, but she'd truly thought that she could better protect him by keeping him in the dark. She'd known that the moment he found out she was IAD, he would do exactly what he did do. Push her away.

But maybe that was because of last night, a little voice reminded her. Maybe he wouldn't have felt quite so betrayed if they hadn't yet been lovers.

She closed her eyes, rubbing a spot at her temple where a headache had begun to throb.

"Are you okay?"

When David touched her hand, Eve jumped. She'd drifted off, and the feel of his hand on hers startled her. "I'm just worried about Tony," she said. "I can't help feeling something terrible is about to happen to him."

David gave her hand a little squeeze. "Everything is going to be okay, Eve. I'll make sure of it. Tony's been in tight jams before, and we've always managed to get him out. We will this time, too."

"I hope so." Eve glanced at her watch, surprised to see how much time had elapsed. "Do you think Fiona is still coming?"

"She said she would. In fact, she said she had an idea where Tony might be."

"Where?"

"Their father's fishing cabin. It's about a two-hour drive from here, way out in the sticks somewhere. There's no phone—"

His words broke off abruptly as Vic D'Angelo ambled over to their table. He drew up a chair, turned it backwards and straddled it.

"So you're IAD," he said in disgust. "I should have

known. No wonder you're so frigid. It takes a cold bitch to work in Internal Affairs.''

"Watch your mouth, D'Angelo," David said with a scowl.

Vic trained his gaze on David. "What are you, her protector? Where's Gallagher? Or has he already skipped the country?"

When David would have said something else, Eve rose on shaky legs. "Let's just get out of here."

D'Angelo rose, too, and grabbed her arm. "We've got a little unfinished business, you and me."

She jerked her arm from his grasp just as someone grabbed his shoulder and spun him around. Before Eve could stop him, Tony punched D'Angelo square in the face. He went sailing backward, crashing against a table amid startled oaths and breaking glass.

Both David and Eve gaped at Tony. Eve opened her mouth, but before she could say a word, Tony turned on his heel and strode from the pub.

When Eve would have run after him, David caught her arm. "Better let me go talk to him." He glanced back, to where D'Angelo was struggling to his feet, wiping blood from the corner of his mouth. "I don't think you'd better stay in here, though. Why don't you go on home? I'll call you as soon as I talk to Tony."

When Eve would have protested, David said gently, "It's pretty obvious he doesn't want to see you right now. I think you'd better give him some time."

Eve nodded miserably. "Then go talk to him. Make sure he's all right. And David?" She caught his arm. "Tell him…" She trailed off and shrugged. She'd wanted to say, "Tell him I love him," but she didn't think he'd believe her, even though she had never meant those words more.

Instead she said softly, "Tell him everything is going to be okay."

EVE FELT SICK by the time she got home. She knew it was probably nerves. The knots in her stomach had tightened painfully when she'd seen Tony and David talking outside Durty Nellie's. She'd paused, wanting more than anything to join them, but when Tony turned his back to her, she knew she had no choice but to do as David suggested. Go home and wait for his call. And pray that Tony would find a way to forgive her for her deception.

Her hands were shaking so badly, she tried three times before she finally fit the key in the lock and opened her door. What she needed was a cool, bracing shower to help clear her head, Eve decided, but as she turned on the light in her apartment, another wave of nausea rolled over her. She stumbled dizzily, catching the back of the sofa to break her fall and feeling grateful that whatever bug she'd picked up hadn't hit her while she'd been driving.

Eve sank to the floor and put her head between her knees, willing away the dizziness. She sat there for the longest time, her stomach churning, her head reeling, and she wondered if emotional upheaval could cause this strong of a reaction. The term "worried sick" took on a new meaning for her.

When she tried to push herself off the floor, the faintness swept over her again, stronger than before, and she fell back against the floor. What was happening to her? she wondered in near panic. There was a strange, bitter taste in her mouth and a sickeningly sweet smell in her nostrils.

Fear exploded inside her as she identified the scent. Roses...

Too weak to stand, Eve rolled over on the floor, until she was facing the dining room table. It was little more than a blur, but she concentrated, willing her vision to clear, and for just a second, she saw the vase of pale pink roses resting on top of the table.

Desperate now, she tried to rise. She managed to get to her hands and knees just as her apartment door opened behind her. A breeze from the lake blew in, and for a moment, Eve thought it might clear away the dizziness, the blackness that was threatening to engulf her.

She managed to sit, leaning heavily against the back of the sofa as she reached for her gun.

A disembodied hand parted her jacket and removed her weapon for her. Eve was powerless to stop it. She moaned softly as another scent drifted on the wind from the open doorway. The same scent she'd smelled in her apartment on Sunday.

The same scent she'd smelled even more recently…

TONY HAD WATCHED EVE leave the pub, glance in his direction, then head for her car. A part of him had wanted to go after her, listen to her explanation for what she'd done even as another part had argued that he'd be an idiot to listen to her. She'd betrayed him in the worst way possible.

It wasn't just because she was Internal Affairs, although in some ways, that was bad enough. What really hurt Tony the most was that she had betrayed his confidence. Apparently, she'd repeated what he had told her about the information left out of the report on Ashley's death, and now it was possible that investigation could be reopened. It was possible Daniel O'Roarke could get out of prison because of what Eve had done.

Tony gripped the steering wheel of his mother's car as he braked for a light. The situation was bad, all right, but he still had a hard time believing Eve could be so manipulative. Could he have been that wrong about someone he thought he knew so well?

Somehow he didn't think so. Somehow there had to be more to the story than he knew, and as mad as he was at her, Tony knew he would never have any peace until he heard her side of things. David had told him earlier that he should find someplace to lie low for a while until the heat died down, and Tony had thought of his father's fishing cabin. He'd planned to drive up tonight, but he couldn't leave town until he knew, without a doubt, that Eve had deliberately deceived him for the sake of advancing her career.

He turned left, circled the block and then headed west toward Eve's apartment. Pulling into the parking area, he killed the engine and sat staring at the darkened window of her apartment. The place looked deserted, but Tony knew that Eve sometimes went to bed early. Still, it was barely nine o'clock, and he didn't want this thing hanging over his head until morning.

Opening the car door, he'd started to climb out when his mother's car phone rang. Tony answered, recognizing immediately his mother's distraught tone.

"Mom, calm down. What is it? What's the matter?"

"It's Fiona," his mother said anxiously. "Tony, she's gone missing."

EVE TRIED TO OPEN her eyes, but the headache that pounded at her temples made the effort seem Herculean. Another try, and she peered through slits into complete darkness. She had no idea where she was or how she'd gotten there, but a strange rocking motion made her head spin even faster.

With another effort, she pushed herself up, bumped her head on something, then fell back heavily to the floor. Panic erupted inside her as she realized she was confined in a cramped space. A coffin was her first thought. Someone had buried her alive!

She swallowed back a scream as she pounded on the top of the enclosure. Whatever it was, it was solid. She couldn't budge it.

Eve lay back, trying to calm her racing heart, her runaway panic. She had to think. Somehow she had to clear the cobwebs from her brain and figure out what to do.

The rocking motion was making her ill again, and as she fought the nausea, she suddenly realized where she was. She was in the trunk of a car.

But how…who…

Why couldn't she remember? She'd gone to the pub earlier. Talked to David. And then Tony had come in. He'd had a fight with D'Angelo….

Or was Eve imagining all that? For some reason she couldn't seem to distinguish between reality and fantasy, but she clung with all her might to her fragile grip on sanity. She couldn't lose it now. She had to *think*. She had to remember.

She'd gone home to her apartment. Something had frightened her there. Some scent…

The roses! Pale pink roses had been left in her apartment, just like the killer had left for Lucy Stringer.

And she'd smelled his cologne, something heavy, musky….

Reality came crashing back with a vengeance. The murderer had been in her apartment, but Eve couldn't remember anything beyond seeing the roses. Somehow the killer had knocked her out, carried her down the apartment steps and stuffed her in the trunk of his car.

Or *her* car.

"Most men would send red roses, but these were pale

pink, the most beautiful shade I think I've ever seen. Very feminine.''

Betty Jarvis's words beat a rhythm inside Eve's head as she tried to find a tire tool, anything with which to pry open the trunk. But they were going fast. Even if she could somehow manage to open the trunk, she would probably be killed or seriously injured if she flung herself from the vehicle.

So what's my choice, Eve thought a little desperately. *Wait and face the killer?*

TONY HAD TRIED not to show his concern to his mother, but he was very worried about Fiona. She'd called their mother earlier that day to say she would be dropping by after work, but she'd never showed up. And Maggie hadn't been able to reach her at her apartment. Fiona didn't answer the phone, and when Tony went by there, she didn't answer her door.

He didn't like the situation at all. He tried to figure out exactly when Fiona had gone missing. David had said earlier she was supposed to meet him and Eve at Durty Nellie's after work, but she'd never showed there, either. At that time, David hadn't been so much worried as he was annoyed, but that was hours ago. Now he would be as concerned as the rest of them, and Tony tried reaching him at home, then on his cell phone, with no luck. He did the same with Eve, but there was no answer at her place, either.

Tony swore, his apprehension mounting by the minute. Where the hell was everybody?

He swerved off the road, turned around and headed back to Eve's apartment. Fiona was missing, and Eve wasn't answering her phone. Every gut instinct Tony possessed warned him that they both were in serious trouble. Fatal trouble. And if he didn't hurry, he just might be too late to help them.

Taking the steps two at a time outside Eve's apartment, Tony banged on the door. "Eve? Are you in there?"

He tried the knob, and when he found the door unlocked, a chill of apprehension crawled through him. He knew that when he opened that door, walked inside, he just might find Eve lying dead....

No, he wouldn't let himself think that way. She had to be all right, dammit.

He entered the apartment slowly. Flipping the light switch, he scanned the room with one sweeping glance. Eve was nowhere in sight, but the apartment seemed different somehow. Her weapon lay on the coffee table, which didn't seem like Eve. She was too cautious to leave a gun lying around. He picked it up, suddenly thinking he might need it.

He glanced around, and just as his gaze landed on the pink roses, he detected a lingering scent. Not the roses, but something deep and musky. An expensive cologne. A fragrance that tugged at his memory.

"You've been with someone else," he accused Ashley. *"I can smell his cologne on your sweater."*

"Don't be silly," she said with a breathless little laugh. *"I gave my stepfather a hug before I came out."*

She'd been wearing a pale pink rose in her hair, and suddenly Tony knew without a doubt who the killer was. What he didn't know was whether or not he was already too late.

EVE COULD FIND NOTHING in the trunk to force open the lid. She'd tried kicking it until she was exhausted, but the space was so cramped, she couldn't get any leverage.

When the car lurched to a stop, Eve braced herself, her

heart pumping. The killer would open the trunk now, and she'd have to be prepared. Surprise was the only element she had going in her favor.

The engine was cut, the car door slammed and the key scraped in the lock. Eve positioned herself as best she could, her muscles taut, ready to spring. When the trunk light came on, she lunged toward the opening, but the killer had anticipated her attack. He stood back and watched her, pointing a gun at her chest as she stumbled from the trunk.

Eve's eyes had been accustomed to darkness for so long that she could see little more than a silhouette. But the gun gleamed in the moonlight, and she knew without a doubt that she was facing Lucy Stringer and Megan Riley's murderer.

Eve could feel the wind off the lake, sharp and biting even for summer. They were in the woods somewhere.

The shadow in front of her moved, placing himself in a patch of moonlight. Eve gasped when she saw his face. "You!"

David MacKenzie said coolly, "You seem disappointed, Eve. Were you expecting someone else?"

Anyone else.

"Why?" she said hoarsely, and realized fleetingly that her first question was the same one Tony had asked her earlier that morning.

David angled the gun toward the right. "There's a path over there. It leads back to a cabin. Let's get inside and then I'll explain everything to you while we wait for Tony."

"Tony?" Eve's voice was hardly more than a whisper.

"He should be here soon, so hurry up. We've got to get inside and be ready for him."

Eve walked slowly toward the path, her gaze darting to either side of her, looking for an escape route. But David didn't let her get that far ahead. He was right on her heels, the gun pointed at her back.

The cabin sat a hundred yards or so off the road, and the best Eve could tell in the dark, it was completely isolated. She glanced back as she climbed the porch steps. "What is this place?"

"The Gallaghers' fishing cabin." The door was locked, and he handed Eve a key. "The light switch is on the right."

Eve turned on the light, and as she paused just inside the door, David used the gun barrel to urge her into the room. She glanced around. The interior was rustic, a typical fishing cabin, with plank flooring, serviceable furniture and plenty of fishing gear littered about. The living area opened to a tiny kitchen and an alcove that served as extra sleeping quarters. There were two twin beds, one of them neatly made, the other piled with clothes.

Eve started to turn away when she heard a soft groan. Her gaze darted back to the bed. What she'd thought was a pile of clothing was in fact a person. *Fiona!*

Eve's heart leaped to her throat as she took in Fiona's appearance. Her wrists and ankles were bound tightly with a rope, and her mouth was secured with tape.

Her gaze met Eve's across the room, and Eve had never seen such terror, such abject horror in anyone's eyes. She started toward her, but David blocked her way. "She's okay. I haven't hurt her."

Yet, Eve thought almost wildly. "Why did you bring us here?"

"Fiona was a mistake. I never meant for her to be involved. I really do care for her," he said with genuine regret.

"You have a funny way of showing it," Eve said, her anger momentarily subduing her fear.

His gaze on her hardened. "Don't be a smart-ass, Eve. I've never found that becoming in a woman, and besides, you're not exactly an innocent in all this. In fact, you can't know how your little charade has helped me."

"What are you talking about?"

"Pretending to be Tony's partner, reporting his activities behind his back. Making him look suspicious as hell."

Eve stared at him in shock. "You leaked that story to the press, didn't you? How did you know about me?"

"Two years ago, you filed a complaint against a cop who was a client of mine. I recognized your name."

"Then why didn't you tell Tony?"

"Because it was just too good, Eve. Like I said, you can't know how much you've helped me out with my plan."

Eve tried to keep the panic at bay as her gaze sought the exits. There were three doors that opened from the living area besides the front door, but Eve suspected they were bedrooms and a bathroom—not an outside exit. A window near the front door was boarded up, and an old-fashioned skylight opened on a hinge overhead, but the beamed ceiling was too high to reach, at least ten feet. And even if Eve managed to make a break for it, what about Fiona? Eve couldn't leave her behind.

David pulled out a wooden chair and motioned her over. When Eve hesitated, he pointed the gun at Fiona. "What's it going to be, Eve? You willing to let her die so you can prove how tough you are?"

Eve glanced at Fiona. Their gazes locked again, and Eve nodded almost imperceptibly, trying to reassure her.

She sat down in the chair, and David pulled her arms behind her, securing her wrists to the rails with a length of rope. Her shoulders and arm sockets screamed in protest.

She could smell his cologne now, too, and the cloying

fragrance sickened her even more. She recognized the scent and knew that he had stood in her apartment on Sunday, plotting how he would kill her.

Through the pain and dizziness, she said, "You slipped knockout drops in my Coke tonight. You've been drugging Tony, too, haven't you? Making him think he was experiencing blackouts."

"It's an old trick, but effective. You can thank him for that. He claimed he blacked out the night Ashley died. That's what gave me the idea." Having secured her ankles, David stood. "I wouldn't feel too sorry for him if I were you."

"What do you mean?"

"Why do you think I've done what I've done?" His voice was anguished, almost desperate. "I'm not a natural born killer, Eve. I didn't enjoy watching those girls die, although the Mancini bitch wasn't so hard. She was getting too difficult to control. All the publicity was going to her head."

"You were the one who persuaded her to go after Tony." Eve worked at the rope around her wrists, but David knew what he was doing. The bindings were so tight her skin was soon raw from the struggle.

"She got the media so fired up they were only too willing to believe the worst of Tony. So is everyone else. Except you, Eve. I knew the moment I saw you with him that I'd eventually have to kill you. And in the end, that's the perfect justice after all, isn't it?"

"Justice for what?" Eve asked softly.

He gave her an odd look. "Justice for Ashley's murder."

Eve felt a rush of new panic at his words. "But Tony didn't kill Ashley. Daniel O'Roarke did."

David gazed down at her, but Eve didn't think it was her face he saw at that moment. "When I saw Ashley's blood-soaked body that night, I knew what had happened. Tony killed her.''

Eve gasped. ''You're insane!''

''Am I?'' His eyes glittered dangerously—not with madness, but with a deep, unhealed pain. ''What if I told you that Ashley and I were in love? What if I told you the baby she was carrying was mine?''

Chapter Fourteen

Eve thought she was beyond shock, but David's announcement sent her mind reeling. He and Ashley had been lovers? The baby she'd been carrying had been his—not Tony's?

Was David telling her the truth?

She gazed up at him and knew that he was. At least what he perceived to be the truth. He really believed that Tony had killed Ashley. All these years, he'd pretended to be Tony's best friend while he'd been plotting and planning his revenge.

"If you're so sure Tony killed Ashley, why did you never say anything?"

"What good would it have done? Who would have listened to me? The Gallaghers take care of their own, don't you know that, Eve? His father and uncle suppressed incriminating evidence against Tony. Even Ashley's own stepfather was a party to it. What do you think they would have done to me if I'd started making accusations?"

"But if you think Tony killed Ashley, what happened to his father? Sean Gallagher's disappearance has always been linked to the O'Roarkes."

David shrugged. "Maybe the O'Roarkes did kill him for framing Daniel. Who could have blamed them? Someone even went so far as to plant Daniel's blood on Ashley's dress. Or maybe Sean was worried what would happen to him once the truth came out about what he'd done, and he just took off. I don't know and I don't care. There's only one Gallagher I'm interested in.''

''What about Fiona?'' Eve asked quietly. ''What did she ever do to you?''

Out of the corner of her eye, Eve could see Fiona's frightened face. Tears were running down her cheeks.

David said sadly, ''She's my one regret. I didn't want this to happen to her, but she saw something in my office today—a picture of Ashley that I usually keep out of sight. I'd left it out by mistake. She questioned me about it, and I knew that it was only a matter of time before she'd figure it all out. Letting her see that picture was the first mistake I've made.''

No, Eve thought. *The first mistake you made was thinking Tony was guilty of murder. The second was in underestimating him. And me.*

Eve renewed her struggles with the rope while she tried to keep her outward expression and her tone calm. ''So why did you kill Lucy Stringer and Megan Riley?''

''Tony got away with Ashley's murder, but he won't get away with these. I've made sure of it. I've planted evidence all over his car and apartment. His gun was used to kill Maria Mancini. There's no way he can walk this time. Justice will finally be served.''

A car sounded outside, and David's head snapped toward the door. ''Finally,'' he said almost angrily.

He walked behind Eve, looped his arm around her neck and pointed the gun at her temple. She held her breath, waiting for the telltale slam of Tony's car door, his footsteps on the wooden porch. If she yelled a warning, she would have to time it right. If he didn't hear her, she wouldn't get a second chance.

But the car door didn't slam, and there were no footsteps on the porch. Silence reigned.

David swore viciously. "What the hell is he doing out there?"

Eve swallowed, hoping against hope that Tony had somehow realized he was walking into a trap. David's grip around her neck eased, as if he wasn't quite sure what to do.

Fiona moaned softly from the bed, and as the sound drew David's attention, something made Eve glance up. Tony was staring down at her from the skylight. Her heart almost stopped, and then quickly she averted her gaze as David turned back to her.

"Maybe you should go see what's keeping him," she suggested.

"And maybe you should shut the hell up." David put the gun to her temple again. "Maybe we don't need to wait for him. Maybe I'll just do what I have to do here and now."

"If you don't kill Tony first, you won't be able to get away with this." She sensed David's hesitation and said, "That is your plan, isn't it? To kill Tony, make it look like a murder-suicide?"

David didn't say anything, but the tension almost dripped from his body. Eve pressed her point. "You have to kill Tony first, David. You know that."

He lowered the gun for a moment, as if considering what to do. Eve threw her weight to one side, toppling her chair. Before David had time to raise the gun again, Tony came crashing through the skylight. Shattered glass flew in every direction as he landed on David. The two of them dropped to the floor, and as they fought, Eve struggled with the ropes.

With all her might, she rocked the chair against the floor, once, twice, three times before the railing splintered, loosening the rope. But before she could free herself, David pounded the gun into Tony's temple. Tony fell back, grabbing for Eve's weapon. David shot first, wildly, missing Tony. Tony's shot connected, but David didn't go down. He stumbled backward, spun and slammed through one of the boarded-up windows. The rotting wood gave way to breaking glass, and then he was gone.

Tony was up in a flash, running after him. Within seconds, the sound of their footsteps died away as they both took to the woods.

Eve flung off the ropes around her wrists, then went to work on her ankles. Finally free, she hurried over to Fiona, removing the tape as gently as she could. Fiona gasped with a sob, "He killed those women. I was in love with him, and he was going to kill me, too."

"I know," Eve said softly. "Try not to think about that now. We have to get out of here."

She managed to get the ropes off Fiona and then helped her to her feet. "Come on." Eve urged her forward, out the door, toward the car parked just behind David's.

"That's my mother's car," Fiona said weakly. "She has a car phone."

"Good," Eve said. "I want you to get in the car, lock the doors and call 911. Then get down and stay out of sight—"

A gunshot sounded in the distance, and Fiona clutched Eve's arm. "Oh, my God. Tony—"

"Make the call," Eve shouted as she took off running for the woods.

HE WAS TRYING to double back, Tony realized. David was trying to get back to Eve and Fiona. Tony had no idea whether his last shot had connected or not, but he knew he couldn't afford to waste another round. He concentrated instead on keeping the trail, not letting David get too far ahead of him.

They were nearing the main road, and Tony thought he heard the sound of an engine. A car could mean David's escape, and Tony doubled his efforts despite the searing pain in his side from the bruised ribs.

He heard the impact of metal against flesh a split second before he came out of the woods. David lay sprawled in the middle of the road, his face bloody and mangled, his body still. Slowly Tony's gaze lifted to the driver. Even in the darkness, he could see Fiona sitting behind the wheel of their mother's car.

He knelt and felt for a heartbeat. There wasn't one.

He walked over and opened the door. Fiona stared straight ahead, her face pale in the interior light. She was shaking all over, her hands still gripping the steering wheel. Gently, Tony pried them loose.

She looked at him then. "Mom always keeps a spare key under her floor mat." And then she began to cry. Tony pulled her from the car and wrapped his arms around her.

Eve came running out of the woods, her face taut with fear. When she spied David, a look of sheer panic leaped to her face, followed closely by relief.

She said breathlessly, "I thought it was you. I thought I was too late…"

She'd come after him, Tony realized almost in wonder. Without a weapon, without anything but determination and a sense of loyalty, she'd come after him. She could have bailed when she had the chance, but she didn't. She'd been covering his back, as best she could. Just like any good partner would.

Slowly she walked toward him, her expression still shaken. "What happened?" she asked softly.

"He ran out in front of me," Tony said. "I couldn't stop the car in time."

Eve glanced at Fiona trembling in Tony's arms and nodded. "That's what I thought must have happened."

Chapter Fifteen

Tony stood in Fiona's apartment the next day, arguing with her.

"I won't let you take the blame for something I did," she insisted.

"I'm a cop. I was pursuing a murder suspect," Tony said wearily. And Fiona had just found out her lover was a murderer, that he planned to kill her. It was justifiable homicide in Tony's eyes, but he wasn't sure how it would have gone down with the State Attorney's Office, and he hadn't been willing to take a chance. It was better this way. His sister had enough to deal with. "The report is filed, so just forget about it. Try to put it behind you."

"But I killed him," Fiona whispered. She turned to face Tony. "I don't know if I could have stopped in time or not, but I don't think I even tried. I saw him on the side of the road. He was looking right at me, smiling as if he expected me to stop. I thought about those poor girls he killed, Mrs. Mancini...all because he blamed you for Ashley's death. How could he have ever thought you'd killed her? You were in love with her."

Tony frowned, not really wanting to think about Ashley. Even after everything he'd learned, it was hard to let go of the memories. Hard to stop believing in the fantasy. But the truth was, Ashley had never been the woman he'd thought her to be. The woman he'd wanted her to be. She'd never been Eve.

"I guess I can understand it in a way," he said, raking his fingers through his hair. "David and Ashley were seeing each other behind my back. He thought she'd told me about them that night and that I killed her in a jealous rage. He's planned his revenge for years, when all along justice had already been served. Ashley's real murderer is still on death row."

Fiona turned to stare out the window. "I really loved him, you know."

Tony sighed. "I know. I'm sorry. I guess we've both had pretty rotten luck in that department."

"You can't compare David to Eve."

"I'm not. But we misjudged them both, Fiona, and maybe there's a lesson to be learned from it."

She took his arm. "I think you're still misjudging Eve. Have you ever thought about how all this has affected her? She didn't ask for that assignment, Tony. She was ordered to do it. What was she suppose to do—resign in protest? And what would have happened if she'd refused the assignment? Another IAD officer would have been sent in her place, one who didn't have Eve's blind faith in you."

"Blind faith?"

"Did she ever once doubt your innocence?" Fiona demanded. "Did she ever once question your integrity? Did you ever once stop to consider that maybe, just maybe, she accepted that assignment because she thought she could protect you?"

"Since when have you become such a big fan of Eve's?" Tony grumbled.

"Since I saw the way she looked at you that first night at the pub," Fiona told him. "Since I realized that you two were made for each other. Don't let her get away because of your pride. Because you're too afraid of getting hurt again. Eve's worth that price, Tony, and you know it.''

TONY WAS SITTING on her steps when Eve got home from work that day. Her heart stopped for a moment, then started back up in double time as she reluctantly approached him.

"How's Fiona?" she managed to ask.

He shrugged. "I think she's still in shock. When it finally hits her, she'll have a helluva lot to deal with. Luckily, she and my mother and grandmother are all very close. They'll help her through this."

"So will you."

He shrugged. "I've got to try and put my own life back together. It's pretty much a mess right now."

"You've been cleared," Eve reminded him. "Vindicated even. The press is treating you like a hero."

He shook his head. "Go figure that one."

"You might even get a promotion out of this if the right reports are filed in your behalf."

"I don't care about a promotion. I think I'd just like a normal life for a change." He rose to face her. "Speaking of reports, though, I'd like to explain about the statement I gave last night."

It was Eve's turn to shrug. "What's there to explain? I didn't see what happened, Tony." But she knew Fiona had been driving that car, and Tony knew she knew.

He nodded briefly, then said, "Can we go upstairs? There's something else I'd like to talk to you about."

Eve tried not to read too much into that, but her hands were shaking as she unlocked her door. Once inside her apartment, she glanced around, still uneasy. The pink roses were gone, but she thought she could smell a lingering trace of their scent. She shivered as she turned to face Tony.

"I know it's all over," she said, "but I can't help thinking what a close call we all had. Fiona could have been killed."

"So could you," Tony said grimly.

"And you could have been blamed for all the murders." She shivered again. "I can't imagine what you must be going through. David was your best friend."

Tony suddenly looked indescribably weary. "He was like a brother to me. Or so I thought. But all these years, he thought I was a killer. Our whole friendship was a lie."

Eve wrapped her arms around her middle. "I still don't understand how he got inside my apartment."

"He had a key." When she glanced up at him in surprise, Tony said, "There was a lot about David I didn't know, it seems. When I met him in college, I thought he was from a privileged background. He had money, a hot car, nice clothes. But all that came from his stepfather. His own father was a small-town locksmith. Evidently, he taught his son all the tricks of the trade. David had the equipment in his apartment, everything he needed not just to duplicate keys, but to make them from an impression of the lock. He had one for your apartment, one for Lucy's, Maria Mancini's house, and dozens more that we haven't identified yet."

Eve thought about David MacKenzie using the trade his father had taught him to move silently in and out of people's private domains. How many times had he been in her apartment that she hadn't known about?

"Among other things, he had an evidence vacuum in his apartment, too," Tony told her. "The kind used by the CSU. That's how he was able to clean up the crime scenes."

Eve shuddered. "He'd been planning this for years."

"Ever since Ashley died."

Eve drew a long breath. "I'm sorry, Tony…about everything. I'd like to explain my part in all this if you'll listen."

"You don't owe me an explanation." He paused, then

said, "Now that I've had some time to think, I realize you were put between a rock and a hard place. You were a good partner, Eve."

Her eyes flooded with tears. "So were you."

"I've been thinking." He took a hesitant step toward her. "Maybe the partnership doesn't have to end here."

"What do you have in mind?" Her heart started pounding. She felt breathless and light-headed, and maybe a little too hopeful.

"What we have is too good to lose, Eve. I've wasted too many years thinking about the past. The wrong past. I don't know how I could have been so blind back then, but my eyes are finally open, and I'm standing here looking at the woman I love. The only woman I could ever want."

Eve made a move toward him, found herself suddenly crushed in his arms. She felt his lips in her hair, and a wave of happiness rolled over her. She couldn't believe this was finally happening, and yet, deep inside, a part of her had always known it would.

"I think I've loved you forever," she said quietly.

He took her face in his hands and gazed into her eyes. "Then I'm the luckiest man alive," he said, just before he kissed her.

Be sure to look for the next
GALLAGHER JUSTICE *book—Nick's story,*

FORBIDDEN LOVER,

will be on sale March 2000.
Only from Amanda Stevens
and Harlequin Intrigue!

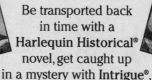

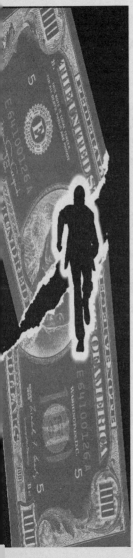